WHIRLWIND
Feyi Aina

FIRST PUBLISHED IN Great Britain in 2024 by
LOVE AFRICA PRESS
103 Reaver House, 12 East Street, Epsom KT17 1HX
www.loveafricapress.com[1]

Text copyright © Olufunmilola Adeniran, 2024
All rights reserved.

No part of this publication may be reproduced, stored or transmitted in any form by any means, electronic, mechanical, photocopying or otherwise, without the prior permission of the publisher, except in the case of brief quotations embodied in reviews.

The right of Olufunmilola Adeniran to be identified as author of this work has been asserted by them in accordance with the Copyright, Design and Patents Act, 1988

This is a work of fiction. Names, places, events and incidents are either the products of the author's imagination or used fictitiously. Any resemblance to actual persons, living or dead, is purely coincidental.

---

1. http://www.loveafricapress.com

Blurb

TOMIWA OYINLOLU IS the successful CEO of Purple Chip Professional Services, the IT firm that everyone wants to work for. One day he meets an exuberant woman in the elevator of his office building and she completely mesmerises him. The thing, she shows up at their oral interview panel as one of the ten short-listed candidates from a pool of over a hundred. It is unfortunate she has a connection to the owner of their competitor, One Tech. Worse, his sister has a spy in the rival company and she won't let him hire the young lady.

The problem is, she is a brilliant programmer, and it seems he has fallen for her.

Cheerful, high-spirited Ademide Akinseye's dream has always been to start her career in Purple Chip Professional Services. On the side, she ushers at parties to make ends meet. The man she encounters on her way to interview attentively listens to her light-hearted chatter about her day, philosophies, and plans to join Purple Chip as a programmer. Then she arrives at the job assessment and realises she's been blabbing to the founder and owner of Purple Chip.

Although the cards are stacked against her, she isn't about to give up on her dreams.

Chapter One

AS TOMIWA OYINLOLU strode through the gold-platted doors of Lion Towers' ten-floor building, his mind was not at ease.

Based on what little information Babs had been able to glean for him, the company eyeing the Kehinde Jules account was not to be underestimated. They had handled a few small to medium-sized projects, and the reviews on their work were good. Astonishingly good.

He was headed for serious competition with them as rivals in the coming weeks.

Feyintola will explode, he thought as he strolled through the wide lobby towards the corridor leading to the elevators. Meeting her this morning was the last thing he wanted to do.

He couldn't fault her, though. She had moved heaven and earth to get them into the bid meetings in Abuja and rung up all her pending favours to ensure they were front and centre. Now they'd passed the first three stages of the bid presentations, the idea of pitching against One Tech, a relatively unknown company, was guaranteed to infuriate her.

Who the heck is One Tech?

How had they passed all the presentation stages with no sponsor? Who did they know on the inside? What was so great about their app?

The elevator dinged as it came to a stop and the doors opened. He pushed away his melancholic thoughts and stepped in, reaching for the control panel when a shriek stopped him.

"Hey, hold the doors!"

Startled, he kept a finger on the *open-door* button and waited to see who needed to get on.

It didn't take long. She flew into the elevator like a tumultuous whirlwind, scattering and splattering his emotions around as she entered arms first, fruity fragrance next, into the rectangular space that had been his alone just moments prior.

Pretty, aquiline-shaped eyes above a small nose and dainty rose-bud lips arrested his attention at once, along with milk-white teeth as she slowed to a stop, placed a hand over her heart, and burst into boisterous laughter. Light and exuberant, it echoed around the spacious passage and had him mesmerized.

"Yeah, they have an elevator! I don't have to rattle up those stairs with all my baggage."

A one-second sweep of her from head to toe revealed a handbag, a laptop bag, a black manila folder, and a lunch bag. Quite a lot of things to be carrying but not so much they qualified as baggage.

'Thank you,' she mouthed as she turned around and smiled at him. "The building is huge and modern. I am impressed."

He released his hold on the button.

"And I'm never late o! The car just developed a fault right in front of the school compound. Today, of all the days I needed to be on time."

He raised his eyes to her face. Was she talking to him?

"I had to take *a bike*," she chuckled. "Yes *o*! I would have been late."

She wasn't. She had on EarPods and seemed to be on a call with someone.

"I'm just praying that Niyi got the mechanic to get it to work."

While she grappled with her phone call, he let his eyes take their time travelling down her svelte frame in the yellow dress and a white, short-sleeved knitted jacket.

She had braids on, whipped up into an elegant bun on top of her head. Hoop earrings dangled past her cheeks, and the top button on the jacket was undone, exposing a neckline hinting at two soft swellings that teased his imagination. It was just enough, better than most of it out in the open, in his opinion. Not that he'd even wanted to look.

"Okay, I'll let you know how it goes," she continued. "Thank you, bye."

The folder was crammed below her chest over her abdomen where the dress followed the shape of her curvy hips to her knees, legs long beneath the hem. A yellow pair of two-strapped, transparent-heeled sandals completed the look.

He loved strappy sandals on beautiful women. They were his weakness. Strapped heels with well-manicured toes on slender legs and a lithe frame to go with.

"Sir." Her voice put an end to his ogling. His eyes veered up and encountered her confused look as her eyes moved from his to the control panel. "I'm going to the fourth floor."

He wasn't the type to stare at girls.

Cars, yes. Buildings, maybe. Women...he drew a line at women. Especially if they were this young, this pretty, or somewhere within the sphere of his work-space environment.

But he was enchanted—it took him a second to realize the lift wasn't moving. "Oh."

She whipped out the electronic visitor's tag she'd been handed at the lobby, but he came alive at once, like a quasi-knight aiming to score some cheap, *unusable* points with her.

He leaned forward, swiped his key card across the scanner, and pressed the number four button without a word. Then, he stepped back to extend a hand across the steel rail running the length of the wall and observe her.

"Or was it five?" she muttered as the elevator lifted with a slight bump.

Flipping open the cover of the black folder, she studied the A4 sheet on the topmost page for a second, raised her eyes to his, and gave an apologetic little laugh. Her pearly whites flashed at him again. Perfect in their row, no spaces or gaps or discoloration. The gesture had been so dainty and sophisticated, he'd held his breath while watching it.

Sweet lollipop, I'm hooked!

Her beauty wasn't the type to make one wild. Like with the girls his brother's friend, Ade, jokingly termed a HOT Run—'Hit Once Then Run.' Girls that weren't the main dish or the side; not even the dessert. More like the accompanying sweet with the bill at a restaurant, according to them.

She was a lollipop. The kind one took time to unwrap and savor and keep.

He had enough on his plate without adding the drama of a lollipop. Plus, he didn't know how to bait a girl and run. It was callous. Offering a job, demanding other things, and bolting out of the door without looking back.

"Fifth floor, I'm so sorry, it's number five. Gosh, I am not myself today! Jelly brain, that's what I am."

Jelly brain? More like jelly-baby, you soft, luscious thing. Ade would have to expand his nomenclature. Desserts and sweets would not just do.

She pointed at the control panel. "Number five, please."

He recalled himself and leaned sideways to press the fifth and eighth buttons on the panel. He'd almost forgotten which floor he was headed to.

Girls like her were a dime a dozen in the job-hunting space. Many of his friends had taken their pick, had their fill, and paid the price. Not him. Casual hook-ups were not his thing. He had more riding on his name and brand than to let one night of careless craziness ruin things.

Yeah, she's beautiful, but hold your horses.

"I'm going for an interview," she said to him.

He froze.

There was only one company in the building interviewing today.

His.

"Purple Chip Professional Services," she added. "It's the IT firm to be in. They're indigenous, pushing frontiers, proudly Nigerian, and breaking boundaries. That's why I like them."

Interesting!

He understood now why she was worried about being late.

"I have always wanted to work with them.

You have?

"Ever since they won that grant from the US and secured the multi-country deal, they've been churning out amazing products. Now here I am, invited for their interview, and I'm late. Can you imagine?"

Unfortunately for her, the test had started.

But the interview, and in that dress, though, yellow? Who wore yellow to an interview?

"Well, test. Says so on their invite here." She tapped the folder.

His eyes lowered to the folder and rose to hers.

"My sister-in-law says that problems are a sign of great things being in store for you."

She was talking. Again!

"So, when your car refuses to start in the morning or you miss a ride on your way to an important interview—" she grinned at him, "—then know that all things are working together for your good!"

She was right. His need to travel down to the ground floor to sign off on a delivery was turning out to be a good start to his day.

"But I'm freaking out! I need to make the shortlist so I can get a chance to talk to the faces behind the greatest software company in the whole of Lagos. I'm a huge, huge fan of their financial management app, *Compound*. Don't get me started on *Compound*. I could think of a few ways to jazz it up, but then, one step at a time, right? I have to get my foot in through their doors first before I think about changing their codes."

His brow furrowed. Jazz up an award-winning software, was she serious? How old was she exactly? What did she know about coding?

The elevator's sudden stop jarred him out of his thoughts, and the doors slid open on the fourth floor. She took a peek out, and he mirrored the gesture.

"Not my floor!" She released a quiet sigh.

Since there was no one waiting to get on, the doors slid back closed again, and he was glad. It gave him more time to stare at her.

His eyes settled on her even-toned, animated face and went exploring again. Symmetry is beauty, he'd read somewhere. The braid bun drew attention to her pretty, expressive eyes and the lips that had been moving a mile a minute, not giving him time enough to admire them.

She seemed to notice him staring and suddenly turned shy, averting her eyes and folding her lips together.

He'd been told often enough that his quiet and stern outer appearance was vastly different from his soft and mushy inner personality. It took a while before people found out the outside didn't quite match the inside. He didn't know what she was reading from his facial expression, but inside, he was umpiring a battle between his yo-yo-ing heartbeat and his logic.

She was pretty. Breathtaking, but he had his rules. He tried hard to follow his rules.

The side-effects of being a rich, powerful guy at the top of his game meant those rules wavered, wanting to be bent often enough, but he had a firm resolve and the discipline to carry it through.

Brand before babes! Brand first, babes later.

Babes— probably never.

She bounced on one spot, eyes on the elevator doors as if willing the carriage to go faster. This was the moment if ever he was going to get a word in.

"You should calm down."

She turned to look at him, halting her fidgeting.

"I'm sure you will do just fine."

His voice had come out rich and sonorous in the quiet elevator, and he'd been surprised at how calm and strong it was, considering the anxious pounding of his heart.

"I'm nervous. I talk a lot when I'm nervous."

"I noticed."

He was convinced she did cartwheels, as well, whenever she was nervous.

"I will. Do fine, that is. I have to. I prepared for this all through my university final year, so..." She chuckled. "But thank you for the vote of confidence, sir."

Sir? The elevator bumped to a stop, and the doors slid open. *Do I look that old?*

"Okay, wish me luck!" She turned to offer him another smile.

She looked genuinely excited, so he tipped his head at her. "All the best."

"Thank you! Enjoy your day," she threw at him as she hurried down the lush red carpeting lining the hallway down to the offices of Purple Chip Professional Services.

He stood in the empty elevator for a moment staring at the spot she'd just exited from.

As he rode the rest of the way to the eighth floor, he wasn't doing much worrying again about Kehinde Jules and the contract, or Feyintola's impending blow-up. He wasn't even wondering what kind of dirt Babs would have been able to dig up about One Tech or if it would even be useful.

He was thinking about the woman who had just waltzed into and out of his life, and how he was going to figure out who she was amidst the throng of candidates milling about on the fifth floor.

He had his rules, but she had bent them.

Chapter Two

FOR ONE WHOLE MONTH, Ademide 'Mide' Akinseye had waited to get the call about the short-listed candidates for the Purple Chip interviews. Ecstatic to find her name on it, she'd prepared eagerly. Only for Niyi's car engine to fall out of commission.

Don't think about it. You are here now and interviewing.

She put the worry out of her mind and focused on getting into the interview room.

A chubby, uniformed female guard sat at a table at the end of the corridor.

"Good morning." Mide threw the brightest smile she could muster at her. "I'm here for the Purple Chip Test."

"Good morning," the guard replied. "You are late. They started fifteen minutes ago. Find your name on this list, sign against it, and put a date."

"Sure." She turned the paper around on the table and looked at it.

Over a hundred names were on the list. Whittled down, she was sure. Yet, so many of them were familiar, some even her classmates. Everyone she knew was looking for a job or hoping to upgrade their current one. Everyone, it seemed, had been shortlisted.

The number floored her. *Keep a smile permanent on your face if you don't want to have wrinkles later in life*—she heard her mother's voice in her head as she scanned the list. It took a conscious effort, especially when she'd lost valuable time getting to the interview venue.

"Ensure to remember the number against your name for reference," the guard added.

"Noted."

After she'd scribbled her signature against her name at number ninety-six, she straightened up, and the guard opened the door to the room. Dozens of candidates were seated at desks in a very long hall, staring down at laptop screens and punching away on keyboards.

Rather than be fazed, she waved at a few familiar faces. Only one or two bothered to wave back. The rest were just scowling at their computers and typing fast.

A slim, fair-skinned woman in very high black heels and a bright red dress was shuffling through a sheaf of papers at the front of the hall. Mide approached her.

"Are you here for the test?" she asked, looking up.

"Yes, I'm Mide Akinseye—"

"Found your name at the door?" She was no longer paying Mide any attention.

"Yes, I'm number ninety-six. I—"

"Find a seat and set up your laptop." She handed her a sheet of paper, eyes focused on a laptop screen. "You have less than thirty minutes to solve this."

"Right." Mide grabbed the sheet. "I can do this," she muttered, turning to stroll past a row of desks amidst a mix of curious stares and blatant indifference.

Searching for a free seat and finding none, she paused in the middle of the aisle and prayed. "All things work together for good—"

There was a whistle in her direction from a young man in a grey sweatshirt at the back left-hand corner of the hall. He waved both hands in the air and pointed at the last seat at the very back.

She hurried towards him. "Thanks, I was just looking for the right space."

He stood behind the seat and pointed both hands down at it without a word.

She wiped off her smile and slid in, setting her handbag down on the floor. She was in an exam hall. She needed to be quiet.

As she brought her laptop out, she glanced on either side of her. The man on her left was sweating despite the air conditioning in the room. The one on her right was chewing on the end of his pencil. There was ample space between them and not enough for anyone to look over any other person's shoulder, but she didn't need to. She was quite confident in herself.

As her laptop booted up, she read the questions on the sheet. There were five.

Number one, given the following data, create a program to return a list of employees who are not managers. Number two, fix the bugs on this report sheet. Number three, write a function that converts a user date format from one to the other....

"This can't be all," she whispered with a frown as she turned the sheet over. "This is Purple Chip; it can't be all. It's supposed to be harder than this!"

"Twenty minutes more."

The lady in red was walking down the tiled aisle between the right and left halves of the hall. Her shoes made crisp-sounding clicks as she swayed, hips swinging, towards Mide.

Mide stared at her. She was pretty, ultra-slim, and curvaceous. She looked like the kind of girl who would work in a company like Purple Chip. The kind of girl Mide wanted to be. A classy, career woman earning a paycheque.

Zoning her and everyone else in the room out, she dug into her bag for her red, round-rimmed spectacles, put them on, and got to work. Four minutes was tops for each question.

From afar, she heard the lady's words.

"The results of this test will be out around twelve o'clock, and fifty of you will get callbacks for the second stage of the written test. That test will be a speed test. We will be picking the first twenty applicants to submit. From that pool, a short list of ten people will report here tomorrow morning for the final round of interviews. Three spots are up for grabs. I wish you all the best."

TOMIWA STEPPED INTO the posh office of Purple Chip's elite reception. He had gained a moment of clarity from his conversation with the girl in the elevator. His company was most sought after. Every Bola, Dotun, and Hauwa was vying for a place in it.

The injection of funds by Mega-Watte two years prior had catapulted them from number thirty-one to a visible number twelve on the list of top hundred companies in Nigeria to work for. Fifth in the Nigerian IT world and winner of a few awards. It had also placed them on a watch list of companies doing excellently, but standing out as an IT company in the twenty-first century necessitated creating an international work environment that replicated—in parts—the Silicon Valley experience.

For the moment, the company occupied three floors in the ten-story building of Lion Towers, and that was just all right.

Nestled within the heart of Victoria Island, the Towers belonged to the Oyinlolu Family Incorporation. Its crop of floors above ground and basement level car park housed companies that paid a fortune just to shelter in the fortress. The topmost floor contained the incorporation's property development business, Filex, and the lavish offices of the Incorporation's MD, Feyintola Oyinlolu, the Filex MD, Goriola Oyinlolu, and the Purple Chip CEO, him.

"Good morning, Mr. Oyinlolu." Enaife beamed as he entered the reception, the corner of her eyes crinkling up to her temples, revealing twin dimples as she smiled at him.

"Morning. Hope you had a pleasant night's rest?"

"I did. Thank you, sir."

Professional and excellent at her job, she was the first face most clients interacted with at Purple Chip. She had taken the company's values to heart and thrown all her efforts into being an exceptional receptionist so he had elevated her to Executive Secretary. 'Receptionist' just didn't do her justice.

He'd often thought that having Afro-Asian roots had something to do with Ena's strong moral code of conduct and impeccable work ethic. But hard work and excellent conduct were part of their core company values. It had taken years, but he'd gotten the crop of staff he wanted through sheer determination, rigorous recruitment exercises, and brutal staff training.

"Miss Tola is waiting for you in the conference room. She's asked for you thrice already."

"Thrice?"

What trouble is she stirring up again? he wondered as he made his way across the wide reception room. *She couldn't have found out about One Tech, could she? The memo hasn't even crossed my desk.*

"She insists you come into the conference room the moment you arrive." Enaife turned her attention to the person on the other end of the line with her. "Yes, Mr. Ferdinand, you were saying…"

Their conversation was finished. Respectfully done, but it left him wanting more information on Feyintola's current state of emotions.

"Good morning Mr. Tom." The voice belonged to Shile, one of the mid-level programmers in the pool on the sixth floor, something of an office assistant to him.

"Shile, how was your weekend?"

"Great, sir." Shile bowed and handed him his usual morning cup of coffee. "Babs also asked me to give you this document, said you needed to see it urgently."

"Where is he?" Tomiwa took a sip as he swept past the receptionist's wide, half-oval desk and the wall behind her carrying the Purple Chip logo.

"Helping Chioma and Ugo out with the interviews. There are a lot of candidates."

The girl from the elevator filtered into his mind for a split second, and he thought about chocolate-layered lollipops. Mouth watering at the thought, he placed the folder on the forearm of the hand holding the coffee mug and flipped through it. Ade would have encouraged him to take a lick. Or taken one himself had Tomiwa shown signs of hesitance.

He missed Ade, a childhood friend of the family. The guy was in the UK on a three-week business trip.

"Where's Abel? What happened to the members of his unit? Why are tech guys doing HR work?"

"It's a techy thing, sir. He said they'd rather stay out of it."

"What does it mean? They're handing out appointment letters to the successful applicants in due time, aren't they?"

"Yes, sir."

"What are my people doing without them? Get Abel downstairs and Ugo up here. I need him. Then tell Chioma the reports need to be on my desk ASAP. She's accompanying me to Brookside."

"Yes, sir."

Tomiwa flipped the file close as he ventured past the glass-partitioned office cubicles to the door at the end of the corridor.

"Who's in this meeting, by the way?" he asked, pointing the file at the door.

"Ms. Feyintola and Mr. Gori. There's also a young guy who looks like an applicant."

"Applicant? Why isn't he downstairs with the others?"

Shile paused a quarter of the way down the corridor. "It's a mystery why the guy is up here and not down there taking the test like everyone else." He shrugged. "He might be here for something else. I don't know, sir. Anything else?"

"Not for now." Tomiwa opened the door with the hand holding the file and strode into the conference room. "Hello, peeps, what did I miss?"

Chapter Three

THE CONFERENCE ROOM on the eighth floor was a twenty by fifteen-square-foot area of expensive indulgence. It was well-designed, well-illuminated, and stocked with a mini-kitchen, state-of-the-art multimedia equipment, and a corner table set up with tea and coffee-making equipment.

The first thing confronting everyone when they walked into it was the large, oval, cherry-coloured conference table in the middle. Crafted out of solid oak with a three-step hand-rubbed finish, it had a two-inch-thick table top, hardwood veneer bases, and a granite centrepiece.

Imported from the States on his sister's insistence, the intimidating table set the tone for discussions whenever they had clients over—Feyintola's way of exerting her absolute supremacy over meeting proceedings. And it was the one thing most clients asked about during the preamble conversations before negotiations.

Tomiwa walked in to find her seated on one end of it, long legs crossed at the knees, looking the part of a prim and proper MD. Her long-sleeved, white silk shirt was tucked into a tailored pair of dark grey pants over grey peep-toe pumps. A shiny, shoulder-length, bone-straight weave hugged her narrow face, a firm reminder of her no nonsense-attitude and serious approach to life.

"Well," she said, hair swinging as she turned to acknowledge him. "It took three calls to move you out of your office."

At thirty-nine, she was the veritable force behind Oyinlolu Incorporation's constant stream of privileged accomplishments, and she was a capable businesswoman in her own right. Tomiwa loved her, but butting heads with her was all it seemed he did at work.

"It's a Monday morning," he replied. "I usually like to get an update from my staff before I come down from the mountain of the gods to visit you earthlings."

"And they say you're the humble one."

"I am the humble one." He pointed the file in his hand at the man sitting on the left side of the room as he strolled down the length of the conference table and its chairs. "How many did it take to move him?"

"Just one, and you didn't even make the call. Didn't you miss me?"

Tomiwa eyed him. "I'm too steeped in work to have time for that."

"I wasn't even gone three weeks, and already, you've forgotten me."

"Weep for your bland future."

Goriola Oyinlolu, their younger brother—called Gori by everyone—was seated in one of the eight black-leather armchairs arranged around the oval table with his legs stretched out on top of it. Having just flown in from the US, Tomiwa was seeing him for the first time in a month.

Thirty-three and one of the best architects in Lagos, he was the youngest, most outgoing sibling in the Oyinlolu clan. His company combined engineering, architecture, and property management under one umbrella business that built corporate real estate. Five years in the market, and they were already making waves designing modern office workspaces and buildings for corporate businesses and Federal government parastatals.

"I called you home because an urgent family matter needed your attention," Feyintola said to them both.

"Urgent family matter?" Tomiwa stopped beside her.

"Now you are all here, I'll explain. Before I do, however, I need my assignment?"

Tomiwa pressed the file in his hands into hers. "Here, all done and typed."

"Took you long enough," Feyintola retorted as she grabbed the file and flipped through it.

"You insisted it be typed."

"I did. It's only professional."

"So glad to see some things haven't changed," Gori cut into their conversation. "What was so urgent it needed my physical presence?"

She didn't look up from the file. "Calm yourself, and take your feet off my granite."

Tomiwa raised a brow at her. "Easy on the snapping, queen bee. It's a Monday morning. You have a whole week ahead of you and plenty of staff to take your trials out on."

"This granite is worth a lot of money," she said, flipping to the next page of the file with interest. "Money that Biggy loves to spend."

Goriola—also called Biggy—looked from Tomiwa to Feyintola. "You asked me to take an exercise vacation!"

"One that burns the fat in your belly, not a whole month's income in one week," she replied. "I work too hard and too long to put up with your excesses."

"That's why we need to consider dates by Skype," Goriola said to Tomiwa. "I already told Ferdinand it's probably how things are going to go down. She hasn't updated her time matrix."

Feyintola turned her head to eye Goriola above the open file. "If you're considering setting me up on a date with one of your corny friends—"

"I think the guy has already called to confirm," Tomiwa said. "I heard Ena on the phone with him."

Gori grinned. "Good luck getting out of it. I already made a reservation for you both at Blue Water. Don't stand the guy up this time around, please. I made him pay for a private booth."

Feyintola hissed, nose buried in the file.

"Come on, Tola. Please don't make us wait any longer to throw you that family send-off festival aka wedding party! We've been planning it for years. It'll be huge. Full of all of Mum's sisters and friends offering their gifts to God for sending Ferdinand to deliver us from you."

"You're an idiot," Feyintola said to him.

"Hey, no verbal abuse in the workplace!" Gori reminded her.

Tomiwa chuckled. His younger brother's assessment of their older sister's lacklustre love life was a long-running joke. He sank into one of the black leather seats beside her and twirled it around to face the silent young man who had been in the room all the while, watching the three of them banter with one another.

"So—" he placed his empty mug on the table. "Who's the applicant?"

"Applicant?" Feyintola slapped the file close. "You mean my genius find?"

"Yeah, whatever. Who's he?" Tomiwa eyed the stranger.

"The second runner up in the esteemed Longman Youth Programmer of the Year award, current Infotech Surf board champion, and recent graduate of the Yaba Institute of Technology." Feyintola sounded excited as she sprung off the table and walked over to stand at its head. "He's a programmer. A damn good one, and a very interesting find."

"Why are we meeting him privately?"

"Yeah, well, he's not here for the interview. I think I should introduce him properly." She paused. "His name is Sesan Bankole Oyinlolu. Bankole being his mother's maiden name. Oyinlolu being—"

"Our surname." Tomiwa's smile faded as he realized why the boy looked familiar. He tilted his head and released a shallow breath as he studied him.

"Which distant uncle's son? Coz I've never heard of him," Gori said from across the table.

"How many distant uncles do you know?" Feyintola asked.

"None."

"None. Exactly."

"Feyin," Tomiwa said, annoyed. "Explain."

"He's immediate family. Close, immediate family. A brother, to be exact—Father's other son."

Tomiwa swivelled his chair around. "Father's other what?"

"Other son," Feyintola repeated.

Gori swung his feet off the granite conference table and sat upright. "Other—what, now?"

"Apologies that you had to meet him like this."

Tomiwa stared at his sister. She wasn't making any sense. Another son? That was preposterous! Their father had just three children. All three of them were in the room. Who was the imposter?

The rest of his questions were swallowed up in confusion as the not-applicant greeted them with a wide smile. "It's great to finally meet you all."

Chapter Four

THERE WAS STILLNESS in the conference room for the first few seconds after Feyintola's pronouncement.

"What are you talking about?" Goriola said.

"Apparently—" Feyintola folded her arms across her chest, "—Dad stepped out on Mum when you were a wee lad of four. The happy consequence of that union is seated right across the table from you."

She tossed an arm in the general direction of the boy's seat. Gori's eyes followed the movement. The applicant swung his chair in Gori's direction, and his right hand flickered back and forth. Two seconds enough to incite irritation.

"How?" Gori exploded. "When?"

"Relax," Feyintola replied. "One would think you were throwing tantrums at the idea of no longer being the baby of the family."

Gori pointed an open palm at the mysterious young man. "Come on, Feyin. Are we doing some kind of genetic testing here, or are we just going to accept somebody from somewhere as our brother because he says so? You do know there are fraudulent people all over this country claiming claims?"

"You know me. I already had him tested."

"When?" Goriola glared at the boy. "Did you vet him?"

"Hush, hush, he's not here for our money, and yes, of course I vetted him. Besides, I think he inherited Tomiwa's genius programming brain as well as Dad's younger day good looks. Not that you managed to port any of those two genes."

"Because he looks a little bit like Dad and can spin keyboards into codes doesn't mean he is an Oyinlolu."

"Nothing will ever make up for him not growing up with us, but he has the trademark wicked grin you used to win Tinu over," Feyintola joked. "So, don't get yourself all twisted up in a knot because you think he didn't take anything from you."

"Feyin!" Tomiwa snapped.

"I ran a DNA test! It's positive."

The not-applicant and topic of discussion proceeded to display a charming smile.

"You had him tested?" Tomiwa said, for lack of anything respectable to say. He had just discovered his father, a man he'd looked up to for years, had cheated on their mother and covered up his disrespect with a hefty sum in inheritance after his death. "When? Against whom? Wait, does Mum know?"

"Against you."

"Me?" His head swam.

"And yes, Mum knows. I told her yesterday."

Tomiwa observed the young man. "Why do I get the feeling you've known about him for much longer than before yesterday?"

"I have. Actually, I might have discovered him about two years ago"

He stiffened, eyes hardening. "Two whole years, Feyin?"

She held up a hand. "I spent all that time watching him and vetting all the information I had, which is more than I can say for you, our supposed IT guru. Are you really on the lookout for geniuses we can add to our arsenal of deviant software programmers, or are you still thinking you can change the world one laidback Computer Engineering graduate at a time?"

"How did you find out?"

"The slush fund Dad kept on the back burner for Oyinlolu Corp had four initials. I wanted to know what the fourth meant. I dug around, and here we are."

Feyintola's quietly spoken words heightened the state of uneasiness in the silent room. For all intent and purposes, their father had been an adulterous man. A liar who had hidden a huge secret from them all.

"He also has a document from Dad—written in Dad's handwriting, by the way—clearly stating exactly who he is and how his mother had him. I was going to pretend like he didn't even exist, but then, a need arose."

"A need. What flipping need?"

His voice was calm, but he knew his sister. He had worked long enough with her to know the wheels in her head were turning backward and she was up to something.

"A work-need."

He studied her tranquil countenance with suspicion. "I source applications from everywhere imaginable. Where the heck did you fish him out from?"

"Right out from under your nose, apparently. His official name is Sesan Bankole. I can see why you might have missed him. Worry not, he doesn't want to work for Purple Chip. He has a chip on his shoulder thanks to Dad."

"And you chose not to share this piece of information with us!"

"This reaction! This is why I chose not to."

"It's a perfectly valid reaction," Goriola reasoned. "Why would you keep it from us? We were going to find out at one point in time, weren't we? That doesn't excuse what you've done."

"What I've done?" Feyintola's voice rose. "Dad is the one you have anger issues with, not me."

"You were not going to say anything till a need arose," Tomiwa said. "That's what you did. Were you even ever?"

"Hey, I'm not the one who had the secret love child and hid him in Bariga. I'm not the one who had a whole other side to life for thirty years. And I am not the one who lied to you both."

"But you found out, and you didn't think we had a right to know."

"I wanted to confirm it was real."

"You were hiding him," Gori yelled. "That in itself is sleazy."

"He is seated right there, why am I speaking for him? Go on, little bro, talk to your brothers. Tell us why you hid from us. Convince them not to hate you for crashing our party of three." Feyintola turned away from Gori.

"Why are you here now? Why didn't you show up years back?" Gori inquired, turning to him with hands on his waist, clearly in the mood for a fight.

Tomiwa wasn't in the mood for one. Their father had lied to everyone, cheated on their mum, heck, even cheated the boy and his mum out of a loving family relationship. It was annoying. Even more annoying—and suspicious, by the way—was his sister being so calm about the whole situation.

"I didn't want to break up your tight little band." The applicant—Sesan—gestured his hands in the air, indicating the three of them. "And I didn't know about you, either. Till about five years ago."

Tomiwa faced him, his face impassive. The boy wanted something. They always wanted something. "What do you want?"

"I don't want anything. I didn't come here looking for you. She—" he pointed at Feyintola who was standing at the head of the table, hip tilted to one side and arms folded across her chest, "—came looking for me. Offered me a job"

"She offered you a—you offered him a job behind my back?" he growled at Feyintola

"And he turned it down. He doesn't want to work for Purple Chip."

"How dare you offer him a job without my say-so?"

"No offense, big brother. I like your codes, and I get that you're the biggest software brand out of Lagos," the boy interjected. "But your style is just not my style."

Tomiwa was irritated by the stream of arrogance emanating from the young boy. "You do know that our dad is dead and no one can vouch for you."

Sesan chuckled. "I figured that out when the letters stopped coming."

"What letters?"

"Dad wrote him a bunch of letters. One every year for twelve years," Feyintola said, tossing a file across the table at Tomiwa. "Failed to mention us, too."

The file flipped open, scattering a sheaf of letters written on their dad's yellow legal pad on the table.

Tomiwa reached for one, recognized his father's handwriting, and narrowed his eyes. "Why was he writing to you?"

"I wouldn't know why he chose to write and not visit. Or why he chose to keep my mother and me in penury for most of our lives when he had this big old fancy tower." Sesan indicated the room they were in. "And more money than a state could spend in its lifetime."

"Because he wanted to keep you a frigging secret," Gori snapped. "You should have stayed a frigging secret."

"Ah, well, you would know him better than I did," Sesan replied. "I never met him. But it's nothing to beat yourself up over. It was mutual, the idea not to show face."

"If you don't want a job—" Tomiwa's voice rose, "—what do you want?"

"Nothing! I didn't ask your sister to come looking for me."

"Guys, guys, guys!" Feyintola unfolded her arms and raised her hands. "Let's all take a deep breath and swallow our prejudices. This is not a meeting to contest the ownership of Dad's estate or decide who heads the incorporation. This is a friendly assembly between siblings to make introductions. No need to bring out the big guns."

Tomiwa took in a deep breath and glanced at Gori before swinging his eyes back to the boy named Sesan Bankole.

"I don't recall your name being on the list the Yaba Institute sent to me. A guy as good as my sister claims you to be shouldn't be missing from their list of the top three."

"I told you already." He levelled cold eyes at Tomiwa. "I don't want to work for Purple Chip. I asked them to take my name off that list."

"You can be sure I will be checking this information out."

"You are welcome to do whatever you wish. Many companies fish top students out of schools."

"That's if you're even a top student!"

"Do offers from IT League and One Tech count? If those don't pan out, NetSoft is still hiring by the hour, and their pay and work environment are top-notch."

"IT League doesn't hire from Polytechs," Tomiwa replied. "And One Tech is a no-name. As for NetSoft, you'll just be lost in a sea of their programmers trying to work your way up from the bottom of the rung."

"I'm not a stranger to pulling myself up by my bootstraps with no help from Daddy. NetSoft should be a fun try-out. I'd rather be lost in there than lost in here. A good leap from there into the consulting world would be even better, so I'm widening my net of choices."

"You're too old to start in KPMG."

"And I hear they didn't even take you. Pity, but then, Daddy had a comfortable slush fund for you to shoot your shots from. You climbed up pretty well."

"I climbed up smart. Everything you see here was built from scratch."

"With Daddy's money. At least, you didn't go all prodigal on him. Good for you."

Tomiwa gripped the arms of his chair, ready to leap out and strangle the boy, but Goriola stood from across the table and held an arm out.

"Don't bother," he said. "Not worth it!"

Tomiwa fumed. He'd had his fair share of arrogant technology whiz kids, and he had a good knowledge of how to put them in their place.

"You're too far above him in age and status to lower yourself and engage him in a verbal fight," Goriola said, turning to Feyintola. "Why is he even here?"

"I hired him," she said.

"You hired him," Tomiwa repeated, anger lacing his voice. "To do what?"

She sent the file he had given her skidding across the table to the boy who stopped it with a flat palm and picked it up.

"To spy on One Tech."

Tomiwa froze. It took him a couple of seconds to ask the question burning in his mind. "Why?"

"I don't need his mad coding skills, and you don't, but they do. I hear they're in the market for a programmer, and I'm looking for a bug. You don't become a dark web surfer without having a deviant side to your personality. Thanks to Dad, he's got plenty of that."

"I meant, *why* would *we* be spying on One Tech?"

"Why would we not?" The stubborn streak in her kicked in. "We didn't work hard to build this company and turn it into the firm it is today so some no-name nobody from nowhere can battle us for contracts."

"So, you want to hire this guy—who you don't know—to spy on One Tech."

"I've known about him for two years," Feyintola replied. "You're the ones just finding out."

"It's ridiculous!"

"What's ridiculous?"

"What you are planning to do. It can't make up its mind between being deceitful and being diabolically stupid."

"Business, my dear brother, is like a bullfight. The chips go to the person who can take the bull by the horns."

"This isn't taking the bull by the horns, it's fighting dirty. I don't like it."

"Have you read the file on One Tech? They may not be popular. They may not have popped their brand onto the horizon like you've done, but they have a crop of very talented programmers with ambition. That's very dangerous," she said. "For us."

"We have what it takes—"

"The first ninety percent of the market goes to talent and hard work. The remaining ten to the people who are willing to wrestle in the sand pit. If we're fighting, I need to know who I'm up against. They beat IT League, for goodness' sake."

"It's crossing a line, and I—"

"Don't care what you think." Feyintola placed her hands on the table and lowered her gaze to his. "You might be the CEO of Purple Chip, but I'm the MD of this whole establishment, and I make the final decisions. This is what we are going to do. Know our enemy from the inside."

Tomiwa glared back, eyes just as determined. His sister had a backbone of steel, but he'd been standing up to her ever since they were kids.

"That's not what we agreed on the board resolution. Every decision needs a two-thirds vote."

"This isn't a board decision. This is sourcing information."

"It's an invasion of privacy!"

"It's no different from this file you had Babs come up with. The plan is already underway. Suck it up, and get on board!" She picked up a biro from the table and stood upright.

"And what would he be getting for his services, our new little brother?" Gori asked. "Since you seem to be rocking his cradle already."

Tomiwa knew how much Gori hated getting caught in the middle of fights between his older siblings, but he was glad Gori was not exactly on Feyintola's side on the issue at hand. The guy she'd hired might share their father's name and bloodline, but he was practically unknown to any of them. He was a dangerous person to employ as an ally.

"He'll get written into Dad's heritage. Since none of the old man's letters had the roadmap to his last will."

"For good reason." Gori sniggered, cutting her off. "I'll bet the old man knew what he was doing."

Feyintola shrugged. "He's our brother, there's no denying that."

"You don't even know him!" Gori exploded.

"We can't even trust him," Tomiwa added.

"Gosh, will the two of you lighten up already? He doesn't want any of our money. What's the big deal?"

"So, what does he want?" Tomiwa turned suspicious eyes in the boy's direction. "What do you want?"

Sesan smiled. "Let's see—fun, adventure, a chance to get back at the guy who cheated me out of the Longman award last year." He ticked the list off his fingers one after the other and shrugged.

"The CEO of One Tech got the Longman award." Feyintola tapped Tomiwa on the forearm. "You're growing old. You didn't even know this."

He scowled. "I don't do competitions. They're childish."

"Well, if they're bringing new talent to the forefront, maybe they are not all that bad."

"Talent and expertise are two very different things."

"Well, I'm more interested in the talent he's bringing." Feyintola walked round the back of Tomiwa's chair to the boy. "Welcome to the fold." She reached a hand out to him. "There's an interview at One Tech this morning. I wouldn't want you to miss it."

"Ten a.m. tomorrow morning, actually," he said, getting up and smiling at her. "It was shifted."

Dressed in a grey, long-sleeved sweatshirt and deep blue jeans trousers—clothes Tomiwa wouldn't be caught dead in—he looked rough around the edges. Like a guy doing his best not to appear financially stifled.

"Good. Thank you for coming," Feyintola said.

"It was nice meeting you. You're every bit as fearless as I was told. Beautiful, too."

"And you're quite the charmer!" Feyintola playfully hit his arm, drawing a curious look from Tomiwa. "Stop by my office and sign the papers. We'll make a photocopy of this little document here, so you can catch up with your new employers. It has everything we were able to dig up on them."

"I don't need it. I already know everything I need to know about One Tech."

"You do?" Feyintola turned to Tomiwa and raised an appreciative eyebrow. "A proactive one, isn't he? If only our execs at PC could be a little more intuitive."

Tomiwa returned the look with a murderous one.

"Sesan, let's go to my office." She flickered her fingers at him and Gori. "See you later, sweethearts!"

Chapter Five

THE PURPLE CHIP RECRUITMENT Oral Interviews began at ten on the dot the very next day. Tomiwa sat with a panel of people in a large air-conditioned room, sifting through a pile of resumes at a table filled with tea, coffee, sandwiches, and sweets.

As he reached for and unwrapped a butter scotch, he thought about the girl in the elevator.

The sweet chocolate éclair.

He hadn't thought about her all day till he picked up the sweet from the saucer on the table. He was still reeling from the surprise of his father's betrayal, brooding about the identity of the brother they had just discovered.

Feyintola had given him the paternity test results the evening before. He'd gawked at it for hours, poring over every little detail. Since their dad was gone, Feyintola had used the half-siblingship test. The closest living male relative was usually the match for such tests, and the results had shown a ninety-eight-point-four percent probability of them having the same father.

He'd called his mother and spent the rest of the evening consoling her. To say she'd been shocked was an understatement.

In reality, he ought to have been upset with Feyin for taking a sample from him without his consent, but their father's deception had overridden all his anger. There had been no indication whatsoever that the man had fathered another child elsewhere.

No warning. No clue. The man hadn't even said it on his death bed.

Tossing the sweet into his mouth, he flipped through the CV in his hands and did a quick rundown in his mind of the candidate seated across from them. The last thing he wanted to think about was how disappointed he was in his father.

'First class graduate, several certifications, previous work experience...' He tossed the file on the table and sat back to watch the applicant rattle on and on about what he could do for Purple Chip.

Tomiwa didn't like him.

"Where are your references for your school IT stint at N–corner?"

"Ref...references..." The young man blinked.

Tomiwa stared him down. "You do know what they are, don't you?"

He wasn't typically the bully in the room, but anger had taken hold of his mind since he'd met his youngest sibling. He knew exactly where the irritation was coming from. He had no time for liars.

He leaned back in his chair as his eyes followed the codes the next applicant was busy spewing onto their whiteboard. The guy had managed to make him forget the troubles in his heart by being near perfect.

He had a brilliant CV, spoke eloquently, had no hidden surprises in his background check, and had scored a ninety-three in the previous test. Tomiwa was relieved to find at least one candidate Feyintola couldn't fault.

LIKE WHIRLWIND 41

The only other person who had scored a ninety-three was female, and they hadn't interviewed her yet. He had a little bias about hiring females. They came with all sorts of drama. Drama he would rather not have on his team.

A female employee with a single relationship status would soon become married, then distracted, and then prone to taking up a lot of family-related—paid, by the way—leaves of absence. He already had two. One on maternity leave, the other planning a wedding. He wasn't too keen on taking on another female, but this was the twenty-first century. The era of gender equality and rage against discrimination in the workplace. If he wanted to peer globally with world-class tech firms, he needed to have good male-to-female representation in his company, and a ninety-three on his test was a strong indication of an employable female.

At least, he wouldn't feel too bad about employing her if she turned out to be as good in person as she seemed to be on paper.

Goodness, your bias kicking up a storm again,. But it was true—he didn't want an employee who got in simply based on gender. It was immaterial to him as long as the employee could code, but no one could know that.

Not especially Feyin, the champion of 'all things feminist.'

The model applicant turned around with a self-assured smile. Tomiwa struggled not to smile back. The codes were clean and well-structured.

"You sure about this?"

The candidate nodded emphatically. "Yes, sir."

"I think I like them. Specifically, your thought pattern. Thorough from end to end."

"Thank you, sir."

"Do you think you're brilliant?"

The question came from the other end of the table. From Feyintola.

Tomiwa drew in a deep breath at the interruption and slowly let it out. *There we go again. Sink my model applicant before I hire him.*

His sister loved using the question to rattle candidates. To see how they did when thrown suddenly off the deep end on the client site with no backup. It would be interesting to see how this one answered.

He looked up at the applicant. "Go ahead. Do you?"

The guy faltered a bit before turning to her. "Ma?" He sounded quite confused by the question. Most of them usually were.

"Do you think you're brilliant?" Feyintola repeated, and Tomiwa could tell without looking at her that she was making her scary CEO face.

The thought made him smile. A lot had changed with the revelation of his father's hidden son, but it was nice to see some things hadn't.

"If you think you are, can you prove it?" she continued.

"Brilliant?" The applicant pursed his lips for a few seconds. "Err...well, I believe the answer to that question is subjective, because brilliance is tied to excellence, and everyone excels differently at different things. I excel at writing codes. It's where my passion lies, where my energy is at its peak, and where brilliance can be seen by anyone and identified as worth mentioning. We can't put a tag on who's brilliant—we can only measure it by how much contribution they bring to the world and what changes they can effect."

They all stared at him, Tomiwa more than mildly impressed. It wasn't the greatest answer, but he had given the best answer they had heard in a long, long while. Most applicants were usually not sure what to do with the question.

"I think we are all done here." Babs looked around. "Miss Feyintola? Mr. Tom?"

The applicant looked from face to face on the panel, seeking a sign of how well he had done. Tomiwa kept his face neutral. It was their usual policy not to let it slip.

"In that case, thank you for your time, James," Babs said. "We will discuss amongst ourselves about your performance here today and get back in touch with you."

"Thank you, sir." He picked up his bag and exited the room.

MIDE PERUSED THE EMPTY corridor. Everyone she had been seated with had been called in. Her initial nervousness had faded into tiredness after more than two and a half hours of waiting and watching people go in enthusiastic and come out looking either disconcerted or angry.

It didn't faze her. She was sure her outcome would be a good one. Grabbing her ringing phone, she flipped it open. Niyi, her cousin.

"Are you done?" He sounded a little worried.

"Not yet. I'm up next, though."

"Look, in case they don't hire you—"

"They are going to love me!"

"Whichever way, you have a job back here with me, remember that."

She smiled. Niyi would never get over worrying about her.

"Just relax. Talk about your journey into the coding world and enjoy yourself. I know you know how to do that."

"Got it, cousin dearest. I'll call you once the interview is done. How were things at your end?"

"Done, he's hired."

"Really?" The inflection in her tone showed surprise. "Just like that?"

"Yes. His name is Sesan. He's good. I think I would know."

"Okay, then. I can't wait to meet him."

"Good luck. I wish you the very best."

"Thanks, cuz." She looked up as she heard her name being called.

THE INTERVIEWS THAT had started off as exciting had slowed to a drag. Most of the people on the panel were itching to get up and leave for lunch, but there was one final applicant they had to see.

Tomiwa himself was glad. He'd settled in on three applicants and only wanted to get through the last candidate for the simple fact they had shortlisted her. He hoped they could wrap it up quickly and be done.

When she walked in through the door, his heart dropped into the middle of his stomach.

LIKE WHIRLWIND

It was the girl from the elevator! The sweet lollipop.

His eyes fluttered, his stomach contracted, and he forgot all about James the model applicant.

In a stylish black skirt suit and red innerwear, she strolled in like she was there to meet with friends and not interview for a job. Her smile had the kind of energy that lifted the general mood in the room by about a mile high, and her braids were wrapped in the same elegant bun she had on the previous day.

He found himself frowning. *Black Suit? Big no!*

She looked almost different. Like she was trying to look formal but it hadn't quite taken. Someone had forgotten to inform her one didn't put a girl like her in a black skirt suit or any formal attire.

She was meant to be in a dress, hair unbound, and feet liberated. Not strapped up in a tailored suit, wobbling about on six-inch weapons of accidents.

He imagined her draped in nothing but gold satin bed sheets with her braids all tussled up, or lying face-down in a bare-backed, sheer-black negligée, or lying sideways wearing his T-shirt and smiling drowsily up at him after having just had a good tumble in bed—preferably with him...

Tomiwa! He cautioned, alarmed. *Control your wandering thoughts!*

Having such inappropriate and sexist feelings in the middle of an interview session had never happened to him before. The idea startled him.

Lowering his eyes to her application letter and resume, he warned himself, looking up only when he was sure he had complete mastery of his thoughts and emotions.

Ademide Aramide Akinseye, he said silently to put a name to the face. *Who are you to do this to me?*

"Good afternoon!" she practically sang as she took the chair across from them.

"Afternoon," Feyintola clipped, in part to bring her down a peg or two. Quite possibly because she was just as hungry as the rest of the members of the panel. "You're our final interviewee."

It didn't work. Ademide was in the chair across from them without the slightest clue how to keep the sunny smile off her pretty face.

Good God! Has anyone ever made you angry? He reached up to flatten his tie against his shirt and sit back to watch her. It was all he found he wanted to do.

"Can you tell us your name?" Feyintola began.

"Yes. I'm Ademide Akinseye. Mide, for short."

There it was, the husky, breathless tone from the elevator that tore his insides to shreds. How could a girl's introduction of herself sound so sexy?

He swung his chair a little to the left and caught Babs' and Ugo's expressions. They were both making no effort to hide their appreciation of the girl. Somehow, it annoyed him.

When he swung it back, she was looking at him, the smile faltering on her lips. He kept his expression as still as possible and stared right back, masking his thoughts. She widened hers for a fraction of a second, cleared her throat, and flipped her gaze back to the other members of the interview panel. She had recognized him. He would have missed it had he blinked.

She seemed focused on Feyintola. He was sure it was going to take her a while to gather the courage to look at him again.

He didn't know to be disappointed or relieved.

Chapter Six

"TELL US A LITTLE BIT about yourself." Feyintola eyed the girl above her thick, round, black-rimmed spectacles.

"I'm a first-class graduate of the University of Ibadan," she began, the smile coming back in full force. "Electrical Engineering, actually. I veered off into Computer Engineering, then web design, and ended up in coding and software design." Her head lulled left to right as she mentioned each one.

"Your resume looks thin. You've got very little work experience—"

"Oh, yes, I know that!" Ademide stopped Feyintola midsentence. "But I've had time to master developing applications. I think I can pull my weight here. So long as you grant me the opportunity..."

Tomiwa closed his eyes. Mistake number one: never interrupt the dragon lady when she's making a point!

The girl continued her talk, unaware of Feyintola's displeasure. She sounded quite happy to tout her prowess.

"I graduated two years ago and had my youth service with the state government, says so right there on the CV." She stabbed a finger at the CV in Feyintola's hands.

He groaned again as his sister glared at the girl over the top of her glasses without a word. Uh-oh, mistake number two: never, ever, gesticulate at the dragon lady!

"Everything I worked on while there is listed according to the timeline. That's practically most of my work experience. Two years pro bono working on various projects and loving the thrill of learning coding languages. I've explored as much as I can lay my hands on, and it's kept me satiated but hasn't paid the bills. That's why I needed this job—need *a* job." She darted her eyes sideways. "Another job. One that pays. One that grants—sustenance."

She slowed to a stop, took in a deep breath, and released it quietly.

"You were working without supervision," Feyintola said, not looking in the least bit impressed.

"My colleagues and I were tasked with churning out applications that did what they were supposed to do. And we did, to an impressive fault."

She was very expressive with her hands. Couldn't seem to keep them still as she spoke. He kept his eyes on them. They were soft-looking hands with slim, long fingers and manicured nails. Hands he'd like to hold. Stroke. Kiss maybe. Someday...

He raised his eyes to hers. She still wasn't looking at him but at Feyintola.

"—so in a way, we were supervised."

"Not by a senior colleague!" Feyintola quipped.

"Our work can speak of our competence."

"I don't see your work here."

"Ma, if you would just—"

"You have a lot of IT stints here and there." Babs rescued her from the badgering before it had even begun. "Mostly undergraduate but supervised by someone very well-versed in software design?"

"I do." Ademide sat up, back straight, and turned to Babs. "We were mandated to do so, in years three and four, most of year five in my undergraduate studies. I guess that counts as part of work experience." She frowned in confusion and looked towards Feyintola for clarification.

"No, it doesn't," Feyintola snapped, and Ademide physically drew back.

Tomiwa turned to his sister. This was more than hunger.

"You weren't being paid, and you weren't being scrutinized as an employee. Work is more than just about knowing how to code and build functional applications. There is an appraisal on the initiative, actual productivity, moral values, interpersonal relationship skills, personal contribution to the company, so much more that employees are appraised on that skip the evaluation an IT student goes through."

"I suppose." Ademide nodded meekly.

He frowned. This wasn't right. They accepted IT stints as work experience all the time, and it wasn't an issue. What was Feyintola's beef with the girl?

"You're fresh off the boat. Not exactly primed for a place like PC. I'm wondering why we should hire you." Feyintola threw the papers in her hands down and peered at her.

"Because I—"

"What attracted you to Purple Chip Professional Services?" he asked, forcing the girl to abandon whatever plans she had of not looking at him.

She did, and their eyes met again, trading silent accusations. *You didn't tell me you were on the interview panel!*

Tomiwa wanted to drown right there and then, staring at her. *I couldn't have told you I was on the panel. What is your phone number? Where do you live? Are you doing anything after this interview? Do you have a boyfriend? You better not have a boyfriend!*

He was hoping she would tell them all what she'd told him in the elevator and more, so Feyintola would be appeased and stop the unnecessary witch-hunt.

"Well," she began. "Purple Chip is one of the leading tech companies in Lagos right now. You are innovative, competitive, and pushing the boundaries of what we know is possible in an ever-changing tech business environment. I would hesitate to ignore a call to service with you because…"

With me?

From that point on, he didn't hear a single word of what she said afterward. He was lost in the wonder of her gorgeous head of curled-up brown braids, expressive eyes, delicious-looking lips, and continuously pleasant disposition. Ninety-three on paper and a beauty in person, the combination was rare to non-existent. At least not in the years he'd spent recruiting staff.

His heart soared a mile a minute just watching her slim hands and long fingers gesticulate, and the force of his heartbeat was like a pounding rhythm he was glad no one in the room could hear.

Babs fired her with a question, and Ugo took his chance, as well, but she tackled them both with a calm kind of confidence proving surprising for a girl he had considered a lollipop. That narrative was changing.

"Do you think you're brilliant?"

He tossed a wary glance at Feyintola. *Not this idiotic question again!*

"Why, yes, of course I think I am," Ademide replied.

His eyes swung back in her direction. *You think you are?* No one had been this direct.

"I possess an amazing plethora of qualities and abilities that I believe will be quite useful to your organization. I love challenges. I expect the best from myself at all times, and I don't believe in giving up when things become difficult."

He couldn't deny he was startled by her. She was entirely too self-confident. James, the previous applicant, had been modest about his opinions of himself. Here she was, declaring herself to be brilliant without hesitation. Proving it with words he couldn't fault.

"The thing about brilliance is that it's not fixed. Anyone can be brilliant if they give themselves the chance to be. Most people give up on things prematurely, and that's where the problem is. When we step out of our comfort zones and tackle things we think are beyond our abilities, we amaze ourselves with the beauty of what we can actually accomplish. The ability to logically think through a problem and solve it or create something that never existed before, that's brilliance. If anything could be called that. I think I am brilliant."

Sitting across the table from her, he found himself abandoning any ideas of pursuing her. She would shut him down in an instant with words that would tear at his self-confidence and bruise his ego. And she'd probably be laughing with him while doing it.

"Tomiwa," Feyintola called his attention. "Your question?"

Question? He couldn't think of any.

Ademide was looking at him again, and her smile was dipping. He knew why.

Feyintola had called his name out loud, and she had realised exactly who he was. He could bet she was regretting having blabbed a little too much on the elevator. What had she been blabbing about again? Oh, yes, about the few ways in which she could jazz up his codes once she got one foot in through Purple Chip's doors. If there was any way in which she could do so, he was interested in finding out.

He didn't ask any question, though; he just handed her the blue felt tip pen and pointed at the whiteboard.

"Solve that, please."

He'd managed to sound way cooler and calmer and more collected than he was, but her eyes were tearing him to shreds for the deception. In hindsight, he could have just mentioned who he was in the elevator.

She glanced at the board, took the pen from him, and reached into her bag for a pair of red spectacles. Jamming them onto her face, she stared again at the board, her smile swapped by a sudden look of seriousness.

He almost keeled over. The idea of spectacles on her was erotic. The lenses magnified the size of her eyes, multiplying his perception of her intelligent look a thousand times over. Its red colour complemented her skin tone, bringing a brightness to her face that charmed him.

In that moment, he couldn't tell what he wanted—for her to work in his company, or for her to be his sweet treat.

Both feelings were meshed into one. The mix of girlish-youthfulness and lady-like maturity made him glance down at her CV again.

Twenty-seven! Twenty-seven put a whole decade between them.

A decade was nothing by today's standards.

When she started to write, he was relieved to switch his focus to her codes. She wrote furiously as if the thoughts were forming faster in her brain than she could write them down. He saw himself once again looking at a replica of James' brilliant codes. Only this time, they were just a little better arranged and very carefully worded.

The handwriting, even, was like a typewriter spewing alphabets on the board.

His gaze wandered off the codes to her face. It was partly turned to him, lips slightly parted, hand racing to finish. She was swift. It was rare.

Mr. Pariola, the finance director, elbowed him and handed him Feyintola's copy of her resume. He sat in interview meetings primarily to ask what the applicant thought he or she would like to earn, so Tomiwa couldn't figure what he was concerned about.

He glanced at him, and then frowned at Feyintola. 'What?' he mouthed.

She pointed angrily at the resume.

His eyes dropped to the well-crafted CV in confusion. Mr. Pariola's finger guided him to a spot at the bottom of the document where Feyintola had written One Tech in bold letters and circled it. Tomiwa stared at the words and looked up at the girl. She had finished.

"Yeah," she said, turning her smile over to him. "I think that's how I would do it."

She stood, hands linked in front of her thighs as his eyes pulled hers into a staring contest. She fidgeted a little, waiting for his approval.

"I have a question," he said, hating the words as they came out of his mouth. He already knew a version, at least, of what the answer would be. "What's your relationship to One Tech?"

"One Tech? Oh, the owner is my cousin."

"Your cousin?"

"Yes. I didn't let on because I didn't think it mattered."

His heart plummeted.

Oh, you sweet, silly girl. But it does!

Chapter Seven

THREE YEARS OF LONGING after a job in Purple Chip, and you blow it the first chance you get.

Mide stood by the fridge freezer in her night coat and favourite thick, blue, knee-length socks, searching for a tub of ice-cream. She was sure she had seen her cousin's wife, Derin, stack it in the freezer compartment earlier in the evening. The girls, her nieces, were fast asleep. It was okay to bring it out and binge without the fear of having to share.

Yeah, she was selfish this way. Derin had bought it to cheer her up, but she didn't feel much like partying. She didn't feel much like sharing, either.

In truth, she wasn't sure anything could make up for the loss.

The front door opened, and Niyi walked in.

Mide glanced at the clock. Eleven-thirty p.m., and he didn't look remorseful.

"Derin is mad," she said to him.

"I'd be worried if she wasn't," he replied, closing the door and locking it up for the night. "Did she leave any food for me?"

She smirked. "What do you think?"

Niyi gave a rueful smile. "I don't know what I did to deserve that woman."

"I don't know, either. She's mad at you, yet she cooks up a storm. I doubt I would be that forgiving."

"If there's food, why are you hustling around in the freezer?"

"Don't feel much like eating." She gave him a miserable smile as she found and dragged the white tub out of the freezer.

"*Haba*, don't let them darken your sun." He dropped his laptop bag and keys on the dining table. "It was just one interview. Plenty more where that came from."

She wrinkled her nose and shrugged as she scooped a large chunk of the cold confectionary and dumped it into a ceramic bowl. "Want some?"

"Needing participants for your pity party?"

"The more, the merrier." She dragged another bowl off the rack in the middle of the dining table, then proceeded to scoop a thick chunk of ice cream into it.

"What's the flavour?"

"Strawberry and cookie dough. Derin bought it to cheer me up."

"Despite my strict instructions for her not to."

"I am going to eat this ice cream, cold or no cold, until I feel better about myself. I've got my lucky socks on. I shouldn't catch a cold."

"*Pele.* You'll find another job, don't sweat it. And like I said, I'd love to have you at One Tech so you don't have to worry about pounding the street pavements, knocking on closed doors."

"I was an idiot. A fool. Going on and on, as usual, chattering without a full stop!" She put the tub back in the freezer and slammed its door shut.

"Stop beating yourself up." Niyi found himself a seat on one of the dining chairs and turned to her. "Tell me what happened."

She sank into a chair beside him.

"There was this guy in the elevator when I got there yesterday. I was late and moaning about how I wanted to come into Purple Chip and fix Tomiwa Oyinlolu's codes. Only for me to get into the interview session today and find out he is on the panel."

"Who?"

"The guy from the elevator," she said with her mouthful.

Niyi nodded. "That's been known to happen to people."

"That wasn't the worst part. Turns out he *is* Tomiwa Oyinlolu. The owner of Purple Chip. Probably the best software engineer in the whole country, no offense to you, and the very guy I was running my mouth off to."

Niyi chuckled.

"And he just stood there in that elevator saying absolutely nothing while I yarned up and down about my simple life. I mean, why would he want to hire me if he thinks I want to come in and fix his codes? Like his syntaxes are not good enough. Like he hasn't developed an app that competes in the market with international brands! What do I know? I mean, the guy is the god of programming in Lagos, why would I think his codes need fixing? And even if I did think it, why would I open up my big mouth and say it to his face?"

"Is that why you think they didn't hire you?" Niyi asked with a narrowed brow as he licked melted cream off his spoon.

"He recognized me the moment I walked into that interview session."

"Are you sure he did?"

"He did. His face just took this zero-shape, like who do you think you are coming in here and telling me you'd like to come in and fix my codes." She groaned. "I was so embarrassed, I practically melted into the chair."

"I'm sure you did great. There was just someone else there who did a little better." He spooned a mound into his mouth. "You did say they had only one spot to fill."

"That's what I thought. Apparently, it was three, and there were like a hundred other applicants."

"But you got down to the final ten. For a Purple Chip job interview, that was great."

"I've wanted this job since like—"

"Forever, I know." He laughed out loud. "You've been dreaming about working in PC for a long time and rubbing it in my face. How come you didn't recognize him in person when you saw him?"

Mide frowned as the thought occurred to her. "You know, now that I think about it, his pictures are rare to nonexistent."

"You sure? I've seen him."

"I follow their company website and scour the net for news about them, but it seems his sister is the face of the company. I recognized her the moment I walked through the door. She's all over the place. He, not so much."

"You might have seen him before. In an article by some tech soft sell titled 'The Purple Chip off the block.' That was like three or four years ago."

"Did I have time to read back then? I was fighting for my life with UI lecturers. It just didn't occur to me it was him. I was so stressed out about the practical part of the interview, I wasn't even really looking at him in the elevator."

"Come and work for One Tech," Niyi drawled.

"I want to spread my wings," she moaned.

"Spread your wings with me. Not saying you can't source any other job if you want to, but just get some more experience on your resume."

"I'll think about it."

"How was Feyintola?"

She sighed, and her shoulders sank. "Really mean and all out for me. The other guys on the panel were okay, but now I get why all those other applicants came out of the room looking like someone ran them through a washing machine. She probably just battered them in there."

"I hope they didn't figure out your association with One Tech?"

She turned down the corners of her mouth and turned to look at him. "Why do you ask?"

"Just curious."

"They asked. I told them you're my cousin. No point in hiding the fact of it."

Niyi dropped his spoon into his half-empty bowl. "They asked?"

"Yeah."

"And you told them who I was to you?"

"Why not? I'm proud of you any day, any time. Because I want to work for them doesn't negate the fact that you are a great programmer."

"Oh!" He kissed his teeth. "Now I know why they didn't hire you."

She furrowed her brow. "Why?"

"It has nothing to do with you threatening to fix Tomiwa Oyinlolu's codes, that's for sure."

"Really, so why?"

"I did tell you I'm bidding for a big contract in Abuja?"

She nodded.

"Yeah, well, it turns out they are bidding for the same contract. Sources tell me it's keenly contested between me and them."

"No way!" Her eyes widened. "Are you serious? You should have told me."

"I didn't want you to give up before you even tried."

"I wouldn't have given up," she declared. "I'd have known how to answer their questions. I'd have been on the alert that they would ask."

"I just thought you would think it would hurt your chances. I didn't want to give you that impression."

She wrinkled her nose. "Their loss."

"Yes, their loss. What are you going to do now?"

She stared at the table for a few seconds, then allowed a slow smile to widen her lips. "Now that I know you're their competition, I'm coming to work for you."

"Finally! I've been begging you to."

"And I'm going to help you figure out how you are going to win that contract."

Niyi sat back in his chair and yawned, wiping his face with his hands. "Like I haven't figured that out for myself."

"I know you have, but I'll help. They're a biased company. How could they not hire me because I'm related to you?"

"Well, they could be concerned about you giving me their company intel."

"Yeah, whatever!" she said with a disappointed hiss that quickly morphed into a frustrated moan. "But I wanted to work for Purple Chip…"

"You're going to be fine."

"I know. In the meantime, I got this one-off part-time job…"

Niyi's face hardened. "Pamela?"

"It's safe. It's ushering at Kola Bamigbe's fortieth birthday dinner. There will be lots of billionaires and company CEOs in attendance."

"Married men with money in their pockets and shady motives on their minds. Why am I uncomfortable?"

"Relax!" she said, rolling her eyes. "It's a thirty-K gig that gets me in the room with potential job providers."

"More like potential Sugar Daddies."

"Niyi!"

"*Na wa o*, Mide, am I not taking good care of you? Do you not have a roof over your head and clothes on your back? Why do you feel you need to take a part-time job? That particular one, for that matter?"

She chuckled. "I'm not doing it so much for the money. Pamela needs twenty ushers. She has only seventeen, and I'm free. Besides, I didn't get the PC job, and I need to take my mind off it."

"Mide, you're an adult. I know I'm not going to talk you out of this, but please, don't do any drinking, don't do any smoking, don't go home with any strange billionaires or job providers, and don't leave the place in a taxi. I'll come and pick you up when the gig ends. Ten, did you say?"

She roared with laughter. "I promise you. I will not do any drinking, I will behave responsibly, and I will call you when I'm done. But I did not say ten."

Niyi exhaled heavily as he stared at her. She could see worried thoughts crowding the back of his eyes like ants. He was her mother's older sister's son, and he had been responsible for her in the ten years she'd been resident in Lagos. He was more of a father figure than a big brother.

"I don't want you to become some rich guy's side chick," he said.

"I won't," she promised.

Goodness, his twins will have hoops to jump through.

Chapter Eight

"WHY AM I JUST SEEING this?" Goriola asked, browsing through the files Tomiwa had just sent to his phone.

They were on their way to some big-boy bash and had been trailing a row of expensive cars into the huge, banana-shaped island estate for over thirty minutes.

"I see Tinuade at the tower much more than I see you, and she doesn't even work there," he replied, eyes scanning his foldable Galaxy Z Note.

"She's your future sister-in-law. *Shey* you know."

"Aren't we getting a little ahead of ourselves?" Tomiwa lifted his arm and glanced at his watch before peering through the window at the night sky and the parade ahead of them.

"What's that supposed to mean?"

"She's number three this year, and we still have four months to go." He turned to his brother and held out his phone and its S pen. "I wouldn't hold my breath."

Gori's well-crafted arrogant expression crumbled into hilarity. He threw his head back and let out a howl of laughter. "You don't think I'm—"

"Sign this, please!" he urged.

"You're one to talk. What with that peek-a-boo you're playing with your tech secretary?" Gori grabbed the metal pen and scribbled his signature on the pad. "I hope the young lady knows there is no future there."

"Chioma is well aware of her duties. I just hope Tinuade won't regret having that ring on her finger." Tomiwa took his phone and pen back.

"And I hope you won't break that girl's heart. It's bad enough you're using her to fence off girls. Worse, that you're keeping her from potential hook-ups."

"And who tells you she wants a hook-up?"

"Stop burning her candle! Must I spell it out in English?"

"At least I'm being honest. Have you completely closed the door to all the other girls? Is Tinu the proud and only owner of your heart?"

"This time, she's the real deal. I'm sure of it."

"Right. So have been the last five or six women." He put his phone away. "Besides, what's this forest all over your jaw? You look like a terrorist. When last did you have a proper shave?"

"This—" Gori pointed both index fingers at his chin, "—is called grooming and style. The ladies love it. You should try it sometime."

"No, thank you. I haven't had anyone complain about it yet."

"You haven't had anyone, period. When last did you have fun?"

"Let's hope Tinuade doesn't return your ring when she sees you with that wild scrubland around your chin."

"What is this unholy fixation you have with my love life? Go get yours."

"I just don't want you to ruin things with her. She's a lovely girl."

"*Joko sibe!*" Gori waved him away. "The gift I brought back for her is a sculpted, rock-hard body plus stamina the strength of a Mexican bull. Spartans don't rate where I stand. Tinu knows."

Tomiwa sniggered. "Gorillas don't, either."

"Ape!" Goriola reached out to give his shoulder a light punch. "I'll let you know what happens after dinner tonight. At least, I'm getting some. Pretty sure you aren't."

Tomiwa snapped his mouth shut. He hadn't gotten any since his three-year stint with Hauwa ended two years previously. The girl had wanted nothing but an Automated Teller Machine to fund her lavish lifestyle. She'd moved on when bigger hooks dangled low enough. The experience had left a bitter taste in his mouth as regards to relationships.

"Be careful with Chioma. Feyintola will kill you if you touch her," Goriola leaned over to whisper.

It made Tomiwa smile. "Goat!"

Despite the ribbing, he adored his brother. Gori's brilliant mind and awesome business skills were hidden behind a laid-back attitude and an affinity for constant jokes. It all contributed to the awesome personality that, in all honesty, he knew ladies liked and Gori had.

And Goriola was well aware of his charm. He was the oil that softened Feyintola's hardness and the cheerful silk cloth that smoothened Tomiwa's cold aloofness. Their father's genes had churned them all out differently, but the diversity was what held the company together.

"Ade's back, right? I miss the guy."

"He should be at this party. His trip to London was a brief one."

"Thank God! I haven't seen him in ages. I'd hate to be stuck on the table with boring old you."

Tomiwa passed him a side-eye, but Goriola was busy peering out of his side of the window as the car slowed to a stop inside the compound.

"See money!" he yelled. "See moneeeyyyy! Kola Bamigbe is forty, world go hear am."

"Maybe I shouldn't have used my boring old car to pick you up, then."

"Hey, Tom, you're boring, most definitely, but your *Velar,* not so much. It's the most interesting thing about you." Goriola was already stepping out of the car upon sighting their friends. "*Hey, K-pee! K-papa! I dey come, I dey come.*"

Tomiwa took in a deep breath and swallowed his unease. He hated parties and noise and flamboyance of any kind. The only thing making this one worth his time was Ade being there. He could spend the evening forgetting about his dad and the little brother who had been added to the family. Goriola seemed to have gotten over it much faster than he had, and Feyintola was chummy with the boy.

As he watched Gori laughing in a circle of his friends, he couldn't help but think he was the only one being too emotional about the matter. His dad was gone and buried. His mother was dealing well with the news. His siblings had moved on.

So, what was his problem?

"John, find a good place to park and keep your phone close. I'll call you fifteen minutes before I head out."

"Yes, sir," the driver said.

Tomiwa stepped out of the car into an atmosphere of glitz and over-blown glamour. Bamigbe had spared no expense.

He sourced his brother amongst the well-dressed crowd trouping into the garden-themed tent party over a long red carpet. Once inside, he found him by a large Grecian ice statue, standing with their host, Kola Bamigbe, a real estate businessman and oil block tycoon dressed in a smart, navy blue, plain and fitted *buba and sokoto* kaftan.

Bamigbe came from old money. Affluence his ancestors had built trading gemstones when the white men first landed on the shores of Lagos. His fortieth birthday party had been the talk of town all week, but Tomiwa felt ill-at-ease attending. Goriola was more the man's friend than he was, but Gori had insisted Kola wanted him there.

He had met Kola on one or two occasions, and they had compared notes on the Nigerian business environment, trading stocks, and nothing more. He had nothing in common with the billionaire. Plus, there would be cameras and champagne and temptations of all kinds guaranteed to veer him off his code of conduct.

But he hadn't wanted to make an enemy out of such a powerful contact. There was no telling where the association would come in useful.

He figured Ade and Goriola's sanguine exuberance would make bearing the party easier, but he'd asked Chioma to link up with Tinuade and meet them there. This was another point of connection. Tinuade was Bamigbe's wife's distant cousin, and Chioma would hang on his arm to keep the sweet treats away. With the revelation of his father's secret

LIKE WHIRLWIND

life, he was more determined than ever to walk the straight path. Pretty girls usually flocked like a herd at outings such as these, and potential wives were harder to find in that pile of rocks when one was considered a big boy.

He wasn't looking for either.

He put his melancholic thoughts away and threw a hand out with a wide grin as he stepped into the persona he used when attending social events.

"Bamigbe!"

"THIS DRESS HAS NO BACK!" Mide whispered as she peered through the hole in the fabric at her friend, Pamela. "There is hardly any material here."

"Quit complaining and get dressed. We go live in fifteen minutes."

She gaped at her friend's disappearing back and lowered the outfit, staring around herself at the many girls of various sizes and shapes all squeezing into the pink and black outfit with undisguised enthusiasm. All of them were young in comparison to herself—nineteen, twenty, even twenty-one tops, none of them above a size ten. Pamela had given her the opportunity because in truth, she had been three girls short of twenty good-looking, young girls, and she could pass for a twenty-year-old.

Mide had obliged her. She hadn't thought twice about accepting because her unemployed status meant her personal income was at an all-time low. Short of taking up Niyi's offer, there was nothing much on the horizon.

Though she was used to ushering, the clothes had gotten skimpier with each job, and this was the worst. Backing out was no longer a possibility. She was already in the lion's den, and the gates to the compound were high and locked tight.

Niyi's warning came clear and bright at that moment.

Please, don't become some rich guy's side-chick!

She had no plans to, but in the outfit Pamela had just shoved into her hands, it would take a miracle to walk out of the party un-propositioned.

She had just spent an agonizing hour being made up in the large bedroom they had been offered by the wife of the inviting socialite. The makeup artist had ooohed and ahh-hed over her flawless skin and painted fewer layers of make-up products on her face compared to the others. Not only did she look nothing like herself, she was dressed in a back-less halter-top dress-shorts made of good quality Ankara fabric ending in little better than bum shorts.

Niyi would kill her. If he saw her.

She turned her face reluctantly to the wall and started to undress. Half an hour later, she followed a trail of nine other girls to the swimming pool area, kicking herself in the leg in her mind several times for not having listened to her cousin.

They were expected to circle the pool area with drinks and flat paper plates filled with skewered chicken, beef, samosas, puff-puffs, and other little delicacies for the guests, but Mide felt the stares. With hoop earrings, her braids piled up on her head, and legs elongated by wooden clogs, she felt naked and exposed. Cold air hugged her back and wrapped itself around her long legs, but she strutted on after the girls.

She had her Ventolin inhaler safely in the pocket of her bum shorts. Two puffs every hour, and she would be fine.

TWO-FIFTY PEOPLE CRAMMED inside a palatial-sized, multilevel house meant the party would be rowdy. Tomiwa stood a few feet from a pool half the length of an Olympic-sized one, staring at the crowd of young people dancing and swimming around inside it.

Occasionally, a huge water ball would sail into the air, and the gleeful screams would drown the sound of the soft contemporary Naija beats strumming around him.

The sitting area was jampacked, the garden flowing with guests, and the tent set up to sit party visitors was filled. Gori had disappeared ages ago, and Ade was in the parking area trying to navigate his car around so someone else could move theirs.

He, Tomiwa, was bored to his teeth.

He tipped his empty wine glass and looked around for an usher carrying a tray of cocktails. There were more than twenty of them milling around the party venue, either under the tent, in the pool area, or walking around the house in colourful native outfits and with smiles of invitation. He'd seen Tinuade link her arm firmly in Gori's elbow the moment she'd arrived and seen the scandalous garments. He had smiled inside, glad to be free of any such entanglements. Chioma was nothing more than an employee, even at parties.

There to keep him in check, and them—the girls—at bay.

They had an understanding; she was merely a front. Word around town was that they were dating, but it didn't keep women from thinking they could try their luck. A few of Feyin's friends had come right out and propositioned him. Chioma had stepped in to help solidify his status as taken. And he was fine with it.

He grabbed an apple sherry from the tray held by a smiling young girl in pink Ankara shorts and turned away. He had his eye on the client with Chioma and his ears on his earphone plug, waiting for Shile's call.

Chioma was working with one of their clients who was also at the party. She was taking notes on his appraisal of their app and booking a clarification demonstration meeting. Well-dressed in a pale lilac sundress, she was fit for a poolside party but reserved enough to keep inebriated men sane. He did his bit to keep his eye on her and his arm around her whenever necessary, but Chioma was an absolute force on her own. Strong in her ability to defend herself.

There had been a time when a client had tried to clutch her backside during a cocktail party. Tomiwa had been prepared to walk over to the rescue, but Chioma had lifted a foot and jammed the pointy heel of her navy-blue stiletto on the client's foot. Then, she'd apologized profusely for the mistake without taking her shoe off his foot. The client had been in too much pain to be angry, but whatever ideas he'd had earlier on had been erased afterwards.

The memory made him smile. Chioma knew how to shut men down whenever they stepped out of line without needing him. She was a whiz at it, too.

He was about to take a sip of his wine when he saw a familiar figure in the ushering Ankara across the swimming pool. His heart lurched a mile high, then began to pound with unequalled force.

Ademide!

It was her all made up in an outfit fit only for the insides of a bedroom.

She was descending the five-step stair that ran around the pool with steady, carefully calculated steps on wooden, brown heels. His mouth parted reflexively as desire gripped him.

The tray in her right hand was balanced with the precise ease of someone who did it often, but it was her caramel-coloured legs that stole the show. Straight, long, and spotless, their narrow contour towards her knees and up the slope to her hips made his breath cling to the base of his throat as she swung each one down the stairs and descended with poise. It was akin to watching a beauty queen in the swimwear category come down from a platform.

He snapped his mouth shut and furrowed his brow as other thoughts took over. What the heck was she doing ushering at a party full of men and alcoholic drinks?

Chapter Nine

TOMIWA'S CURIOSITY swelled with his anger. Why was Ademide here? Was it because they hadn't given her a job? Was it because she had no money? Was she a runs-girl or a hook-up babe? Why was she here?

The questions burned his brain for answers, but he wouldn't get them unless he approached her and asked.

He swallowed a shaky breath as she turned towards a group of loud men and paused so they could sample the array of drinks on her tray. He got a glimpse of her bare back and the knot at the nape of her neck and froze. She had nothing underneath her outfit! He hadn't even thought to examine the ushering uniform till he saw her.

Frustration swirled within him for a moment. One tug was all it would take. One tug by an inebriated idiot, and it would all come undone. There was definitely no bra underneath that item of clothing!

"Drat!" he seethed quietly between his teeth.

One of the men said something, and she stood there with the tray in both hands, bare shoulders high and lifted, mouth open in laughter. The men laughed right along with her. He couldn't hear it from this distance and with the noise of the music, but he could see it, and he couldn't bear it.

Her laughter in the elevator was one thing about her he'd been unable to forget. The soft and joyful sound had filled him with a need to know her some more after their encounter. Now watching her share this laughter with other men, sharp pangs of jealousy crawled around his insides, seeking release. She had no right to be there with those men, or with the other bimbo-girls in pink halter-neck pinafore shorts serving drinks.

She belonged in an office. With a regular job tasking her brain with syntaxes. Coming up with cutting edge solutions for the next coding phase of the IT world.

Not waiting drinks, flaunting her body, and taunting men!

When the tray was empty, she strode away from the group with strong, confident strides and headed back up the stairs towards the table where the cocktails were set up. Halfway up the stairs, a jovial-looking man in traditional attire stopped her with a finger on the outside of her arm. She listened to him for a moment and then nodded and left. But not before he trailed his finger down her elbow to her hand and tucked in a business card.

Tomiwa tightened his fingers against the stem of his empty glass cup with a soft growl as jealousy seared his insides. *What the heck does he want from her?*

His gaze followed her backside as it swayed gently with each ascent, then travelled up her bare back till she turned and headed towards the concession stand to set her tray down for more glasses. She crossed her arms across her body and rubbed her hands down her bare arms vigorously while she waited for the tray to fill with drinks.

Was it cold? Was she cold?

He wanted to shrug off his jacket and go and wrap it around her. Anything to hide her figure from the throng of married eyes ogling girls at the party. Why on earth had she come there?

It didn't matter there were others. She wasn't like them. Not in any way.

She picked up the tray, and his gaze followed her movement back to the staircase till she began her descent once again. This time, right across from him.

He panicked. *Drat!*

Conflicted whether to dissolve into the crowd or stay and get a drink from her tray, his brain froze up. His legs, too.

Move! Dammit!

He couldn't. His eyes had found comfort in his leisurely admiration of her smooth brown skin and alluring makeup, and his heart was banging like a marching band drum to the crazy thoughts filling his heart at the sight of her descending the stairs.

No, he wasn't going anywhere until he'd talked to her. Until she noticed him.

As her feet hit the last stair, she looked up, and their gazes locked. Her eyes widened in recognition, and she slowed to a stop. He stared back.

Too late to pretend he hadn't seen her; he downed his drink in one gulp, and his brain released his feet enough for him to lunge with easy strides towards her.

She stood still, watching him walk over.

What are you going to say? he mused. *Ask what she's doing there? Apologise for not hiring her? Chastise her for the crazy outfit? Send her home and offer to drive?*

The thoughts were ridiculous. He had no right to send her home or fume about what she was wearing. It was none of his business. She was a grown girl with a right to do whatever she wanted.

Her surprise morphed into a frown, but he was already in front of her and trying to control his erratic heartbeat as his mind scrambled for something to say. She couldn't know he found her madly attractive. She didn't know he was gutted they hadn't hired her.

"I need a drink," he said.

Of all the wonderful things that you could have said, Tomiwa Oyinlolu. You need a drink?

Her gaze met his, and her innocent look melted his insides. *Sweet Chocolate!* She was a joy to behold. A combination of aquiline symmetrical eyes in an oval-shaped face with a small nose and moist, titillating lips. She was the first girl since Hauwa left to muddle his brain.

She recovered from her shock and looked down at the tray. "Uh...there's Margarita, Cosmopolitan, Negroni, Apple Sherry...there are stronger ones down at the bar." She looked up at him. "If you—if you want."

"These are good."

She didn't say a word, and he couldn't help his brief show of disappointment. She'd been so talkative in the elevator and so expressive at the interview, why was she mute? It was a pity he couldn't hire her. Or tell her why.

Dropping his empty glass cup on the tray, he picked up a glass of Apple Sherry and met her gaze once again. "Thanks. See you around."

See you around?

There were a billion things he could have said to her, like, *I'm sorry we didn't hire you* or *Here's my card, call me and I'll find you a job.*

Rather, he'd said he'd see her around. Where? They didn't move within the same social circles. He wasn't hiring again any time soon. How was he hoping to see her again?

"Need me to go over and get you her number?"

Chioma's gentle voice in his ear broke his thoughts and made him search the crowd for the fair-skinned assistant. In that brief moment, he'd masked his expression and replaced it with aloofness.

"Of course not. What did he say?"

"They love the app. It was a good thing you asked Ugo to take over the training when you did. They were about to ditch it for lack of understanding. Babs didn't take enough time to listen to their complaints."

"Good." He resisted the urge to turn around and look at Ademide. "Have you had something to eat?"

"I'm fine, and you? Need me to get you anything else, sir?"

"Not hungry. Have you seen my brother anywhere around?"

"Yes." She showed up in front of him just then and slid her arm into his elbow, turning her face away from his as she did. "He's ehm...inside. With Tinu."

He heard the resignation in her tone. "Making friends?"

"More like entertaining them," she said with a small laugh.

Gori, the life of the party, he thought and put his other hand over hers where it peeked out of his elbow. "It's not going to last," he assured her.

She sniggered. "She's crazy about him."

"I'm not entirely sure it's reciprocal. My brother doesn't hang onto relationships for long, but I'm concerned about you. I'd rather you fell in love with someone else. Someone worth your time and effort. Someone with a bit more prudence."

"Well, the heart wants what it wants."

"Your heart doesn't have to want him. There are other options."

They climbed up the poolside stairs together. From the outside, they looked like a beautiful couple, and everyone who knew him had the impression they were together. At work, however, they were nothing more than boss and employee.

In private, at functions, or in his car, they were friends. He knew she understood he wasn't remotely interested in her or in any girl, for that matter, and he knew the secret she was keeping from everyone.

"I hope I'm not hurting your chances," he said, recalling Goriola's comments to him in the car.

"Of course not, sir. Maybe I'll give up one day. Who knows? Till then, I don't want to think about relationships."

"Fine. Let me know when you meet someone."

"I will, sir. Why don't we go inside?"

"Are you sure you really want to go inside?" He was worried about her finding Gori and Tinu arm in arm, or worse, locked in a passionate kiss.

She smiled up at him. "You don't want to go inside? You want to stay here and watch her, or you want me to go and get her number?"

He was quiet for a moment as he thought about Ademide. What Chioma didn't know was that she wasn't just some plaything he wanted to explore; she was an intelligent programmer he wouldn't mind working with.

"I already have her number," he said. "Let's go inside."

As they stepped into the party proper, Tomiwa laid eyes on his brother. Goriola was with his friends, gesticulating wildly with one hand and holding Tinuade in a circle of his other. He stopped talking and kissed her long and hard to the jeering of friends.

Tomiwa felt Chioma stiffen beside him.

He sighed, let go of her arm and prodded her forward. "Come on."

Chapter Ten

TOMIWA FOUND HIMSELF in Feyintola's wide corner office the following morning, filled with remorse at the thought of Ademide at Bamigbe's party and the despondent way she had looked at him. Like he'd broken her heart.

"So, you're still going to cut this girl," he began tersely as he relaxed in the chair across the table from her.

"Yes! Her family owns One Tech."

"That's ludicrous. What has that got to do with anything?"

Feyintola eyed him. "Everything."

"So what if she's related to the owner of the company we are bidding against. Does it matter?"

"It does."

His sister looked disinterested in the conversation. She studied the papers on her desk and the open laptop in front of her without paying him any attention.

He frowned. He was losing the battle to her, but Ademide's image in the halter neck by the poolside looking deliciously desirable spurred him on.

"Come on, Feyin. We have the resources to take on four programmers. More if we wanted. And Lord knows we need more hands right about now. What's to say she doesn't know enough about what makes her cousin's app so good?"

"It's a definite conflict of interest, Tommy, you know that."

"How's that any different from you sending that boy to go work for One Tech? The girl is a gold mine of admirable qualities. It's not too late to call her back and offer her employment. I see her right now, standing in front of potential clients, pitching *Purple Ledger* to them with confidence. Inspiring trust with her fresh, youthful looks. Making sales."

"Really? I see her pitching her tents with One Tech's *Profit X* and bashing us in the face with it."

Tomiwa recalled her in the middle of the men at the party, and his fist clenched over his armrest. "Not if she works for us."

Feyintola eyed him above the rim of her rather large frames. "You actually assume she's going to tattle on her cousin if she works for us? You think she is going to turn her back on loyalty to her family, open up to us about One Tech's plans, and feed us all the info that will aid us in pulling them down because she works for us? Are you sure you are not thinking with that thing between your legs?"

He took in a deep breath and closed his eyes at the subtle hit at his conscience. In truth, he'd fantasized a bit about kissing her when he'd picked up the drink from her tray. "Why would I hire a girl simply to sleep with her? Prettier girls have walked in here for interviews."

"And now, Gori is dating the girl who would have been my executive assistant." Her eyes were calm behind her frames.

He returned the stare. "If I wanted her in that way, I wouldn't want her here. You didn't even like Tinuade. She wasn't a top contender."

"True, but this particular girl is family to our current enemy and very attractive. I don't know why we are still having this discussion."

"Because she is good," he growled. *And she doesn't deserve to be parading about half-naked at a party full of drunk men.*

Feyintola went back to her laptop and typed a few words in quick succession.

"Feyin—"

"James is equally good and very much better for us," she replied without looking up. "And we've hired him."

"James is an intense and excellent programmer," Tomiwa said, ignoring the fact James had blown him away. "But he will be slow. Ademide is carefree and spirited. It tells me she will be smart enough to find the quickest and most efficient way to get things done. That is a skill most programmers do not have."

"She had time enough to doll up her face and find a pretty dress to wear to the written interview. I don't think she was here for anything serious."

"Come on, she had ninety-three percent on the test! Eighteen points higher than the only other girl who's ever scored high on our tests, and eleven higher than the average for guys. I don't want her because I think she's pretty." He paused and took a deep breath. "I want her because she's brilliant, and I think she could pull her weight here."

"So you think she's pretty," Feyintola replied. "One more reason why we are not hiring her."

"Feyin, good grief, you are something else," he exhaled in one breath. "I can't believe I'm losing this kind of talent to a lesser tech company because you think I'm going to sleep with her."

"That possibility is not next to impossible, Tomiwa." She reached for a folder on the table. "Not because I don't trust you, but because your hormones are clearly on overdrive. They are controlling your emotions and not letting you think."

He narrowed his eyes at her. "What? What am I, twelve?"

"You are single and pushing this a little bit too much."

"I'm not going to date my employee! I've never done it before, and I'm not about to start."

"Chioma—"

"Is not my booty call. Ademide is—"

"Not an option. We cannot hire family to our competitor. It's simply not done."

"She is—"

"We are not hiring her, Tom, so suck it up!"

He shook his head, done trying to reason with her. Unfortunately, an applicant had to have four out of six votes from the interview panel to be hired. Ademide had scored three: he, Ugo, and Babs.

Back in his office, he reviewed Ugo's work and sent corrections to him. He was supposed to tackle the errors they had piled up for him, but he couldn't get the girl out of his thoughts.

He logged onto his Instagram page for the first time in over a year and looked her up. She was a tad difficult to find, so he pulled up three more windows: Facebook, Snapchat, and X. A few more clicks, and he had her pages up and running on his laptop screen.

There you are.

In thirty minutes, he had learned all he wanted to know about her. Especially her relationship status.

"You horrible cyber-stalker!" he muttered to himself as he scrolled through her pictures and read a couple of her posts. She was an avid reader, listed swimming and chess as her hobbies, had a crazy ton of friends, and loved parrots. *Oh, man, you're breathtakingly photogenic...*

If one good thing could come out of not hiring her, it was in how he could proceed to seek her out with no fear of work ever coming in between them.

This cheered him up, to a large extent.

MIDE HELPED NIYI WITH his lunch basket while he juggled his laptop bag and file folders. They were walking down the compound of the office complex where One Tech was located and heading for the main door of the building.

She had tried to shake off her melancholy about losing the Purple Chip slot and was looking forward to starting at One Tech. Her friend, Grace, who was also job hunting, had called to see if Niyi was still hiring. Unfortunately, he wasn't.

"I'm glad you've decided to oblige me."

"Am I starting today?" she asked, convinced he had not fully gotten over his displeasure at her appearance over the weekend.

He'd driven there to pick her up and thrown a fit at the sight of her in the ushering outfit. It had taken Derin a whole day to placate him on her behalf.

Mide hadn't cared. She'd spent the day replaying the moment she'd run into Tomiwa Oyinlolu at the party, wondering if she should have said anything and obsessing at the look she'd seen on his face as he selected a drink from her tray.

Disappointment?

His eyes had lowered to her outfit, and his let-down had been visible. The embarrassment had eaten her up so badly, she hadn't mentioned it to Niyi. She was sure the CEO felt justified in having rejected her. She could as well have been a Korean courtesan, the way he'd looked at her.

"I already know what you can do, so I don't need to waste time interviewing you."

"Isn't that going to be like cheating or something, unfair to the other guys in your company?"

"Trust me, you're as good as most of them. Maybe even better. Except, of course, Sesan."

"Sesan. That's your new hire, right?"

"Yes." Niyi beamed. "He's good. Just two days in, and my developers are all sitting up. A little competition is healthy for business growth, I guess. He could easily replace me if I'm not careful, but I won't tell him that. His java scripting is off the hook, he has crazy-patient debugging skills, and he's learned PHP. Even I haven't learned PHP. He has the kind of flair for learning languages I haven't seen in years, which means he is flexible. He also understands business processes, which means he knows exactly how to create the stuff that solves client problems!"

"Okay," Mide said, trying hard not to be intimidated by the praise. Niyi had never praised her this way. "But you built *Profit X* on a web-based platform with JavaScript. You don't need new language skills. It'll be a colossal waste of time."

"Yes, but his PHP knowledge means he can test the app on the server-side of things better than my guys can. He brought up twenty-seven errors on his first day of work. And fixed them!"

"OK, wow."

"Wow truly is the word."

Mide changed the basket from her right hand to her left. "I was talking about your food basket. What in the world did Derin pack for you?"

"I wonder o. I always tell her not to bother, but that woman can be so stubborn!" They climbed the staircase to the rented three-room office belonging to One Tech. "Every day, I look like a kindergarten boy going to school."

She laughed out loud. "Not at all. Do you know how much a decent plate of food costs nowadays? Seven hundred to a thousand bucks. This is cost-effective, and the meals will have less oil and salt."

"You sound like Derin already," he murmured, opening the door to a shout of, "Good morning, Mr. Akinseye."

"Hi, Kemi."

Kemi was the slim, very efficient office manager Niyi had hired to handle the reception and keep the petty cash book and office running. She was handling a lot, and he tried to pay her as well as he could.

Mide was meeting her for the first time, but felt like she already knew her. Niyi praised her all the time to Derin's dissatisfaction. Every detail about the girl had not escaped his notice.

"*Don't worry,*" she had whispered to Derin. "*Niyi is not dating that girl. If he were crushing on her, he wouldn't talk about her to us.*"

"Kemi, this is Mide. Please prepare her documents. Entry forms, acceptance letters, medical, the works. Then open a file for her. I'll give you everything you need."

"Sure, sir." Kemi stood and smiled at Mide. "Welcome to One Tech."

Mide smiled back. She was happy. Kemi was nothing compared to Derin in looks and height, but she was warm and sweet. Most importantly, she didn't give any vibes to indicate she was interested in her boss beyond her official duties. Derin could rest easy.

"You can give her the basket," Niyi said and paused before they walked into the main office.

"What is it?"

"The boys are going to go gaga and stare at you. Just ignore them. They stare at every female that walks in here like they don't have mothers and sisters at home. I've told them severally it's quite unprofessional, but they can't help it."

She chuckled. "Why do they stare?"

"They complain a lot that the testosterone levels in the office need some oestrogen dousing, and I've been promising them I'll hire a female programmer to balance things out."

She let her mouth drop open. "Oh, so that's why you've been begging me to come work for you. To be your office eye-candy, *eh?*"

"Of course not! I had no intention of hiring any more staff, but Purple Chip forced my hand. You're going to be something of a distraction. Perhaps it will motivate the guys to work harder. If I see them becoming too distracted, I'll camp you in my office. In any case, you know a lot about the application because you helped from the start before you went back to school for your final year. So, who better to hire?"

"Are we going to talk about a salary?"

"Of course."

"How much?"

"It's a one-man company, and you live in my house."

"How much?"

"I definitely can't match Purple Chip's starting quote, but—"

"Niyi!" she drawled. "How much?"

"One ninety—" His brow was furrowed in a hopeful frown, "—five?"

She stared at her cousin. "That is tiny."

It was less than half of Purple Chip's starting salary. True enough she was living in his house and eating his food and knew how tight things were, but she needed to start life at some point.

In truth, working with Niyi would be better than nothing. There would be work experience Feyintola wouldn't fault at Purple Chip's next interview sessions. She would have money to sort online certifications and probably get a place of her own if Niyi would consent. There would be a level of freedom.

The last gig with Pamela had been upsetting enough for her, and Niyi. She'd made up her mind. No more ushering at parties, no more sourcing business cards from potential job providers, and no more part-time jobs. She'd work at One Tech and use the time to figure out her next move. This way, no arrogant guy would look down on her and disdain her abilities.

"I'll take it," she said, and he heaved a sigh of relief. "Thank you for looking out for me."

He nodded. "Come on."

She followed him into the office pool.

Chapter Eleven

TOMIWA STROLLED TO the conference room unsure what his sister had called the meeting for, but whenever she called, he had to go.

Babs and Ugo were already seated. So was his new younger brother, Sesan.

Feyintola gave him a reprimanding stare. "You're late."

He lowered himself into a seat and glanced at the One Tech spy. "Why are we here?"

"Strategy meeting." Feyintola picked up the projector's remote control and switched it on.

He sat back and turned the chair around to observe the display board.

Three reasons why Purple Chip will not survive the next five years. Written by Ademide Akinseye.

He chuckled.

"You find this funny?" Feyintola clipped.

"I do. Why should it interest me?"

"Because it's followed up by an X thread bashing our interview process."

'Purple Chip's off-the-shelf, customizable investment app hit the market to nationwide acclaim and rave reviews. It won awards for its ingenuity and bravery at a time when the laws regulating the nation's foray into the digital currency market were under various uncomfortable reformations but blurs the

lines between gambling and addiction...' Tomiwa stopped reading. "She didn't specifically mention *Compound*!"

Feyintola scrolled to the relevant tweet and read it out loud. "Compounding money based on machine algorithms on an app blurs the lines between gambling and gaming because it edges out proper critical thinking, research, as well as personalized advice from seasoned financial professionals..."

He hung his head.

Compound had almost gotten the axe, but he'd been forced to swim with sharks to keep his company afloat. He'd lobbied Feyintola's government pals to keep a step ahead of government decisions and socialized to get *Compound* everywhere in the media. Then he'd hired several student interns to start X threads and drop Instagram videos with content that highlighted *Compound*'s practical usefulness.

Everything had panned out. The app climbed charts and was genuinely instrumental in helping Nigerians hedge their funds against erratic regulatory changes and constant inflation.

Now, Ademide was taking a stab at it because she had an issue with them.

"She didn't get a job with us, and now, she's throwing a tantrum!"

"It's nothing new," he said, reading further. "She's not the only one vexed by the interviews."

He couldn't help but picture her in the Ankara halter-neck shorts coming down the stairs. "I didn't know she was a writer, too."

"Tomiwa? She endorsed a puff piece that casts lots of shadows on both *Compound* and Purple Chip. Where does that leave us with client-confidence in *Purple Ledger*?"

"Higher." He turned his face to hers. "Those who haven't used the app will. Those who haven't heard of the app will download it. She just gave us free publicity."

"How dare she? I've a good mind to sue her for defamation. The final presentations are in a month," Feyintola said "We don't need this happening so close to presentation day. It's a multimillion-naira deal, and a lot is at stake."

Tomiwa caught Sesan's bored look. "Why is he here?"

"I told you, he's my bug."

"Forgive me, I still don't see the point of him spying on One Tech. A lot is at stake, and you want to entrust the sourcing of intel to a guy we barely know."

Feyintola smiled. "Sesan, please tell them what you've found out in one week."

Sesan sat up. "Well, their system has exactly all the features your system has, including a mobile app and offline access. The only thing they are still working on is making it more user-friendly. Where yours has a friendlier user interface, theirs has a nicer look and feel."

Feyintola raised her eyebrows at Tomiwa. "So, what are you going to do about that?"

"Tear down the current graphics and rebuild in three weeks on the word of your emissary?" He sniggered. "You must be joking!"

Sesan chuckled. "You can't do it. I was told you were the best in the business."

"Pretty pages that don't get the job done don't interest anyone," Tomiwa replied coolly.

"And we are doing a lot to make our system even more robust than it is," Babs stepped in. "I'd take user-friendly over look and feel any day, any time."

"And putting stuff like what exactly?" Feyintola asked. "Because it has to be cutting-edge features the other side doesn't already have."

"What do they have that we don't?" Babs asked.

Sesan shrugged. "I'd say you let me compare, but your boss wouldn't like me poking through your codes to find the gaps."

"I'd say the gaps are none of your business." Tomiwa's voice was cold. "You don't work for Purple Chip."

Feyintola held up her hand. "Now, boys, let's play nice. I'm looking for a weakness, something we can play on. I need their proposal. I need their quotation. I need to know who they know on the inside of Kehinde Jules. And I need to know what feature they have that Kehinde Jules thinks is their unique selling point. Can you get that for us?"

Sesan nodded. "Why not?"

"Okay, Babs, Tomiwa, what would you want to know that can help us better prepare for this thing?"

Tomiwa could sense Babs' eyes on the skin of his face as he stared blankly at Feyintola. He had no plans to say anything, and he expected his staff to follow suit.

"A list of what other industries and companies they plan on targeting," Babs said before glancing sideways at him. "If that's all right with you, Mr. Tom."

"This doesn't sit right with me. My software is well-tested, and we're constantly improving it. We don't need to steal ideas from someone else's ERP solution to win."

"Tomiwa, this is business. You think the other side is not fighting as hard as we are?"

"We don't need to spy on them!"

"People don't win in life by playing nice. Even your so-called little applicant has figured that out!" Feyintola snapped. "You know what, you build the software, and let me worry about the business side of things because winning sits right with me. We are not breaking any laws."

"Then I don't need to be in this meeting!" He pushed his chair back and stood up. "Babs!" he called as he headed out of the conference room.

Babs stood but sat back down when he saw Feyintola's face.

"You stay and listen," she said to him. "Then go back and tell your boss exactly what we discussed and what he needs to do so we can be on top of things."

"Yes, ma'am."

BACK IN HIS OFFICE, Tomiwa scoured the X-app for the threads rousing a whirlwind in Purple Chip's direction.

"It's an X whirlwind, boss," Babs said.

"A what?"

"A twitter storm directed at Purple Chip," Ugo explained. "People jumped on the thread and poured their hearts out!"

"They say the interviews were rigged. That we already had in mind who we wanted to employ," Shile added. "Then Ademide nailed *Compound* by pointing out a tiny flaw."

Tomiwa grinned. While Feyin had found the whole situation annoying, he'd found it amateur.

Ademide was hitting back. Lashing out at him for having spurned her application. Perhaps the entire write up would tell him what she felt was lacking in his codes.

"Are you sure you want to read it, sir?" Shile asked, worried.

"I'm already reading it. Look up the word *pachydermatous* for me."

MIDE GOT ON IN ONE Tech with everyone except Sesan Bankole. It irked her to see him more indifferent about her than when she'd first started.

At strategy meetings, he countered every suggestion she gave and questioned every modification she made to the app.

"It's a strategy," Chuka told her. "When someone argues too much with you, he probably likes you."

"How come you don't argue with her all the time?" Femi inquired.

"Like I said, it's a strategy. There are many strategies. Mine is to be as sweet and as uncomplicated as I can ever be." He grinned broadly at her.

Femi scoffed. "That's why you'll remain in the friend zone. Keep being sweet."

"Everything I'm doing will pay off. Right, Mide?"

She didn't respond. She was looking into Sesan's screen from her seat.

He fixed her with a stern scowl. "Can I help you?"

"How are you declaring local functions inside other functions? I've been driving myself crazy all week trying to figure it out." She dragged her chair nearer to his so she could look see better.

"Kotlin," he replied. "It relaxes all of Java's restrictions."

"Ahh, that makes sense." She leaned closer to him, peering over his arm.

"What are you doing now?" he asked, shifting away from proximity to her.

"Learning from you."

"So, it's not like you want me to take you out or something?" he muttered with a distrustful frown.

She burst into loud laughter. "You think I'm looking at your work because I want you to ask me out?"

"That certainly gives me some measure of relief."

"The Dappler is married to his laptop, he's not into girls," Akin said from the other end of the room. "He's not into girls."

Mide was still peering into Sesan's work. "Have you considered the other variables?"

Sesan stopped typing. "Yes, as a matter of fact, I have. Don't you have work to do?"

"I'm done! Waiting for the boss to review and send it back." She sipped on her smoothie and smiled at him.

"So, you think you should help me with mine?"

"No, I think I should learn from you. I hear bitcoins are the new dollars, and SD-WAN or a SASE provides me with more anonymity and security than a VPN-TOR merger ever will."

He gave her a fierce look, snapped his laptop shut, and stood from his seat. "I am going to sit over there. Don't follow me!"

She watched him set up his laptop beside Ross and glare at her when he was done. She chuckled.

"What do you see in him?" Chuka asked, baffled.

"He's a very good programmer!" she announced as Niyi came into the pool and signalled her.

"Plus," she added, standing up. "He's done outstanding work with machine learning. His algorithms generate algorithms of their own, so we should all learn from him."

"Mide, you're with me, we are going out," Niyi said when she came into his office.

"Out? Where?"

"The Jules' Incorporation office. I'm meeting the head of their procurement unit this afternoon, so we need to head to the Island."

"Okay. Let me get my bag."

The drive to the Island took an hour and a half in which Niyi bounced ideas off her about how to approach questions concerning their final offer price.

"I hope this call means they have agreed to use us for the whole project, or at least a major part of it," Niyi said. "In truth, I knew I'd bitten more than I could chew when I learned that the other product in competition with ours was *Purple Ledger*."

"They'll be pricey," she said. "Ours must be affordable. No matter how rich a company is, they will definitely want to save money."

It took them another thirty minutes of waiting outside the procurement chief's office before they were finally ushered in.

"Mr. Lewis." Niyi reached out to shake the hand of the burly, slightly overweight man. "Thank you for meeting with me."

"Ah, no, the pleasure is all mine." He glanced at Mide.

"This is my junior software analyst, Miss Akinseye," Niyi said.

"Family?" Mr. Lewis inquired with raised eyebrows as he took Mide's hand.

"Family." Niyi sat opposite the man.

"You are meant to submit another copy of your proposal including your offer price."

"Yes, we have it right here." Niyi turned to Mide who handed the folder over to Mr. Lewis.

"That's great. This submission doesn't mean that the company has approved you. The board will still meet and deliberate."

Niyi was surprised. "I was of the impression—"

"No, Mr. Akinseye. There will be an unveiling party, a mixer. The date, time, and venue will be communicated to you via email."

Niyi grumbled about the politics of bureaucracy as they left the building. If the Jules wanted to have a party to make the announcements, who was he to judge?

"Aww don't worry. Let's just go finish up our presentations and concentrate on that. What harm will a little party do?"

Niyi turned to her. "All that time we spent rehearsing in the car."

"Don't worry about it!"

"So how about it, you want to accompany me to this mixer?"

"You bet." She grinned at him. "I have a dinner dress or two."

"There is the state's National Technology Dinner and Award Night coming up this Saturday if you're willing. You're welcome to join us."

"You know I love parties!" she cooed, slipping her arm into Niyi's elbow.

"I do. I just don't want you ushering at them."

Chapter Twelve

THE AROMA OF FIREWOOD-cooked jollof rice and roasted chicken permeated the hall as the MC cracked dry jokes and the National Technology Dinner and Award ceremony went underway. It was being held at a popular hall on the mainland. All the *Who's Who* in the Science and Technology Industry were there.

It was an annual event put together by the state government's Ministry for Science and Technology department, attended by government officials, lecturers, professors, and administrators from different universities and secondary schools. Stakeholders in different local and nationwide businesses in the tech industry were also present.

The hall was packed, and the Akinseyes found themselves seated at table twenty-seven at the rear end of the hall with a former schoolmate of Niyi's, a local government chairman.

"You'd think an idea like that would be common knowledge," their table companion was saying. "But it defies explanation."

Niyi and Derin burst into laughter, right along with their amiable companion.

Mide fingered her gold neck chain and glanced briefly at the six-foot-high AC unit beside their table. She'd been feeling the familiar allergic tickle in her throat all morning but hadn't wanted to decline Niyi's invitation. Though she'd taken an anti-histamine tablet, she was sure her subtle but constant perceiving of cigarette smoke in the office all week was partly to blame. Along with the thunderstorm the night before.

Derin pointed stylishly at a table up in front. "Aren't those the Oyinlolus? Right up there at table six."

Mide's gaze veered towards table six. Tomiwa Oyinlolu was sitting at the table opposite his sister, Miss Feyintola Oyinlolu, in a lovely deep blue dinner jacket with black lapels and a black shirt underneath. And he was typing away on his phone, seemingly absent from the party going on around them.

She hissed. They looked posh, well-dressed, and snobbish. She was glad she'd put up the article on the X app. Swallowing her annoyance, she averted her gaze from their table.

In truth, she was more disappointed than angry. Her heart swelled with the weight of the emotion, and her chest started to hurt. She had put all her hopes into working at their company, but they hadn't even considered her worth hiring.

He, the elevator guy, hadn't considered her good enough.

She'd passed their written interview, and she was sure she had excelled at the question she had solved in front of him. So why had they dropped her?

"*You should calm down*," he'd told her in the elevator. "*I'm sure you will do well.*"

And she had, and he hadn't taken her. No doubt, working in One Tech the past two weeks had been great, but Purple Chip had been her dream.

"Darling, it's not polite to point," Niyi whispered.

"I'm just showing you what they're doing. They are sitting with Kehinde Jules, and I can bet I know what they're discussing."

"Well, what about it?"

"I'm just showing you."

"I've been seeing them all night."

Mide took a sip of water as she felt dryness cling to the base of her throat. Her cousin and his wife were now arguing, and she didn't want to get in the middle of it.

"Do you think they are trying to cut a deal?"

"My work will speak for itself. I don't need to cozy up to anyone to sell my software." Niyi sounded a little offended.

"*Profit X* is a great product," Mide said to them both. She didn't want to talk about any of the Oyinlolu siblings. "We'll fix all the kinks before D-day. We'll be ready."

"Thanks for the vote of confidence," Niyi said.

Their companion turned in his seat to get a better look at the Purple Chip siblings.

"Ahhh, Feyintola Oyinlolu," he murmured. "They call her the ice-breathing dragon."

"Why is that?" Derin wanted to know.

"She's tough in business with hands in many pies. Mining, quarrying, and construction is a male-dominated field, but she's leading the pack."

Derin eyed the subject of their discussion. "She married?"

"Married? The lion has not been born yet who can tame that lioness."

Mide tried to follow the conversation, but her chest was hurting. It was getting harder to breathe without pain. She didn't want to use her inhaler with Niyi watching and getting all riled up.

Her subsequent wince, however, invited his concerned look. "Are you alright?"

"Yeah, I just need a bit of fresh air. I'll step out for a bit."

"I told you to take a scarf," Derin said as she stood to her feet. "The air conditioning in halls like this can be quite frigid."

"I didn't have one that matched my outfit. I'll see if I can have a word with the servers or maintenance guys on my way out."

Niyi nodded his understanding. There was worry in his eyes, but she laughed it off.

"Don't be too long," he cautioned.

"I won't. But if I see a rich, handsome hunk, I might just go home with him."

"Not before he pays his dues, please," Derin joked as she saw Niyi's face.

Mide grinned, took her purse, and made her way out of the hall. Her throat was tightening.

AT TABLE SIX, TOMIWA kept a casual ear on the conversation his sister was engaging the younger Mr. Jules in. Earlier on, she had risen to collect the award for their company amidst a thunderous ovation, and she had looked very chic in her sculpted black and white evening gown.

"You seem a bit nervous about the pitch, Feyin, why all these questions?"

"Me, nervous?" She hit the back of her hand lightly against his chest. "We're up for whatever you throw at us, right, Tommy?"

"Sure." Tomiwa lowered his phone and flashed a grin across the table at Kehinde Jules Junior before letting his eyes rove around the rather large, rather full, and very noisy hall

"I'd have awarded the contract, but—" Kehinde shrugged, "—protocol's protocol."

"And you have to follow it, I get, no hard feelings." Tomiwa turned to him. "But you've seen our portfolio. We have everything in place to ensure we give you the very best."

"I have."

"And Tomiwa is quite capable, as you well know." Feyintola picked her wine glass and sipped from it.

"I know that, too, but I don't make the decisions here. One Tech's *Profit X* has some unique features that I very well can't discuss with you."

"Features?" Feyintola inquired. "Perhaps you could be a bit more specific."

Kehinde laughed modestly. "Well, I can't tell you what they are."

"They are features, aren't they, and clearly, we don't have them."

"Come up with an above excellent presentation in three weeks, and I guarantee you won't have anything to worry about."

"I am sure we don't have anything to worry about. Tomiwa darling, weigh in on this."

Tomiwa felt his sister's nudge and lowered his phone so he could look up at their client. "*Purple Ledger* has a wide variety of applicable uses. You've seen a short demo before, Kenny, why the hesitation?"

"I have, but as I said, we need to shop around a little."

"For what? We are the biggest and most reliable IT brand in Lagos, and you know we don't deal with small fry."

"I don't doubt your quality," he replied. "But everyone is cutting costs these days. We need something a little—less expensive."

Tomiwa's wandering attention picked at the sound of that. "Less expensive?"

"Perhaps the words should be, more affordable."

"How much are they bidding?"

"Tommy, you can't expect me to give you that figure. I'd be ratting out my company."

"Surely, Kenny, you can't seriously expect us to bid lower and compromise on quality." Fehintola seemed taken aback.

"There's always a way around everything." Kehinde shrugged. "Might help your pitch if you considered it."

Tomiwa's phone rang just then. He flipped it open and put it to his ear. "Kenny, we spent months paying staff, running overheads, and building an app you can't argue with. Good things cost money. Good staff, a whole lot more."

"And we have a reputation to protect. Our brand includes the kind of premium we place on our products," Feyintola continued.

"I'm not the only decision-maker."

"Shile," Tomiwa said into his phone, taking his mind off the conversation on the table. "Talk to me."

As he listened to Shile's patient explanations, Kehinde Jules Junior took his leave from their table. Across the room from them, Ademide Akinseye was getting up to leave, too.

Feyintola nudged him as he cut the line.

"Isn't that the little spy from One Tech?" She watched Mide exit the building from the left-hand flank of the hall.

"Fire on the mountain at Black Copper Limited," he said, scrolling through his phone without looking up or responding to her. The only thing on his mind was figuring out what the problem was before the owner got wind there was an issue. "The site is down, and the window of opportunity for agents to cash in big-time might be discovered soon. I have to sort Shile out."

Feyintola wasn't listening to him. "Did she think she could just sneak in and we'd just hire her without knowing who she was?"

"I doubt she was sneaking in. She genuinely wanted to work for us," he murmured.

"Who wanted to work for us?" Goriola appeared at the table decked in a wine and black tux and looking quite out of breath. He was late, as usual, and without his fiancée.

"You're here early," Tomiwa said.

"I'm here at all. Who are you both gossiping about?" He lowered himself into a seat.

"The little spy from One Tech that wrote the ridiculous article."

"Oh, the pretty girl from One Tech I've been hearing so much about. Babs said she was very good. Ugo said she was the best-looking thing he'd seen in ages." Gori poured himself some wine.

"Good, my foot. Babs and all the other guys in the room were enraptured by her flirtatious giggling," Feyintola said, irritated. "Ugo was practically drooling. I was convinced he was going to ask her out next."

"One Tech probably had the same idea you did and sent her," Gori continued. "He can't claim to not know she was applying."

"That's what I told Tom!" Feyintola said, rolling her eyes. "But we are smart, and he is not. He hired Sesan."

"Then you must beware," Gori replied, tucking into his forest cake. "He might be hiring Sesan to spite you."

"He doesn't know Sesan is an Oyinlolu," Feyintola quipped, picking up her wine glass. "And it should stay that way. Senator—" She sprung to her feet and beamed at the heavy-set man in brown native lace and agbada. "I've been looking out for you all evening."

Tomiwa stood to his feet. "Things sound a little more serious than I envisaged. I'll just be outside."

"Take your time, bro," Gori replied and winked at a lady on a table across from theirs.

Chapter Thirteen

TOMIWA WEAVED HIS WAY in between the tables while nodding to familiar faces and avoiding the hands waving him to a stop. He made his way out of the hallway through a side entrance and ambled down the hotel's side corridor in between an avalanche of waiters bearing trays.

Spotting another door, he exited the main building, and it led him into a darkened balcony with a short staircase to his right.

"Okay, talk to me—"

"There is a variance, boss."

His footsteps skidded to a halt. "How much?"

"We are still computing the figures, but it looks like six figures."

Drat!

He felt a headache coming on. Black Copper Limited was one of their four biggest clients. Any downtime with the system in place over there meant the company's staff would have their fill of not making any financial returns to the company.

That wasn't good. It could mean a loss of confidence in *Purple Ledger*.

"Concentrate on fixing the bug, and we will worry about the money later." His conscience bugged him about Ademide's comment and Feyintola's warnings. He'd been too cocky. Now, he was paying the price. "Have you done all I said?"

"Yeah, Abel and Ugo are on it. I called in James and asked him to work on that report page."

"Good!"

He shut the door to the poorly lit balcony, relieved to be away from all the party noise.

"Calm down. I can hear you better now. Remember, don't touch any other thing but that line and we'll be fine. Get Ugo and Abel to test for other errors and just mail them to me as soon as you find them."

"Noted, sir,"

"Run the script as per instruction. I need this site up and running like five seconds ago because we can't afford to give them any more time to pilfer more money. Once I give this party another fifteen minutes, I'll be on my way to you. There's one more award we have to collect. It will look bad if I'm not there. It's a state thing, and you know how Feyin is about government officials."

As he listened to Shile's response, Tomiwa heard someone breathing heavily beside him.

Turning left, he saw a feminine figure huddled over the banister in a corner of the long balcony.

"Okay, Shile," he said without taking his eyes off her. "I'll catch you later. Let me know how it goes."

He cut the call and took a few steps closer to her.

"Are you all right?" he asked, thinking the braids looked familiar.

She raised herself, and he saw her face.

Ademide Akinseye!

His heart did the dropping thing again and added a little backflip. In the dimness of the balcony, he hadn't recognized her at first. And she wasn't smiling or laughing or talking or doing any of the adorable things he knew she often did. She was breathing heavily.

"Are you alright? Do you need help? Do you want me to get someone?" he asked, alarmed.

She waved a hand.

"No, I'll be fine. It'll pass," she whispered.

Raising an inhaler to her mouth, she took a slow, painful puff. He could tell it was painful because she shut her eyes and began to cough.

Asthma? She's asthmatic?

"Do you need me to do anything?" he asked again as he watched her struggle to breathe. "What do you need? Please, tell me."

She managed a faint smile. "Nothing!" Her voice sounded hoarse.

"You don't look fine—"

"I'll be okay," she whispered, and he almost didn't hear it.

"You don't sound fine."

"I—" she paused, grabbed her throat, and grimaced. "I—" she began again, then her knees buckled.

He was beside her in two bounds, catching her before she hit the ground. She looked like she couldn't even stand, much less talk. He put her right arm around his neck and lifted her up.

"Hey, I'm taking you to the nearest hospital!"

She tried to shake her head, but the sounds coming from her throat were terrifying high-pitched gasps.

"Oh, my goodness!" Tomiwa sucked in a deep breath and swung her legs onto his other arm. "Help!" he yelled.

Two passing security guards had seen them and were hurrying towards him. He managed to lift her down the stairs, the awful thought of anything happening to her while she was in his arms filling him with fury.

"*Oga wetin?*" the first asked as they watched him hurry down the stairs with her.

"Take my phone and call my driver, tell him to meet us at the gate immediately. I think she is having an asthmatic attack. His name is John. Look in the last dialled numbers."

The second guy helped him carry her legs while the other guy took the phone and hurried after them. Tomiwa could hear him shouting directions into the phone.

"Is there any hospital nearby?"

"*One dey down the street*, Precious Life."

He was confused about calling for her cousin who was probably still inside or taking her straight there with hope they had the equipment to deal with whatever was wrong with her. They had to. This was the Island.

He looked down at her. She was still breathing in that awful way and trying to raise her inhaler to her mouth. His driver drove up just then, and the gateman opened the door for him.

"Find Mr. Niyi Akinseye," he barked at the one with his phone. "Tell him where I took her. Ask him to meet me there as soon as possible."

He turned to his driver. She was panting now, her mouth partly open. "John, drive like a madman. The hospital is just down the road."

When the driver drove into the compound of the hospital, Tomiwa opened the door while the engine was still running and helped Ademide out.

The gatemen were trying to direct them to a proper parking space, but he ignored them.

"Emergency," he snapped, swinging her into his arms in one swift move. She was hyperventilating, taking short, sharp breaths and releasing high-pitched sounds from her throat.

One of the gatemen raced to open the giant hospital glass doors.

"Dr. Gbadebo!" he yelled into the hospital reception. "Emergency, come quickly."

Tomiwa struggled with her into the reception. The nurse at the counter stared at him blankly, and the other was seated, taking an elderly man's height and weight.

"Help!" he shouted, mildly irritated by their slow response. "She's having an asthmatic attack!"

For a second, he worried he'd brought her to the wrong place.

The nurse at the counter handed him a surly gaze, then she was gone and back in a second with a stretcher on wheels. The doctor came out just as Ademide was being laid on the stretcher.

"What's happening?" he asked, a stethoscope casually draped around his neck.

"Asthma," the first nurse said.

He took one look at Ademide and yanked the stethoscope off his neck. He tried to listen to her chest above the neckline of her dress.

Tomiwa watched with concerned eyes. The doctor sank the equipment lower and tried to listen through the bodice of her evening gown, but her face contorted into a grimace. Her chest kept heaving as the high-pitched sounds from her throat increased.

"I'm not getting any breath sounds. Get me IV hydrocort, aminophylline, water for injection, and everything to set a line. Where's the oxygen tank? Someone get me the neb, stat."

He was wheeling the stretcher as he spoke. Another man, probably a nursing orderly, came and together, they pushed the stretcher against the wall of one corridor.

The doctor turned to Tomiwa. "What exactly happened?"

He shook his head and shrugged in confusion. "I don't know. I just found her like this on the balcony and brought her here. We were at a function at the Raven Hotel down the road."

"Who is she to you?"

He stared down at Ademide. Sweat poured down her face as she struggled to breathe. He didn't know whether to say they weren't close and she was his prospective employee, or she was someone he had been interested in before the incident.

"A friend…" was what came out of his mouth.

"How long has she been asthmatic, and how long has she been having this particular episode?"

"I'd say about ten, maybe fifteen minutes. I wasn't there when it started."

"Is she on any meds that you know of?"

He shook his head as he watched them roll a screen over to shield the stretcher away from prying eyes. "I don't know. I didn't know she was asthmatic."

The first nurse hooked a rubber mask oozing a strange white mist over her mouth and nose. The second brought a tray filled with tubes and needles and cotton swabs and tiny bottles of fluids he was guessing were injectables. While the first nurse stuffed two pillows in between Ademide's back and the stretcher to raise her up, the doctor donned his gloves.

"Nurse Joy," he said. "Find the zipper to this gown, pull it down, give her chest some space to expand."

"Yes, Doctor."

"Did you get the SP O2 reading?"

"Ninety-three sir, temperature thirty-six."

The doctor was tapping her wrist and tying a tourniquet across her forearm.

"Find me that oxygen tank and get it here immediately." He turned to Tomiwa. "What's her name?"

"Ademide."

She was writhing in agony.

"Ademide—" The doctor turned back to her and slid a cannula into a vein in her wrist with the calmness of one who did it often. He secured the flaps with thick straps of white plaster. "Ade, can you hear me?"

Tomiwa took in a deep breath and watched, his whole being doused in worry.

"Step back, sir," one of the nurses said to him as they raced around in his first-ever experience of an emergency reaction in a Nigerian hospital.

He took a few steps back and covered his mouth as he watched the hospital staff attend to her. Everything seemed to be happening in slow motion, but he could tell they were working as fast as they possibly could.

Please, God, don't let her die, he was thinking to himself as he suddenly realized how much he wanted her to live.

Someone as brilliant and full of life as she was deserved to live.

Chapter Fourteen

TOMIWA SAT IN THE RECEPTION waiting area with his thighs spread apart and his hands clasped in between them. His tux jacket lay across a thigh, and he had been sitting for an anxious thirty minutes waiting for word from his driver, or the doctor.

In his race to get her to the hospital, he had forgotten his phone with the gateman who had called his driver on his behalf, meaning he couldn't reach anyone. Feyintola would be wondering where he had gone off to. Shile would be flying blind with the problem on hand, probably almost going crazy trying to reach him, and Niyi Akinseye, CEO of One Tech, would be wondering where his cousin was.

He had spent a good part of fifteen minutes alternating between trying to find his driver and trying to get information from the nurses on how she was currently doing. John hadn't come back yet, meaning he hadn't been able to locate the guard who may or may not have made off with his quite expensive Galaxy Z-Note phone. But the phone was replaceable, the contacts and other information downloadable.

"Mr. Oyinlolu?"

He looked into the eyes of the matronly-looking nurse who had sat him in the waiting area. "Yes?"

"Your friend is stable now. You can check on her."

He heaved a big sigh of relief, and she smiled in an understanding way.

"She's very lucky," she said. "Good thing you got her here in time."

He stood and followed her out of the reception into the corridor that led to the emergency room.

"You can go in." The nurse's tone was kind.

"Thank you, ma."

The emergency room was built to hold two patients at a time, but Ademide was the only one in it tonight. Taking a deep breath, his suit jacket slung over one arm, he stepped into the room.

There was medical equipment everywhere and the sharp smell of disinfectants and antibiotics in the air. He remembered then why he hated hospitals and did everything he could to avoid going to them. When his father had died, it had been swift. He had been brought to the hospital dead on arrival, and Tomiwa had come to associate them with sadness.

Today, however, he'd had no choice.

She was lying on the stretcher bed, propped up with pillows and covered with a white bed sheet. The mask was back on her face, spewing out the thin white mist. The soft buzzing from the machine on the table was the only other sound in the room. Though he couldn't see her nose and mouth, he could tell she was smiling at him.

"Hi." He took slow steps towards the stretcher, morbidly relieved she wasn't breathing like she was about to give up the ghost anymore. "You had me worried there for a minute."

He was shocked at the calmness in his voice despite the worry that had gripped him.

"Please, don't ever do that again," he added.

She chuckled through the mask, eyes crinkling at the sides. It was a relief to hear. The whirlwind he had met on the elevator was somehow still in there.

"How are you feeling now?" he asked, forgetting she still had the mask on.

She nodded and stuck out a thumb at him.

"Glad to hear it," he said looking around at the pristine, white-tiled walls and stainless-steel medical apparatus.

She pointed at the chair next to the stretcher bed. He pulled it out and sat, placing his jacket over his left thigh, watching the soft bulge of her cheeks at the edges of the nebulizer's mask. Then he lowered his eyes to the needle in her right hand and traced it up the IV line to the bag hanging above the bed. The mask attached to the nebulizer was making a hissing sound, and it put him ill at ease, but he shrugged it off.

"Hope that doesn't hurt." He looked back down at her.

She shook her head and kept staring at him. He stared back and couldn't resist a smile. Her eyes lit up more.

A nurse came in just then to switch off the nebulizer, the same one who had been taking a height and weight measurement.

Ademide took the mask off, looking grateful to have it gone. There were beads of sweat around her mouth and nose, and the nurse gave her disposable wipes to clean herself with.

He turned his face away to give her some privacy. They had exchanged nothing but a few words in an elevator and a job interview room. They were not friends, nor were they a boss and employee. They were strangers, and he had denied her application to work in his company. It was awkward he was the one sitting there with her and not anybody she was more familiar with.

"I'll be back in thirty minutes for your next dose," the nurse said and walked away.

Ademide lay back against the pillows.

"Thank you," she whispered.

"You're welcome," he replied.

She looked so fragile with the oxygen tube hooked into her nose and over both her ears, he felt guilty all over again. Contrasting images of her in the elevator, at the interview, and at the party with the tray of drinks in her hands hounded him.

He worried she was probably upset with him but was being too nice to actually say it. If they had offered her the job, she wouldn't have needed to be ushering in skimpy clothing at a frat-like party. "I'm sorry I didn't give you the job."

She chuckled briefly and turned her eyes to the ceiling. "It's okay."

Her voice was a hoarse whisper. The sexy throatiness he loved was gone.

"Need me to call anyone for you, your cousin, perhaps?"

She turned to him with widened eyes and shook her head. "I don't want him to worry."

She was whispering, and it was scary.

"Your voice. What's wrong with it?"

"It'll get better."

"But it doesn't mean you're going to—"

She gave him a slow, lazy, sleepy smile. The kind he'd always imagined she would.

"Not with all that intravenous cocktail they just gave to me." She cleared her throat. "I'm really grateful you were there, and that you didn't listen to me."

He eyed her. "I think you should rest your voice."

"It's going to get better. I should apologize, by the way."

He frowned. "For what?"

"For saying your codes weren't good enough."

He remembered the X-app write up then, and their conversation in the elevator. He remembered every moment they had ever met. The problem was, she was right. He was only human, and his codes were not always on point. Shile was tackling an issue at this very moment.

"They're not always. Perhaps when this is all over and you're much better, we should get together, and you can show me how to jazz them up."

She chuckled, and the doctor walked in just then.

"Hey, Ade," he said. "I'm Dr. Leke Gbadebo. Dr. Leke, for short."

He was young, in Tomiwa's estimation, but quite handsome now that his face was not etched in tension. He had handled himself brilliantly under the initial pressure of their arrival, and Tomiwa had to give it to him. He was very good at what he did.

"You gave us quite a scare there. How are you doing?" He stood over the stretcher she was on and stared at the clipboard in his hand.

"Good," she whispered and turned her smile over to him.

"How's the chest? Tight?"

"Not so much anymore."

"Throat open?"

"Yes."

He nodded and turned to the nurse. "Let's check her vitals once more. Her voice is still a little raspy, make sure she gets nebulized in another ten minutes. That IV line should run for an hour. Then they are good to go."

"Yes, sir." The nurse reached for the blood pressure kit and clipped a tiny box-like peg over Ademide's left index finger.

Tomiwa stood and stepped aside so the doctor and nurse could attend to her.

They listened to her chest, checked her eyes, and administered another IV injection. The doctor was overly nice. He asked her questions about how long she'd been having asthmatic episodes, bustled around her like an eager young schoolboy, and she rewarded him with smiles that were more than enough to let any guy think she was interested.

Tomiwa stood in his well-tailored clothes, holding his jacket and watching the scene. He was trying not to dislike Dr. Gbadebo.

"Ninety-seven," the nurse announced. "BP, one-twenty over eighty-five."

The doctor grinned. "Looks like your oxygen levels are back up, and your BP is stable. But I'm going to keep the tube in place. A ninety-nine is what I'm looking for, but for the moment, you seem to be doing okay."

"Thank you," she said and kept her eyes on him.

He smiled at her one last time, looked up, and nodded at Tomiwa. Then he walked out of the emergency room.

The nurse walked up to Tomiwa. "Sir, there are forms to fill, and we need to have a deposit for all our treatment now that she's stable."

"Sure. Give her everything she needs, I'll pay for it," he replied.

"Mr. Oyinlolu." Ademide's voice went above a whisper. "You shouldn't."

"You should rest your voice," he said to her and followed the nurse out of the emergency room.

Outside, he paid the deposit of fifty thousand with his MasterCard. Luckily, his wallet had been in the breast pocket of his jacket. He gave them the little information he could remember from her CV and from scouring her Facebook page and other handles. He had been feeling a little guilty when he'd gone snooping, but the information was coming in handy now he had to fill her medical forms. He was a little glad he had put in the effort.

Then he went in search of his driver and found him in the car park. John had been able to get his phone from the gateman but hadn't been able to locate the girl's guardian. Tomiwa was also grateful to see he had found Ademide's purse and phone in the back seat of the car. They could both call the people they needed to call and inform them they were fine.

He called Shile, whose fourteen missed calls were alarming, and Feyintola to let her know he was attending to an emergency. What it was, he didn't bother to tell her. The crisis at Black Copper Limited had been averted, and Shile had just been worried he hadn't picked up his calls.

The only thing left was to fish out the employees who had taken advantage of the downtime, and one of them had already been discovered. Tomiwa was glad he could rest easy and stay to see whether Ademide, or Ade as the doctor had fondly called her, was going to be all right.

When he got back to the emergency room, the mask was back on her face and emitting thin white wisps of mist.

They disconnected her from it ten minutes later, and she sat up in the stretcher bed, looking and sounding noticeably better. Her voice was still a little hoarse, though.

"The nurse told me you paid a deposit for my treatment." She stared up at him, a cross between happy and disapproving. "You didn't have to do that."

"It's the least I could do." He handed her the purse. "You dropped this in the back seat of my car."

"Thank you. I'm immensely grateful for your help—"

"Oh, forget it," he said and sat down on the chair. "You should be calling your cousin so he doesn't get worried."

"I already did. I borrowed one of the nurses' phones. He is not worried."

Tomiwa looked confused. "So why isn't he here?"

"Because I didn't exactly tell him I was in the hospital." She gave him a playful grin. "I told him I'm with a friend, and I'll come back home much later. I don't want him to worry. He does, a lot. He'll call my mum. She'll race down to Lagos and not sleep for days. I don't want to worry anyone. And honestly, I would like to return your deposit myself. I don't want to put that burden on him. He's a family man."

"What makes you think I'm going to give you my account number?"

She eyed him. "I can't let you do this. I can't let you pay for me."

"I'm not going to take the money back from you, so forget it." He pointed at the machine beside her. "What's that, and what does it do?"

"It's a nebulizer." She cleared her throat. "It takes the drugs I'm meant to ingest and turns them into a mist I can inhale so they go directly into my lungs and work faster."

He searched her eyes. "How long have you been asthmatic?"

This knocked the smile off her face. "Since childhood. It doesn't usually flare up like this, but I'm allergic to cold and dust and certain flowers, freshly cut grass, pollen—" She shrugged and smiled up at him. "Weird way to live, right?"

"What happened at the party?"

"Must have been the AC." She rubbed the back of her neck. "Dust, or the live flowers, or a combination of both. I'm not sure."

"That was really, really scary. Don't ever do that again!" he said.

She burst out laughing, making him smile.

"Are you always this chirpy? I mean, the little I've seen, you're always smiling." He was thinking about the interview. And the elevator.

"Today is a bad day. I just don't let it get to me is all."

He nodded and looked down at the space between his feet. "I'm glad you are okay."

"Me, too."

"For what it's worth, you are an incredible programmer, and you came in a close second."

She stayed quiet for a moment.

"This is going to sound weird, I'm kind of like hungry. Those drugs—they make me ravenous."

He laughed and stood. "I'll get you something from the vending machine."

"I'm sorry I'm sending you on an errand," she whispered.

"That's okay." He looked down at her. *I'm happy to do anything for you*, he thought to himself. "Just rest and get better," he added out loud.

Chapter Fifteen

MIDE EXHALED THE MOMENT he stepped out.

"This is the most embarrassing day of my life!" she wailed and covered her face with her hands. "Why do I keep meeting him in the most ridiculous of situations? And after I maligned his app on social media."

She had always wanted to work with and learn from Tomiwa Oyinlolu, but it seemed like life had other plans. It was surreal how she'd met him, been rejected by him, then become angry with him. Now, she didn't know what to think. He had saved her life and paid a hefty sum for her medical bills. Perhaps he wasn't as cruel as she had thought him to be.

And she'd succumbed to the dreaded illness again, in front of a man she wanted respect from.

Taking a deep breath, she wiped tiny tears from her eyes and swallowed every other large one. She couldn't cry, her makeup would get smudged. Not like it already wasn't.

In truth, she hadn't been hungry. She had just wanted to get him out of the room so she could have a few moments to process what had happened. She had known an attack was imminent, but she had mistakenly taken the almost empty canister of Ventolin instead of the full one. On that balcony, all she'd been inhaling was empty air.

Letting out a deep sigh, she thanked God he had been there to get her to the hospital on time and wondered what he must think of her now. How glad he must be to have narrowly escaped employing a sickly person.

The thought brought more tears to her eyes, and she fought it, determined not to give in.

"I'm happy, I'm healthy, I'm hearty," she muttered to herself. "I'm brainy, I'm beautiful, and I'm bold. Every dark cloud has a silver lining, and there is a rainbow after every rainstorm—"

It wasn't working—the tears were threatening to spill. It was happening all over again, and she was the sickly child no one wanted to be friends with, or hire, for that matter.

Her mother had taught her those words to calm herself, but she hadn't been able to get through the whole passage on a day she'd needed it the most.

He walked in just then, and she dabbed the tears with her fingers and smiled at him.

"Hey." He was holding a bottle of Lucozade Boost and a packet of Super Bite sausage. "The nurse said to avoid a cold drink so I took one that was room temperature. Are you all right?"

She nodded. "Yeah, I'm—I'm fine."

Her eyes remained glued to her hands for the moment it took him to walk over to her bedside. She hadn't wanted to let him see her cry.

"This is all they had," he said as he sat down.

"It's okay." She wiped another tear. "The nebules make me hungry so I'll eat anything."

He watched her for a while. "I didn't think there was a chink in your armour."

"What?"

"You wear an armour. The smiles, laughter, and talkative disposition all seem to be part of a persona. The identity supporting the character handling a huge challenge. I have never met you without them until today."

He put the sausage down on the tiny table beside them.

"I won't pretend to understand what you're going through, but—" He twisted open the cover of the drink and handed the plastic bottle to her, "—everything works out for the best, right? A certain someone said that to me in an elevator on one crazy day of her life, and I took a lesson from it."

She sniffed and took the drink from him.

"Hey, don't cry. Don't be sad. I know that a smile gets you through the most trying of times, but you should know it gives strength to the people around you. Don't let that smile die."

Taking a huge sip of the drink, she swallowed it along with the tears at the base of her throat. Her smile was completely gone. She didn't think she could summon it up again.

"It's admirable how you don't even let it show that you're dealing with something this huge."

She wiped the tear off her cheek. "It's not a big deal."

"It's an illness that stops you from breathing. Don't be modest, it's a big deal."

"But surmountable," she replied, hoping to change the topic. "I didn't know who you were when I was mouthing off in the elevator."

"I'm glad you didn't. You would have cautioned yourself, and I wouldn't have known there was someone on Earth who could jazz up my codes. Nor that *Compound* makes money off gullible millennials who have an app addiction problem."

She chuckled and glanced at him. He'd read the article. "I'm sorry. That was mean."

"Yep. There's a smart phone addiction, and it's unfortunate that I've contributed to it."

"I shouldn't have written that."

"It was rather entertaining."

He wasn't as intimidating as she had imagined he would be. He was certainly posh, but not in any way a snob. Hours earlier when Derin had pointed him out, she would never have imagined he could carry her in his arms or that she'd be seated right next to him trading corny jokes.

"I was just angry. In truth, I call you the Lagos god of programming," she said and put a hand over her mouth.

"The what?"

Behind her hand, she bit her lip. *Goodness gracious, where is your filter?*

"I don't know where that came from. I just open my mouth, and things fall out of it."

He laughed out loud. "I'm flattered. I think your cousin is pretty good, too."

"You are the one everyone I know wants to work with. I have friends who cried because they didn't get picked for the interview at your company." She passed him a side-eye, hand still over her mouth.

"Well, everyone starts from somewhere, and for the record, I'm just plain, ordinary Tomiwa. Not Mr. Oyinlolu, not the Purple Chip whizz kid as you addressed me in that article, and certainly not the Lagos god of programming. Just call me Tomiwa."

She nodded and cleared her throat, hoping the hoarseness in her voice could go completely and stop embarrassing her.

"I'm Mide," she said, dropping the hand over her mouth. "You know me as Ademide Aramide Akinseye, but when I was younger, they called me Mide-Mide, or Mide squared, Double Mide, M squared, M times two, Miss Cheeky, Chatterbox International, Miss Smiles, Miss Mouth, what have I left out?" She glanced up, saw him watching, and covered her embarrassment with a nervous chuckle. "I talk too much, I know, I've been told."

"I find it entertaining."

She went quiet under his intrusive gaze and wondered how to broach the subject of releasing him. "I'm sure you have like a billion things to do besides sitting here keeping me company. I'm keeping you from the Tech Award dinner. You should leave and go get your other award. If they haven't called your name already."

"And leave you here?" He sounded appalled. "Never. I'm waiting till you're okay, and I'm taking you home afterward."

"You don't have to."

His eyebrows rose with his answer. "I want to."

She smiled. She just couldn't seem to stop smiling around him. "Thank you."

"You're welcome."

"I didn't recognize you in the elevator. I don't think I've seen your pictures anywhere before."

He sighed out loud. "I'm not a fan of having my pictures taken."

"I guessed as much."

"I did have one magazine interview, though, about two, three years ago. My picture should have been in there."

The nurse came in just then holding a tray filled with needles and syringes and small plastic tubes. Mide saw him stiffen at the sight and follow the tray with his eyes.

"How are you feeling?" the nurse asked. "It's time for your next dose."

"How many more of that is she having?" he asked when the nurse put the tray down on the bedside table and pulled out the rubber mask and tube. "Doesn't it have side effects? All that medical concoction she's inhaling?"

The nurse shrugged. "It does, but the benefits outweigh the effects. Better for us she takes it and stays alive. There are no drugs without side effects."

Mide made a face as the nurse took the oxygen tubes out of her nostrils.

"This is the last one for today," the nurse said with a kind smile. "After that, she can go home with her medication. I'm taking off the oxygen tube."

She lay back and let the nurse put the face mask over her head after she had filled the machine's cup with the required medicine. Tomiwa took the Lucozade bottle out of her hands and placed it on the table beside the sausage.

He had invited her to call him by name, but she still couldn't do it. He was older and was someone she deeply admired. It sounded wrong, somehow.

He stretched both his arms up in the air and leaned back against the chair, bringing out his phone from his pocket. "I'm just going to send out a few quick emails while you dose up."

Dose up—it sounded like she was fixing to get high.

"Sure."

She relaxed and let the nurse pull the nebulizer's mask over her face.

When he lowered his head and got busy on his phone, she watched him.

It was funny how in the space of three meetings, they had become close. She was supposed to take him to task for snubbing her application over a business turf war with her cousin, but she couldn't. Not when he had been so nice as to save her life and pay for her hospital treatment.

She was probably never going to see him again, but she promised to find a way to send him a thank you note or a cake or something.

And as she inhaled the salbutamol, she felt herself getting sleepy. She was severely tired from all the meds and from struggling to breathe. Sleep was the only thing on her mind.

Chapter Sixteen

AN HOUR LATER, WHEN Mide was feeling much better and ready to leave, she found Tomiwa Oyinlolu waiting for her in the reception. He rose to his feet the moment he sighted her, but she walked slowly over to him, feeling self-conscious about her inability to hurry.

"Are you okay?"

She nodded weakly, her heart pounding at an alarming rate. Her hands were vibrating a little. Scared he would see, she folded them under her armpits. "Thank you for everything."

"You're welcome. Can we leave now?"

She nodded. Her physical state had little to do with being awestruck in the presence of programming royalty. It had more to do with the side effects of the bronchodilators she'd been given. Being familiar with the symptoms, she was hoping to not have to repeat the treatment at home by herself the following day, because it would worsen the trembling, and drive Niyi nuts.

"They expect me to come for a follow-up tomorrow, said you already paid for it."

He shrugged. "It was part of the package."

"I might be unable to make it. This is the Island, and my regular doctor is on the mainland. Besides, it's not a new condition. There is a specialist I see."

"As long as you are okay."

"I am."

"So, can I take you home now?"

She was too tired to even argue. "Yes, please."

He took off his jacket and handed it to her.

She frowned. "Why are giving me your jacket?"

"You look cold. Plus, it's cold outside, and it will be in my car. The doctor said you need to keep warm because cold is a trigger for asthma. I don't want you to land back in here, or in any other hospital, for that matter."

He draped the jacket over her shoulders with large and gentle hands. It was big, warm and harboured subtle remnants of a minty, lavender-based cologne. She whispered her thanks, and they walked quietly towards the front entrance.

"You are not chatty tonight." He opened the reception's glass door for her.

She shook her head and stepped out. "I'm tired."

If it was cold, she didn't notice. His jacket kept her warm, and it seemed he was content with just strolling along the hospital corridor beside her.

"I'm sorry I took you away from your award night."

"That's okay. I'm not sure I wanted to be there anyway."

"Why not?" she asked, clearing her throat.

"Been to quite a few, would have rather been elsewhere. My sister was made for dinners and awards. All the fancy stuff that comes with company brand representation. I'm not. So, did they give you any medication for your voice?"

"Yeah. I have it in my purse."

He stretched an arm out to the right. "Car is over here."

He held the car door open for her when the driver arrived and helped her in. It felt strange. Weeks ago, he had been an unattainable entity she had heard so much about but didn't know. The next thing, she was in his arms, being rushed to a hospital.

"Does it happen often?"

His voice broke into her thoughts when they were settled in the car and the driver was manoeuvring his way out of the hospital compound.

"The asthmatic episodes?" She looked up at him in the dimness of the car. "No, not so much as when I was younger. I had it bad then. It's a lot better now."

"This was bad."

She nodded without a reply.

"Is there a way to prevent it?"

"Yeah, keeping away from my triggers. Dust, cold, grass, rain, and so on."

"What is it, exactly? What happened to you?"

"Just an extreme allergic reaction. My body was fighting an allergen and fighting it so hard, it shut my airway down."

"What allergen, dust?"

She shrugged and looked out of the window. "I don't know. Something in that hall, or maybe the food, the AC..."

He stared at her. "I can see you don't want to discuss this."

"I don't."

"We won't."

TOMIWA STARED AHEAD for a few silent minutes. There were things he wanted to tell her and questions he wanted to ask, but it wasn't the right time.

"You are a very good programmer," he said instead.

"Is that supposed to make me feel better about you not hiring me?"

The accusation came like a punch in the gut. He supposed he had been expecting it.

"I mean it. Your codes were meticulously arranged and well thought out from end to end. We just had three equally brilliant male programmers."

"You don't hire females?" she asked and coughed. "I'd better stop talking. I'm sure I sound like a frog at the moment."

"Yeah, you should," he replied, happy not to have to expand on his reasons for his bias against women. "Rest your voice. Where do you stay?"

She gave him the address. He repeated it to the driver and then sat back.

"I meant what I said about you, and I don't readily give compliments. You're good, and I would like to recommend you to a friend of mine—"

"I already have a job," she said in a voice that sounded like it was breaking again—like she had somehow developed a cold.

"Oh, good, where?"

"One Tech."

"Ahh," he said and uttered a chuckle.

"Yeah, you didn't want me, but they did."

"Touché," he replied.

"I always had an offer there. I just wanted to try building a career outside my family. That's why you didn't hire me, right, because of One Tech?"

His smile faded. "We didn't hire you because we felt there would be an obvious conflict of interests. Your cousin's company and mine are bidding for the same job. It would have been wrong and unfair to put you in the middle of it."

"I understand."

When they got to the front of her street, they both got down. Looping round the back of the car, he walked over to find her taking off his jacket.

"I'm grateful you were there tonight." She handed it to him. "I can't thank you enough."

"Oh, don't worry about it." He folded the jacket over his arm. "Can I call you?" he asked, and she looked taken aback. "Just to make sure you're okay. Can I call you tomorrow?"

"Do you have my phone number?"

"I believe I have your CV."

"Ahh!" Her smile turned into a chuckle. "Sure. I'll expect your call. I'm going inside now."

"Better, goodnight. Just ensure you rest well and take extra good care of yourself."

He returned to the car without waiting for her response, but paused at the open car door to confirm she'd gone in. She had.

All he had to look forward to was calling her the next day.

"I'M STILL MAD AT YOU," Niyi said to Mide the very next morning as she pulled out a chair and sat at the dining table. "You had a severe asthmatic attack, and you didn't call me."

"It was not so severe. Besides, someone took me to the hospital."

"If anything had happened to you, what would you have wanted me to tell your mother?"

"Relax, nothing really serious happened."

Just then, she coughed and had to blow her nose into a paper towel.

"Do you hear the sound of that cough? And nothing serious happened?"

"I'm sorry. I just didn't want you to worry."

"Stop side-tracking me!"

"I'm not side-tracking you." She looked helplessly in Derin's direction.

"Niyi, stop hounding her." Derin put a bowl of chicken pepper soup in front of her and rubbed her shoulder. "Let's just thank God she's fine. Drink it up, dear, it'll make you feel much better."

"Lots of ginger?" Mide asked, picking up the spoon in the bowl.

"As much as you need right now," Derin replied and left for the kitchen.

Mide sniffed and pulled the bowl closer. Niyi was staring at her so intently, it was unnerving. She was sure he could see right through her to the things that had happened the night before, but she chose to ignore him.

"Who helped you to the hospital?"

"A random stranger," she replied, slurping a spoonful of the pepper soup without looking up.

He leaned closer. "Does he or she have a name?"

Her gaze moved sideways and encountered Niyi's worried look. She was not going to mention Tomiwa Oyinlolu's name. Not in any vein. "A friend."

"Which friend?"

"You haven't met him yet."

"Him? Ademide!"

"Leave this girl alone, *haba*!" Derin joined them at the table with her mug of coffee. "She is old enough to have male friends who can take her to the hospital whenever we are not around."

"If anything had happened to her, what would I have told her mum?" he said to Derin and turned round to face Mide. "I'd like to be notified if for any reason you have to go to the hospital. And with any male friends."

"Yes, sir," she replied, slurping some more of her soup and hiding a smile.

Niyi glowered at her. "Please don't ever let it happen again."

"Okaaay!"

Derin made a face behind the back of her husband's head. "Don't mind him. Just ensure you bring this said friend home once in a while so we can meet him."

Niyi twisted his head to look up at his wife. "Are you encouraging her to date strange men and bring them here?"

She glared playfully at her husband. "Do you want to have her living in your house forever? She is twenty-seven, for goodness' sake, old enough to get married. You ought to let her live."

Niyi exhaled in disgust and turned to Mide. "At least give me his name."

She pursed her lips and blew over the soup.

"Mide?"

"I don't think it's heading anywhere. It was just a one-time thing. He just took me to the hospital and brought me home. *C'est fini.*"

Derin started laughing. 'Is he fine?' she mouthed above her husband's head.

Mide thought hard. In between trying not to die and having drugs pumped into her, she had not considered what Tomiwa Oyinlolu looked like. "He's rich, and he runs his own company. Not sure if he's married, though—"

Niyi looked mortified. Derin looked tickled.

"Mide," he said. "Your mum entrusted your welfare to me. I have been doing my best to protect you, and I always will. But please, be careful who you give your heart to."

She eyed him. "I didn't say I was giving him my heart. He just brought me home."

"Just let me know whenever anything happens to you. I promise I won't go ballistic."

Yeah, like you are currently not *doing.*

"Okay," she said out loud, taking another spoon of her pepper soup. Her phone rang just then. She was charging it in the living room and was grateful for the interruption. "I'm going to go get my phone."

She was glad to get away from Niyi. The last thing she wanted to tell him was how the random stranger had turned out to be their mutual work rival. She wasn't exactly sure how he would receive it.

When she picked up her phone, it was an unknown number. With a sniff, she pressed the answer button. "Hello?"

"Am I unto Ademide Akinseye?"

"Yeah, who is on the line?"

"Tomiwa Oyinlolu."

She froze.

He went on, hardly bothered by her silence. "I was with you last night. I took you to the hospital and brought you home."

"Oh," she thawed out, chuckled, and ended up coughing hard.

"Are you okay?" His concern reverberated through the phone's speaker.

"I'm fine," she said and forced herself to swallow the mucus that had come up with the cough. It was disgusting, but she was too keyed up and tense to ask for a break to spit it out.

Tomiwa Oyinlolu had promised to call. She couldn't believe he had lived up to his promise.

"You have a cold."

"Yeah, it just decided to descend with a vengeance this morning."

"I'm so sorry about that," he replied quietly. "I just wanted to ensure you were okay."

"I am," she croaked, slightly embarrassed.

"That cold sounds very bad."

"It's not that bad." She tried to get the hoarseness out of her voice by clearing it, but she went into a small coughing fit.

"It is bad. Are you taking any lozenges?"

"They are more like sweets than anything. They don't work."

"In that case, what are you taking for the cold?"

"Antibiotics, honey-flavoured tea, pepper soup, steam."

"Steam?"

"Yeah." She caught sight of Niyi watching her. "That's—I—put my head over boiling water tinted with a splash of eucalyptus essential oil or vapor rub. The menthol-infused steam from the water clears my—" She broke into fits of coughing.

"Mide..." His voice was soft on the other end of the line. "I know we hardly know each other, but I'm a tad concerned about your health."

"I'm good." She cleared her throat.

"I'd like to see for myself."

"Mr—" She turned away from Niyi and whispered, "Mr. Oyinlolu—"

"Tomiwa," he corrected. "Please."

"Okay," she said as she closed her eyes and pictured calling him by name. It still didn't sound right, so she shook her head. She was not going to be addressing him by name directly. "I'm going to be fine. I've gone through this before like a thousand times. A severe attack and then a cold that just lasts for a while and goes away."

"What are you doing tomorrow evening?"

She drew a blank, then recalled he was waiting for a response. "Resting."

"I support that. I take it as you are free in the evening?"

She frowned. *What does that even mean?* "I'm supposed to be resting."

"Sure, so I will send a driver to pick you up. Around five p.m., if that's okay."

At this point, she was a little baffled. It sounded like she was being propositioned for a date. "Are you asking to take me out of my house?"

"Yes."

"Why?"

"To ascertain that you are fine, and to clarify the few issues between us. We will be having dinner at six p.m. at the Blue Water Hotel on the Island. Do you have any preferences?"

She was confused. Was it a date? If it was, she wasn't sure yet how she felt about it. She needed to give him an answer, though. He was waiting. "I don't eat seafood. Allergies."

"Fine. We'll avoid seafood, and—any other thing you don't like. I'll see you tomorrow at six. If that's okay with you."

"Yeah," she said after a long pause. "It's okay."

She was slightly flabbergasted at how they had gone from a random meeting in an elevator, to a work interview in his office, to cat fights on social media, to chatting like friends in the hospital, to his jacket on her shoulders, to a date.

"I'll see you tomorrow. Do take care of yourself," he said. "And, steam."

She cleared her throat. "I will. Thanks for checking up on me."

"It was my pleasure."

When she cut the line, she stood staring at the phone for a while.

The CEO of Purple Chip had just asked her out on a date, and she'd said *yes*.

Was she crazy? She hated the guy!

Chapter Seventeen

MIDE FOUND HERSELF tapping one finger on her laptop keyboard as soon as fifteen minutes to five clocked. It was Monday evening, and she was thinking about her upcoming date with the tech magnate.

She was worried he would show up and worried he wouldn't. Both scenarios scared her. What would they discuss aside from asthma? Being asthmatic was not even a subject she wanted to talk about. There was the fact she'd dragged him on social media. That would come up.

She took in a deep breath and let it out slowly.

He is just checking up on me, she told herself. *He asked me on a date to check up on me!*

The thought freaked her out. There were many things she'd always wanted to ask him. This was going to be the opportunity.

Glancing at her watch, she stood from her seat and started to shut her laptop down.

"Where are you going?" Chuka asked when he saw her get up.

"Association of monitoring spirits," Akin muttered from his end of the office.

"It's been an entirely rough day for me. My voice has been gone half the time, and my throat and eyes have been itching because someone in this office has been smoking."

She made a point of looking ahead at Sesan who completely ignored her. "I want to go home and rest."

"We still have a mountain of work to get through," Chuka grumbled. "And your part of it is very key."

"I will continue it when I get home. After I've had some much-needed rest, thank you very much." She hurried to Niyi's office.

"That's why you don't hire girls," Femi said to him. "Weak vessels."

"This one is not weak," Chuka said, to her hearing. "She is just playing hooky with her work and taking a French leave. Which one of you is smoking?"

There was no answer to his query.

Mide knocked on Niyi's door and opened it.

She dropped her things on the chair in his office and ran into the bathroom where she coughed up a lot of phlegm and took in deep breaths of air to calm her breathing. There was pain in her chest, and she was tired of coughing.

"Are you taking the cough syrup?" Niyi asked with concern when she came back out.

"Yes, but it makes me sleepy. I want to take some time off this evening. I know there is so much to do, but—"

"Go," he said without hesitation. "I don't like the way your voice sounds."

"I kind of like it," she teased. "Chuka said it's husky and sexy. I think my man-friend will like it."

Niyi scowled at her. "Just go before you lose it completely."

She grinned, loving the huge kick she got out of teasing him.

"It's drizzling outside, how are you getting home? Taxify? Would have loved to take you myself, but I'm still stuck here. Might even pull an all-nighter."

"Don't trouble yourself. I'll take Taxify and get some work done once I've rested." She picked up her handbag and laptop bag.

She hated lying to Niyi, but she very well couldn't tell him she was going out with Tomiwa Oyinlolu.

"Rest. Tomorrow is another day."

"Yes, boss," she said hoarsely.

"Please go and take some lemon tea with honey when you get home."

She thought again about spending the evening with the CEO of Purple Chip versus resting at home with a cup of lemon tea. The benefits were vastly different. "I hear you."

With that, she left his office, waved goodbye to the guys, and blew a soft kiss at Chuka. He caught it and winked at her. She smiled and hurried down the staircase, putting her umbrella up once she stepped out of the building.

It was drizzling hard, and she didn't have to turn to know Femi and Chuka were watching her from the window. They had heard part of her conversation with Tomiwa's driver on the phone, and she knew they would try to confirm if it was a taxi guy picking her up.

She lifted a hand in a backward wave when she got to the gate and the gateman let her out.

A silver Mercedes Benz GL 450 pulled up as soon as she stepped out. It was the same one that had dropped her at home days prior, so it was Mr. Oyinlolu's driver. As she got in, it occurred to her the date was happening.

A date with the owner of Purple Chip.

A date, at all!

It had been two years since she'd broken up with Biyi, her former fiancé, and that long since she'd gone out with anyone. Somehow, his mum had convinced him asthma was infectious, and she would give it to him and pass it on to all their children. Plus, she wasn't so sure Mide would even live very long, or survive childbirth.

Their horrible breakup had left her feeling very hurt and confused about her future. Did having asthma ban one to a lifetime of loneliness? Did it mean she wasn't good enough for any guy because she had it? Did it even mean she wouldn't live long?

Her father had died from asthma-related consequences, and she had promised herself she would never get involved with any guy. But she had done so, and it had caused her a heartbreak, so she proposed she would flirt with guys, laugh with them, and go out with them if they ever pressurized her, but she would never commit.

Neither would she let it be known she was living with asthma.

Somehow, this date with Tomiwa Oyinlolu had happened in reverse order.

There had been no chance of flirting in between meeting him in an elevator and trying to get a job in his company. There was no way he could like her following her bashing of his company on X. She had also experienced a full-fledged attack right in front of him, so there was no hiding her health status.

Now that she was meeting up with him, she was hoping her allergies wouldn't flare up and embarrass her. A nebulizer was packed up in her laptop bag just in case. She had snuck off to use it in the office restroom earlier in the day.

So, when the Benz stopped in front of her, she had panicked, especially nervous about the date.

"Good evening, Miss Akinseye," the driver said the moment she shut the door. "I'm John. I will be taking you straight to the Blue Water Hotel lobby this evening, per Mr. Oyinlolu's instructions. He'll be waiting for you."

"Oh, hi, I remember you." She had scrutinized him well before she settled down into the car. He was indeed the driver who had taken her to the hospital. "Thank you for the other night."

"You are welcome, ma."

She leaned into the back seat of the SUV and exhaled quietly. The vehicle was air-conditioned and too cold in her opinion. In moments, her nose was congested, and she was finding it hard to breathe. Later, she sneezed, brought out a paper towel, and spat out the offending phlegm with worry.

"Would you like me to adjust the temperature of the air conditioner, ma'am?"

"Yes, please, take it up. It's a little too cold."

"Yes, ma."

Mide watched him fiddle with the controls, sure Tomiwa had warned him about the temperature in the car. She was touched he was concerned about her having another attack. The chesty cough she had, however, was her main worry. It just could not show up when she was with him.

THE BLUE WATER OVERLOOKED the Atlantic Ocean on its south side and seemed glamorous from the front. Mide viewed it from the backseat window of the Benz as the car drove through the hotel's spacious compound.

"Beautiful," she found herself whispering out loud.

The only time she'd been at a hotel had been to usher at an event on Pamela's behalf. The hotel had turned out to be more a motel than anything, and she'd been too busy waiting tables to enjoy the sights.

"We are here already, ma," John said. "You can get down here and walk to the entrance. He's waiting."

It had stopped raining, so she folded her tiny umbrella and stuffed it inside her handbag. It would have been great had she been able to drop her things at home before coming, but going home first would have meant she would be late.

True to his word, he was waiting when she got to the lobby. She hadn't even needed to ask the front desk officers. She found him seated on one of the plush, modern-looking armchairs to the left of the front desk, looking distinguished as he scribbled across his phone with its accompanying pen.

Upon sighting her, he sprang to his feet and folded up the phone before sauntering up to her.

"Good evening," she said, nervous.

"Evening. How was your day?"

"Good. And yours?"

"Great, let me help you." He made to pick her laptop bag from off her shoulder.

"Hey, no, sir. You don't have to—" she protested, stepping back.

"Come on," he replied softly. "What kind of ape country do you think I come from to let you carry all this baggage by yourself? You should have dropped it in the car. John would have taken excellent care of it."

"I didn't know that," she said, releasing the laptop bag to him.

"We are having dinner at the Blue restaurant on this floor." He swung the bag onto his shoulder. "No seafood as you have so graciously expressed, and definitely nothing you do not like."

"Thank you."

He nodded with his eyes on hers. "I'm glad to see that your voice sounds so much better."

"I told you not to worry, sir. It's—I'm much better."

"Please, don't refer to me as *sir*. It's kind of aging, and I'm not even yet forty. Come along."

He led the way down the expansive corridor leading away from the lobby. She followed, glad to get the awkwardness of their initial encounter out of the way.

"I hope this is not rude, but how old are you exactly?"

He turned to her with an amused smile as they strolled across the corridor's luxurious blue and gold carpeting. "Thirty-seven. Hope that doesn't scare you."

"No," she said, wondering if it was a trick question. "Why would it?"

"You're twenty-seven. Some would call it cradle snatching."

She laughed. "How did you know how old I was?"

"You applied to work in my company." He opened a door and led her into another corridor.

"You have my CV," she said, feeling a little slow.

"A decade is a lot. What do you think?"

"Well, I'm hardly a tot in a cradle, and ten years won't seem so bad a dozen years from now."

"Really? You see us together a dozen years from now?"

"Please, give yourself some credit. I'm just saying that age is relative. It depends on how you want to look at it. When I'm forty, you'll be fifty. If we were together, we'd both be in or around forties, and no one would be the wiser. Besides, men tend to get better-looking with age, and you are hardly the type of guy I'd call a cradle snatcher."

He grinned, opened the door to the restaurant, and turned to let her in. "So, what kind of guy would you call me, then?"

"Uhm, you're a successful, loaded business entrepreneur. I'm a girl with a dream just starting out in life." She shrugged and gave him a coy look as she passed beside him into the half-filled restaurant. "My cousin would say sugar-daddy."

He burst out laughing at her answer and pointed to a cordoned-off area in the back where a waiter was raising a hand and beckoning to them. "You want everyone in this restaurant to label me before this night is over."

"My apologies. Nobody heard me, and you don't look that old, so don't worry."

"I am glad you think so." He stepped towards the private seating area and nodded at the waiter. "Evening."

"Welcome, sir, ma," the waiter said and took the laptop bag from him. "My name is Friday, and I will be attending to your table this evening."

"Thank you, Friday." Tomiwa pulled out a chair on one side of the rectangular table, looked up at her, and pointed both hands down at it. "Please."

She stared at him. She had seen that move done before. By one of his staff, on the day of the interview test when she had run in late and had been looking for a seat. He had probably borrowed it from his boss.

"You are very chivalrous. Has anyone ever told you that?"

"You would be the first," he said as she lowered herself into the seat. "And it's refreshing to hear you think of me as something other than an affluent pachydermatous boar."

Her mouth parted, and she gasped as her past social media activities came to light. "You read that, too."

"I did." He let go of the chair and walked round the table to drag out the seat opposite her.

"I'm sorry. I didn't intend for you to read that."

"I'm also on the X app. Difficult as it may be for you to believe. And I do follow interesting threads."

"Once again, I apologize."

"Apology accepted. I don't think anyone has ever called me a name I had to look up before," he said good-naturedly.

She shook her head. "It's a wonder you didn't let me pass out on that balcony."

"And confirm my pachydermatous nature?"

"I've come to realize you are rather gallant."

"I haven't done anything out of the ordinary, Mide. This is a date. You're the princess, and I'm the guy trying to charm the glass slipper off your foot."

"A date?"

"Yes, you're intriguing." His bright eyes challenged hers. "And this is my chance to get to know you more. Outside of work, that is."

Chapter Eighteen

FOR THE FIRST FIVE minutes of the date, Mide regretted every nasty word she'd ever spewed about him on social media. Especially because he'd turned out to be affable.

He had a stern-looking countenance, but it seemed that was as far as it went.

"How's your chest?" he asked.

She took in a deep, full breath. "Better. As you can see. You didn't need a date to ascertain that."

"I did. I wanted to hear you laugh and talk too much and assault my senses with your gregarious fashion sense. None of which seem to be happening tonight."

She watched him for a moment before eliciting a quiet chortle. "Okay, I'm talkative, and I tend to laugh a lot, but what in the world do you mean by gregarious fashion sense?"

"Who wears yellow to an interview?"

"It's—I—I wanted to stand out." It had been the most tenable outfit she'd had in her wardrobe.

"You certainly did, and not just because of your dressing." He leaned back into his chair. "You had a ninety-three on my test, and it's the highest I've ever recorded. That was very well done."

"Thank you," she said, more than humbled by the praise.

"I miss the yellow, though," he continued softly. "I was hoping you would wear it today. Not like what you are wearing is disappointing, but I was hoping for a red dress, or an orange sweater, or a purple pair of trousers, something captivating and gregarious."

"I'm coming from work, and we had this dinner, and..." she trailed off, finding herself unable to relax with him as she had the previous day. *Is he flirting?*

"You were supposed to be resting!"

"Yes, I was—"

"Sir, ma'am." Friday butted into their conversation, making them both turn to him. "What would you like to drink this evening?" He handed them the food and drinks menu.

Mide took the drinks menu, glad to focus on anything but her rattling mind. They had been having an easy conversation so far, but nothing she had prepared in her head to ask him was coming to mind.

She looked up above the menu to catch his eye. "I don't think I should have anything cold. Maybe tea, lemon tea to be precise with a dash of honey."

Tomiwa turned to Friday. "Do you have hot tea?"

The waiter straightened up. "I'm not too sure we serve that in the evenings, sir."

"Please try and make it available. Just talk to Chef Michael, and tell him Mr. Oyinlolu requested it. I'll have a blue special with ice. How do you want your tea, Mide?"

She looked up at the waiter. "Hot water, not boiling, the juice of a whole lemon with half a tablespoon of honey in it."

Tomiwa looked from her to the waiter. "Did you get that?"

"Of course, sir," Friday replied. "Hot water, not boiling, juice of a whole lemon and one teaspoon of honey. And for you, the blue special with ice. While I get your drinks, could you please look at the food menu and decide on your starter and the main meal of the evening?"

"No problem. Thank you, Friday," Tomiwa said.

The waiter bowed and left holding the drinks menu.

They were both quiet while they studied the meal menu.

Mide read through the list, but nothing was jumping out at her. Her thoughts were more along the lines of questioning why he'd asked her to dinner. Wanting to see how she was doing was a lame enough excuse in her opinion, and Tomiwa Oyinlolu didn't strike her as a person who did things randomly. A lot of thought had gone into the decision. The reason was what eluded her. She was intriguing? Not enough reason.

She felt his gaze on her after a while and looked up to find he was studying her and not the menu. Her heart worked itself into a frenzy, and she found herself leaning back into her chair, letting her gaze peruse the artwork on the walls around the private sitting area. She was going to ignore the heat creeping up her neck into her cheeks.

"Lemon tea helps you with the cold?" he inquired.

She was forced to look at him. "Yes, and mint tea, and apple cider vinegar, and mentos sweets, and vapor rub, and sweaters, and hot water bottles, and Maltesers, and steaming—"

"That many things?"

"That many things, can you imagine?" She shook her head in pretend wonder.

"What do the Maltesers do?"

"Bribe me to stay in the hospital. When I was younger, sometimes I'd be hospitalized for days, and I hated it. But they would give me a packet of Maltesers to melt in my mouth, and I'd do absolutely anything they wanted me to. Even take injections."

His gaze was soft but intense. "I hate hospitals. Not sure there is anything you can bribe me with to get me to stay."

"But you were there with me on Saturday. You didn't seem uncomfortable."

"There was a need. And you looked so fragile on that gurney, I had to put away my fears."

She looked back at the menu. Nothing was striking a chord. In fact, she had lost her appetite and was just full of questions that were eluding her at this particular moment.

She covered her mouth and coughed a little.

He narrowed his brow. "Did you steam last night?"

"I did. Sometimes, my chest just gets congested after an episode, hence the cold."

She coughed and then sneezed. Unfortunately, some mucus came out of her nose with the sneeze, and she was mortified. She covered her nose and reached in her handbag for a tissue. "I am so sorry."

Tomiwa seemed more concerned than disgusted.

"That's okay," he said, handing her a serviette from the container on their table. "You don't have to be. I understand you have a cold. Everyone gets colds now and then."

"Not like me." She wiped her face and wished she could disappear from that restaurant right then. The embarrassment was suffocating. "This cold could last like for the next two months before it goes away completely if I am not careful."

"You assured me you were fine!" he sort of growled.

"It's just congestion and allergies. Nothing to worry about." She was still covering her nose. "I'm sorry, I have to blow my nose."

"Go ahead."

Mide turned to the side to blow her nose. It sounded horrible, even to her.

"I don't want to ruin dinner for us," she said. "I'm so sorry."

"You won't. Your tea will soon be here. That should help."

She passed him an embarrassed look and blew her nose again.

"I'm not in any way offended," he replied. "Just worried."

TOMIWA WATCHED AS THE waiter put the tea down and served his blue special. Her tea had come in a very large teacup with fancy detailing around the edges. His special was a rum and ginger beer infused beverage with a splash of an energy drink and sweet spices.

He felt guilty. She still needed rest as far as he could see, yet he had been unwilling to let the opportunity go. Finding her on that balcony had been a blessing in two ways.

One, he'd gotten the chance to save her. Two, he'd gotten a point of contact with her that did not necessitate any creative fabrication.

She allowed him to pick a chicken dish for their main meal with sides of coconut rice and a salad. Then he sent the waiter away.

"So why did you ask me out?" she asked, surprisingly direct in her inquiry.

He sighed dramatically, knowing she had probably been dying to ask. "I'm not sure your cousin will let me into his house to check in on you."

She stopped halfway into a sip of her tea. "He's not the kind of person who would do that."

He raised his eyebrows. "Did you tell him we were having dinner tonight and mention my name specifically?"

"No." She smiled and put her cup of tea down. "Actually, I don't think it's the idea of you he doesn't like. Any guy would be subject to scrutiny by him."

"Hmm," he said and sipped his drink, enjoying the sweet, syrupy, and ginger notes.

"The thing is, my cousin is very protective. Asthma is not exactly an ailment that one jokes around with. He just wants me to be safe."

"I understand. I'd be, too, if I were in his shoes."

"I was just wondering—because it's not normal to go for an interview at someone's company, fail to get in, and then be asked out by the MD slash CEO after lambasting him on the X platform— why did you ask to see me? I didn't tell Niyi because I just didn't think he would understand or that I fully understand what, exactly, this is."

He stared at her. "My apologies for camping us in this private area, but my brother and sister frequently have meals here, and I wouldn't want them to see us together and conclude I'm giving away trade secrets. Like I said, I don't want you in the middle of whatever is happening between my company and your cousin's company. We just don't need that drama."

"I assure you, I'm not in the middle of anything. I wouldn't be here if I didn't want to be."

She wanted to be. His ears perked up, but he hid his delight. Nothing good came from showing one's hand prematurely.

"I'm glad you are. And as to your question, truth be told, that stint at the hospital was a little scary for me. I was, and still am, concerned about you."

She nodded.

"I feel a little guilty about not giving you a place in my company. Especially when I saw you serving drinks at Kola Bamigbe's party." He ended his words by looking at her.

Her eyes widened. She looked down at the table between them. "I-I didn't know you would be there."

"Do you do that often?"

"Usher at parties?"

"Was that what it was?"

A tiny frown settled between her brows. "I did nothing but serve drinks."

"I saw."

Ade had gone home with one of the Ankara girls, prompting him to search for Mide. He had been both disappointed and worried to find her gone.

He thought twice about saying the next words out of his mouth but didn't see the need to filter it. "I searched for you afterward. You weren't anywhere to be found."

She let the frown fizzle out of her face and looked like she was contemplating whether or not to respond to his query. "My cousin came to pick me up. He ensured I left there in one piece."

He stared at her, trying to ascertain if she was hiding anything.

"I'm not a runs girl. If that's what you think."

He shook his head. "I didn't say that..."

"My cousin would never allow me to—he picks me up from parties, I don't go home with anyone."

He exhaled with relief. "That's a wise, good decision. Why were you ushering?"

"Why do you want to know?" Her tone had turned defensive.

"I'm—" he shrugged, "—just concerned."

"I ushered a lot when I was in the university. It paid my way through school."

"What about your parents?"

She sighed. "My dad passed away when I was little. I've been living with Niyi off and on, ever since I finished secondary school."

"And you don't want to impose too much on him."

"I don't."

He wondered if he should tell her his dad had died and left them a surprise that was working in her company at the moment gathering intel for them on his sister's orders.

It wasn't information that would endear her to him, so he pushed it out of his mind and focused on her. She had been hard-pressed for money. It was why she'd been ushering.

He recalled she'd mentioned needing a paying job at the interview. It was understandable she didn't want to be more of a burden on her cousin than she felt she already was.

"Niyi did his best, but I had to supplement. Not that he liked my knack for sourcing odd jobs to make ends meet, but he knows I want to make my way in life. He was especially scandalized by that night's outfit, too, but I had agreed to usher, and...I needed the money."

He scrutinized her face for an endearing moment. "For the record, I liked the outfit. It showed off your finer assets."

She blushed and lowered her eyes to the table.

"Finer assets being your legs, and a very delectable view of your backside."

The image hadn't left his brain since the night of the party. Her curvaceous hips and endless legs toured his mind from time to time.

"I had no say in picking the outfit. I just usher, I don't—" She looked up at him. "I don't do anything else."

"I know. You don't seem like the type."

He'd seen the pictures on her Facebook page. She was a decent girl.

"Now that we've talked about that," he said, sipping his drink and lowering the glass cup. "We can just pretend for this one evening I am not the CEO of Purple Chip and you are not from One Tech. Let's forget the myriad of things that brought us together and just be a guy and a girl having dinner and conversations without a care in the world. Can we do that?"

She eyed him and raised her eyebrows, all shyness slipping in that moment.

"You want me to pretend you are not this hugely successful CEO—" she held out a hand to him and then pointed at herself, "—and I am not the girl who tried and failed to get a job in your company."

"The beautiful, intelligent, and strong girl with plans to debug my codes once she gets one foot through the doors of my company, if I may correct. And yes, would that be so hard?"

She chuckled. "Nope! That way, my brain can just wrap itself around the fact I am not and can no longer be your employee—"

His mouth widened into a huge grin. "You really wanted to be my employee?"

"Are you kidding me? Since like the day I discovered coding."

"Let's just be Tomiwa and Ademide, then," he said. "Forget the labels."

"Okay." She picked up her teacup. "I'll toast to that."

He smiled and reached across the table with his glass cup. "Likewise."

"So," she said, taking a sip. "Tell me about yourself."

"I'm Oluwatomiwa Oyinlolu. What I love most to do is to solve complex problems for different companies using technology."

"Okay. What school did you attend?"

"The prestigious University of Lagos with a second class upper in Computer Engineering, and then the University of Virginia with a double Masters in Systems Engineering and Business Administration. I play tennis and basketball, whenever I can. I hate reading or cooking. I code." He shrugged.

"Tell me something else about you. Something nobody knows."

Dear girl, he thought as he smiled at her.

"Something no one knows," he said out loud. "Okay, well..." He paused as he stared at the table between them for a long moment. "I think you are perhaps the most attractive girl I have ever met." He looked up at her. "That's something nobody knows."

She seemed stunned. "Thank you, erm, I am honoured that you find me attractive, I—but I didn't mean about me. I meant about you."

"Oh, I am only thinking about you at this moment."

"Don't. I want to know about you."

"Okay." He sighed out loud. "Let me try again. I started my company with zero-naira zero-kobo because I didn't want any of my father's money."

She gazed up at him with an attentive expression.

"I had nothing but my wits, my guts, a few rich contacts whose companies had issues and a determination to prove to my father that technology was a key factor for business growth. He was very sure the fad would pass away. Now, it's a multimillion-naira company, part of the Oyinlolu Corporation but a separate entity on its own that's a turn key investment, and most people think I got lucky because my father handed me some naira notes on a platter of gold."

"That's impressive," she whispered.

He shrugged. "I hope to write a book one day, teach Nigerians how to start and run successful tech companies in this complex Nigerian business atmosphere. Talk about the real truth of how I made it, and why coding isn't exactly my strongest suit."

"It's not? What is your strongest suit?"

"Diagnosing business problems. It's the why of why I code. Finding and solving problems for people who run businesses."

"That's an interesting way to look at software coding."

"Coding, for me, is like breathing. I don't see myself on this earth without it. We're here to solve problems, and that's part of what I plan to put in my book. Rather than hope, I've actually begun writing it."

"That's great. I wish you all the very best."

"Throwing my elevator words back at me?"

She chuckled. Her laugh was joyful. Likeable.

"I've always wanted to pick your brain. I'm really glad for the opportunity to sit across from you today."

"Pick away. Only, we are not talking about work today, and I'm not going to be the only one sharing. Your turn."

"My turn to tell you something no one knows." She took in a deep breath and thought for a couple of seconds before she spoke. "I have never been inside a hotel restaurant before. This is my first time."

"Are you serious?" he said, his voice brimming with laughter.

"I'm not. I was drooling with my mouth open when we drove up the hotel driveway and asking myself if I was still in Lagos when I walked into the building."

"Oh, goodness," he said, letting out the laughter. "And you're not afraid to reveal that to me. Thank God for me in your life, then."

"Yes, o!" she replied, sipping her tea. "Thank God for you now being in my life. At least now, I won't ever say I've never been in a hotel restaurant before," she replied with a playful smile.

"What about all those ushering gigs?"

"Usually happened at event halls, or in people's homes. The only hotel I've ever been at was on the mainland, and it was a third of the size and opulence of this one. More like a motel than anything." She leaned across the table at him. "Please don't tell anyone."

He smiled and leaned into her.

"I won't," he promised as their food arrived.

Chapter Nineteen

AS MIDE TYPED AWAY on her laptop the following morning, she tried—unsuccessfully—not to think about her date the night before.

Niyi had tasked her to work on the framework for the programming language for all the future projects they would have to execute at One Tech, but she was thinking about a second date with Tomiwa Oyinlolu.

He hadn't given any indication there would be one, and she had tried not to give off the vibe she wanted a repeat of their evening. Future dates meant the first date had gone down well with him, too, but she was doing her best not to have her hopes raised and dashed.

It was futile.

Tomiwa Oyinlolu had been the most courteous host, and she had been charmed by his gracious manner. The food had been nice, and her host surprisingly easy to be with. Plus, he found her attractive! That thought had been bubbling around in her mind all morning.

Down to earth was not a phrase she would have put in the same sentence with the CEO of Purple Chip before yesterday. *Going on a date with* would not have made it in, either.

When she sneezed and proceeded to blow her nose very loudly, it drew a disapproving frown from Sesan.

"It's just allergies, I'm not contagious."

"I can see you have lost all sense of poshness since this illness began," Chuka said from his position in his seat. "How can you blow your nose like that in front of everyone?"

"Well," she replied, clearing her throat and reaching for another piece of tissue from the box on her desk. "I'm a tomboy in a dress with a cold."

"Any which way," Akin said glancing at her. "I'll take you any day over a model."

"Thank you," she said. "Those are the lies you tell all the girls, right?"

"What girls?" Akin scoffed without taking his eyes off his laptop screen. "There's only you."

Chuka's look was contemptuous. "Akin, stop hitting on Mide. Her cousin is somewhere in the building."

"His job is just to collect yams. He's not going to marry her himself, is he?"

"I will repeat," Chuka said. "Stop hitting on her, or your salary next month will be dicey."

"*As if na you dey sign cheque*," Akin replied.

Mide blew her nose again, making Sesan look up and frown.

"Are you going to step outside?" he asked tersely.

"No." She smiled sweetly at him and rubbed the antibacterial sanitizer on her table on her hands. "I am not going to step outside because someone in this office smokes. It's making my allergy worse. I'm not going to stop blowing my nose until that person owns up and stops smoking. Entirely."

She had a sneaky feeling it was the Sesan who was the smoker. He took long breaks every three or four hours and stepped into the balcony supposedly to think and make calls.

And, he was the one person she knew who was into Orbit chewing gum.

The door between the office pool and the reception opened just then, and Kemi popped her head in. "Mide, there is a delivery for you."

"Me?" she said, startled. "I didn't order anything."

"Do you want me to bring it in?"

"Yes, please."

Kemi came in a minute later, carrying a huge rectangular box that had been cloaked up in a pretty, transparent gift wrap.

Mide's mouth dropped open as it made its way towards her. Even the Dappler stopped his work for a brief moment to frown at the delivery.

The huge box was filled with all sorts of things. Her name was printed in pretty colourful letters on one side of it. The most prominent feature was the huge bouquet of red roses sticking out from under the transparent plain and pink hearts cellophane wrapping.

"I didn't order that!" she said as Kemi set the box down on an empty table.

"Of course you didn't." Chuka reached for the box. "Someone sent it. Bae, perhaps?"

"I don't have a boyfriend."

"Don't mind him, he is just being antsy because he didn't think of it first," Akin replied.

"An idolizer, then?" Chuka stood up and grabbed the accompanying card right off the package. "Well, now, you probably will have to say yes to him."

"*Amebo*," Kemi teased. "Is it yours?"

"*I was listening to all the many things*," Chuka read out loud and flipped the card over. "*Get well soon.*" He looked at Mide. "Idolizer, definitely. What was he listening to?"

A slow, perceptive smile spread across her face.

"No name." He handed her the card. "He expects you to know who he is."

Yeah! Tomiwa Oyinlolu!

Chuka bent to look at her face. "You know who it is, don't you?"

She kept the mischievous smile on her face, and without saying a word, stood up to dig through the treasure box of gifts.

"And you won't say," Chuka added.

The bunch of artificial red roses was tagged, '*Because the real ones might make you sneeze.*' She chuckled. It had a mild floral smell, too.

There was a huge jar of honey, several packets of Mentos sweets, Maltesers, three different types of fruit-infused tea, a large hot-water bottle bag, a tube of vapor rub, a bottle of silver bird oil, and a beautiful green, turtleneck cashmere sweater. There was also a big bottle of apple cider vinegar, a bottle of fruit wine, and a round piece of six-inch strawberry cake wrapped in cling foil.

"Whoever it is, he's not romantic at all," Chuka declared.

Mide packed all the items back into the box absent-mindedly. The gift was both precious and expensive. He'd been listening.

"You are just jealous. What's your definition of a romantic gift?" Femi called out from behind them.

"Well, it doesn't include tea and vapor rub."

LIKE WHIRLWIND

"It's a get-well-soon gift pack, you idiot!" Femi replied.

"Okay, can we all get back to work?" Sesan snapped at all of them from his corner of the office. "Sideshow's over!"

The subject of their conversation, Mide, was already back at her desk, typing away.

"Aren't you going to call him?" Chuka asked, curious.

She shrugged. "What makes you think it's a he?"

"Is it a she?" Chuka asked, staring at her with worry.

"Well, I'm not calling him, or her, in front of you all."

"FEYIN, NOT ANOTHER one of these meetings," Tomiwa exploded when he got into the conference room. "I told you before—if you're going to spy on One Tech, leave me out of it."

He stopped short at a large image of Ademide's face on the projection screen. The sight made his heart take a tumble in his chest. He opened his mouth and closed it gently.

I really must get a grip on this runaway heartbeat of mine every time I see her.

"Why is her face on the screen?" He turned to his sister. "Finally planning to hire her?"

"At all."

"Has she dragged us to the curbs on X street again?"

"No."

"Has she produced a sensational TikTok video that hurts *Purple Ledger* and shoots our confidence to pieces?"

"Tomiwa—"

"Has she written another tell-all-tale about the shady shenanigans in Lion Towers?"

"Don't be ridiculous!" Feyintola seethed.

"Then why is her face on the screen?"

"This is something you need to hear. Sit."

Tomiwa exhaled as he noticed Sesan in the room. He slid himself into a black leather-clad chair and turned it around to face his half-brother. "We're going to be having our meetings with him in the room now, aren't we?"

"Yes," Feyintola replied. "As long as it concerns securing this project."

"What's the occasion?"

"It has to do with the modules," Babs began. "Sesan here has furnished us with data on every single module in their solution in comparison to ours."

Tomiwa placed his forearms on the granite conference room table. "And?"

"You know we were thinking the Jules are purely an engineering company and we didn't develop the compliance module as much as we should have. They have a few reports on their compliance module—"

"That's missing in ours," he finished, realizing that's probably what Kehinde Jules Junior was talking about.

"How soon can you get it done?" Feyintola asked, looking at him.

"A day," he replied. "That's not tough to fix. Why is her picture on the screen?"

"This module—" Feyintola said with a gleam in her eye, "—was developed by none other than your pretty little applicant on the screen."

He tilted his head and raised an eyebrow. "And how is that important?"

"It means she is good."

"I recall trying to convince you that she was, but no, we have to do things your way."

"I don't want her working here, but she is good enough for what we want her for. She helped to develop the first drafts of the solution that's competing with *Purple Ledger*. That was before she even finished school." Turning in her chair, she faced Sesan. "I want you to date her."

Tomiwa's heart somersaulted before he realized his sister was addressing their half-brother.

Sesan's brow rose. "Date her? Mide? Akinseye?" He gave a dry, throaty chuckle.

"Yes, that's the next step. If our plan is to work, she has to like you. Because when she does, she will tell you everything her cousin is thinking about doing, and it will be like having a fly in the wall of their office."

"I'm already a fly working in their office."

"But you are not a fly living in their house, are you?"

He opened his mouth to speak, but Feyintola beat him to it.

"She lives in his house. She's handling the presentation slides and building their programming template. Date her, and you have unlimited access to his house and anything else he's thinking about doing."

Sesan narrowed his brow at Feyintola. "In two and a half weeks? Why don't we just bug their house? It's pretty easy to do nowadays."

"I need her distracted, as well. It's not just about knowing their plans; it's about destabilizing them."

Tomiwa wasn't liking the train of the conversation. "Feyintola, you come up with the most outrageous of plans, and sometimes, I don't even know where your mind is at. How is he dating her going to change things in three weeks?"

"I am not dating her," Sesan declared.

"Why not?" Feyintola quipped. "She is a pretty girl."

Sesan stared at Feyintola for a minute before he spoke. "She is not my type."

Babs and Tomiwa turned incredulous looks in his direction.

"We don't get along much."

Feyintola looked confused. "She's a girl, and she's pretty. What else are you looking for? You don't need to get along, you only need to pretend to. You can always dump her when we're done."

Tomiwa's eyes flew to Feyintola. "I am so sure she won't give him the time of day."

"Kick up the charm!" Feyintola said to Sesan. "I'm sure you can do that."

"She's pretty and intelligent, but she has got some less-than-desirable qualities."

"Such as?" Feyintola asked.

Tomiwa leaned back into his seat, quite interested in hearing what he had to say.

"She doesn't mind her business. I don't like that. She laughs too much and too loudly, is a tad clumsy, says the most outrageous things, and attracts too much attention. And on the subject of her nose, she has this nasty cold that won't go away. I'd rather not fall sick, thank you. She is not my type."

Tomiwa struggled to keep his face straight. *Thank God for that.*

"So, what is your type? Docile and idiotic?" Feyintola countered. "She's a project! You don't have to like her. Dump her when you're done."

"She is a person, Feyin," Tomiwa exclaimed. "A human being. You don't play around with people's feelings. I was going to tell you how ridiculous this whole plan of yours sounds, but I know you're just going to do your own thing, and it will be a complete waste of my time."

"Besides, I think she has a boyfriend," Sesan added.

Tomiwa went dead faced. *A boyfriend? Seriously? Who?*

"Displace the boyfriend!" Feyintola said.

"I can't displace someone I don't know. He sent her this box full of stuff, and she couldn't stop smiling. My guess is she's really into him. Not sure she will be open to dating me."

Tomiwa's heightened heartbeat calmed. Somehow, this piece of news made attending the meeting quite worthwhile.

"I'm giving you everything I need to give you. Do I need to date her?"

"You can start with being her friend," Babs offered. "I think it will serve the same purpose."

At Feyintola's lethal stare, he closed his mouth and looked elsewhere.

"That girl knows everything the One Tech CEO will not readily share. She was working with him long before he hired anybody. You need to date her. Shower her with attention, break down her defences, buy her a bigger box. She likes to talk, get her talking. Heck, get her drunk, for all I care. Just do whatever you need to do to get it done! Pronto!"

She grabbed up her files and walked out of the conference room.

Get her talking, get her drunk?

Tomiwa eyed his sister's back as she stomped out of the conference room. He was annoyed, but he couldn't let it show. He got up and tapped Babs's shoulder. The man jumped up and followed him out of the conference room, through the reception, and past Feyintola who stood giving Ena instructions.

As they took the elevator to the topmost floor, he was quiet. The meeting was over, but he was a little clearer on where he stood with Mide and why it was necessary to let her know she had to be wary of Sesan.

"Sir," Babs paused with his pen on his notepad. "Pardon my asking, but why is he doing this?"

"Who?"

"The—uhm, the new guy. Feyintola's spy."

Tomiwa stopped at the door of his office. "They have an understanding beyond what you and I can comprehend, but the answer to that question is what I want us to find out. The why—that he is doing this."

He turned around to face Babs. "Put a cyber-tail on him. I want my phone to beep with his every frigging footstep. He sneezes, I wanna know. He makes a peep, I wanna know. He sends a mail, I wanna know. He gets a text, I wanna know. He pays a bill, I wanna know. He goes to the bathroom, bet you, I want to know. I want to know every single thing he does, every place he goes, and every person he talks to. I want his whole damn life on my phone!"

Babs nodded. "I'll get right to cloning his phone, sir."

"Get to it." He glanced at his wristwatch. "Tell Shile to pick up my dry cleaning, and give James the compliance module to sort. I want to see what he does with it."

"Are you still going for the meeting, sir?"

"Yeah. Tell Chioma to prepare."

Chapter Twenty

NIYI DRAFTED SESAN to help Mide handle the application's Power Point presentation slides.

"They are the new guys," Akin grumbled. "Why would you pick the new guys over us?"

"Because they seem to have their brain cells firing faster than you old guys. Can you market *Profit X* for over an hour?"

Akin hung his head.

"If we win this, you're going to have to hire more hands to help with system support and implementation," Mide said. "The five of us can't pick up the slack. It's a lot of work."

"Six," Niyi replied. "I'm with you."

"Even then, it's inadequate. There will be synchronization issues, and we will need lots of testers."

"I've sent out feelers for IT students. Right about what I can afford now. Where is Sesan, by the way?"

"He stepped out," Chuka said. "Something about a family issue."

Mide's phone rang just then. She glanced at the screen and smiled at the name.

"Can I take this?" she asked Niyi.

"Sure. We were about wrapped up here anyway, and I have to meet a new client. I'll be back in three to four hours, and we can go home. Start work on the slides with Sesan when he gets back, and please tell him to see me next time before he leaves the office."

"Yes, boss," she said before she stepped into the balcony and shut the door.

She noticed the unmistakable smell of cigarettes immediately and sighed with frustration. "Hi."

"How are you doing?" Tomiwa's voice was soft on the other end of the line.

"Beautiful. Someone sent me a box full of asthma essentials yesterday. I was pleasantly surprised."

He chuckled. "Did you like it?"

"I did, thank you. I'm sorry I didn't save your number, so I couldn't call."

"That is okay. How are you feeling now?"

"Much better." She cleared a dry, tickly feeling at the base of her throat.

"You are still clearing your throat."

"I am standing outside my office. There is something in the air."

"It's taking a while."

"Yeah, it can take a while to completely get over it, but I'm very much better." He was quiet for a moment. "I was thinking we could do dinner again."

"Dinner again?" She folded an arm across her stomach and looked out into the streets below "When would you like to do dinner again?"

"As soon as you can possibly get time off work."

She shrugged. "You pick a date."

"Tomorrow night?"

"Hmm...Friday night, I'll be working. Not sure I'll be able to get away."

"Saturday breakfast?"

She smiled. "You said dinner."

"Breakfast can extend till dinner." He let the statement hang in the air. "And vice versa," he added, filling her mind with immoral, illogical possibilities.

She closed her eyes. This was Tomiwa Oyinlolu, her cousin's rival. "Are we at the stage yet where dinner extends till breakfast?"

"Saturday dinner alone, then?"

"How about Sunday evening? I will be sure to be free then."

"Okay. Do I have permission to call you before then?"

Mide's brow furrowed at the strange request. They had crossed the lines of phone calls and dinner—why was he taking them both into the past? "You are so proper, I forget you are Nigerian!"

"Ah, well, I don't want to be a pest."

"Asking for permission makes our conversation a stilted interaction that we're way past. Please call me, anytime."

He kept quiet.

"Are you there?"

"Yeah. I am going to call you every night from tonight till I see you on Sunday."

She didn't want to admit it, but the words were upturning her insides. "You don't need to ask. It's okay."

"Great, then." A short pause settled. "I'm not stepping on anyone's boundaries, am I?"

"No."

"You're not taken? There's no boyfriend showing up on Sunday wielding an axe and causing a commotion?"

She chuckled and found herself imagining the scenario. "No!"

"No bae, no... what do you Gen Z call it again? Boo?"

"Goodbye, Tomiwa. I have to get back to work. I'll expect your call."

"I won't disappoint."

"I'll see you on Sunday."

"I'll count down the hours."

When she ended the call, she leaned back against the door and stared at the sky as a warm, prickly feeling washed all over her. *He's growing on me.*

She took in a deep breath and searched her heart for a reason.

Was it the gift? The fact he was rich and handsome? That he'd forgiven her X-rant, or the fact he was a well-respected tech entrepreneur?

Is he fine?

Derin's question lit her mind with curiosity. It wasn't his physical features tugging at her heart nor his confident and capable leadership traits. It wasn't his money, either.

It was his chivalry!

The polite, courteous way he treated her. The tender, quiet tone of his voice whenever they had conversations, and the devotion in his eyes when he looked at her. She was no fool. She knew what he wanted. The question was, was she ready for it? Was she ready to let another guy into her world to grapple with her illness and open up her fears about it?

Was she ready for a relationship?

"Mide!"

She sighed. "Coming!"

———◆———

WORKING LATE INTO THE night the next day, she was getting nowhere trying to win Sesan over to her side of their argument on what direction their presentation should take.

"You work on the introduction and the company profile. I'll do the modules," he offered.

"I don't think we should do a module-type presentation. They would like to see a busy CEO's mobile version of the app and its features."

"I don't agree with you," he replied, nose buried in his laptop. "Most companies don't know what they want. Going briefly through all the modules will help them decide."

"I agree, but what I'm talking about—"

"Is not what we are going to do," Sesan said without looking at her.

It occurred to her just then how much of a sharp contrast there was between him and Tomiwa.

Why is that thought in my head?

"It won't kill you to be nice occasionally," she said.

He raised an eyebrow. "Because I don't agree with you?"

"It's the way you say things, and I'm not just talking about today. You can be very—you know what? Forget I said anything." She picked up her mug of tea and sipped from it.

He kept on typing. Then he turned his laptop around and showed it to her. "This is what I'm talking about."

"It's nice," she said after staring at the screen for a while.

He frowned at her. "Nice was not the adjective I was looking for."

"Nice is all I have."

"Nice is basic, and what I have just created is way above basic."

"Don't let me stop it getting to your head."

He snorted, and they were quiet as she sipped her tea and forced herself to stay awake. Her cousin was in his office, looking through their work for the day. Femi and Ross had stayed over supposedly to test, but they were stretched out on the floor of the office, catching some sleep.

"Why do they call you the Dappler? What does it mean?"

"Horses," he said. "The dappled grey horse is a sign of freedom without restraint. It was my surfing name."

"On the dark web?"

He glanced at her. "You're sure curious about that a lot."

"I am."

"And you're pretty," he continued, out of the blue.

She narrowed her eyes and watched him type on. "Where's that coming from?"

"From the truth. I'm not trying to flatter you, but it's late, we've been working for hours, and most of your makeup is all gone. Yet, you're still pretty. Why did you choose coding?"

Mide made a face. Though she was usually agreeable to be with, she didn't want to talk about how she got into coding. "Needed something to do one time when I was hospitalized for a while. Niyi put a laptop in my hands and taught me programming syntaxes."

"He did you a favour, you're rather good. Let me see what you have on the busy CEO."

She turned her laptop to him, and he scrolled through her slides for less than a minute.

"It's not enough. I expected something more intellectually stimulating."

Halfway between angry and irritated, she put her mug down. "Do you just get a kick out of being saucy all the time?"

He eyed her. "Do you get a kick out of laughing all the time like a hyena let loose in the wild?"

"Goodness gracious! Sesan Bankole! Me, a hyena?" She looked around at the silent room wishing she could hit him over the head with something hard. "It's two a.m. in the morning, and I'm not in the mood."

"Neither am I. Half the slides have to go. Short, sweet, and straight to the point is the watchword."

"First you say it's not enough, then you say the slides are too much. Pick a side!"

"Here's what we'll do. Halve your slides, tweak the rest into a video animation, and replace those removed slides with mine. That way, we can mutually agree on a cohesive presentation. Deal?"

"Does it look like I have a choice?"

"Great. Have lunch with me tomorrow so we can finalize," he said suddenly but kept on typing on his laptop.

She made a show of turning to look at him. How could someone be on the opposite sides of a line at the same time? "Did I hear you right? Was that you, or an artificial clone of your very impertinent self, asking me out? After insulting me?"

"Scratch it. I don't know where that came from," he replied and kept typing.

"I'll pretend I didn't hear it, either. I'm going to do thirty minutes, then I'm going to Niyi's office to sleep."

———◉———

TWO DAYS LATER, MIDE found herself at a restaurant called The Hallow Point seated across from a very affable-looking Tomiwa Oyinlolu. They were two weeks away from the pitch meetings, and she had been needing a break from work all week.

Not that she hadn't also been looking forward to seeing him.

Recalling Derin's question again, she found herself changing her mind about his level of attraction. He was a huge upgrade from her last boyfriend. Effortlessly sprouting the well-to-do look in a powder blue T-shirt underneath a black, casual jersey jacket.

Inconspicuous as he always tried to appear, it was obvious just looking at him there was quality and opulence in the outfit. Possessive emotions swarmed her heart. It seemed he got better-looking with each meeting they had. With his jacket hugging his shoulders, and his beard and hairline neatly trimmed and blending into the brown tan of his face, he had enticed a couple of looks on their way in.

This had sent looks veering her way, too. Probably to assess or ensure—she couldn't decide which—the girl with him was good enough to be seen with him.

The first time they had gone out, it had just been a dinner invitation. An opportunity to check on her and inquire of her health, as he had put it. This time around, it was clearly a date. She'd taken a careful look at her clothes and selected something nice.

She didn't own designer brands, but she had a good tailor with an eye for pretty fabrics.

And he was happy when he saw her. His eyes said as much.

"Ah an, where are we going?" Derin had remarked after looking her over twice.

"Just out, with friends."

She had made her tone as flippant as possible, but the woman had raised eyebrows at her black, short-sleeved, Lycra tie-top fused with a multi-coloured, flared Ankara skirt. The Lycra had accentuated her modest pair of breasts, giving them definition while the skirt's fullness gave her the hourglass shape she'd been gunning for. A gold bracelet and wristwatch completed the look.

"Looking like that?"

"It's a Sunday evening, I just wanted to look nice."

Derin had looked at her again. "With heels? For your friends or for our mutual friend—the sender of the gift basket?"

Mide had tittered with laughter and hurried out through the front door right, past Niyi who was relaxed on the three-seat sofa watching a football match.

"At some point, I'm going to have to meet him!" he'd yelled as she opened the front door.

Now, she was seated across from Tomiwa sipping a Limoncello Spritz and perusing the menu, the thought made her smile.

"I was rejoicing at not taking you to the Chinese restaurant next door, but this is equally as bad. Fried rice with shrimp sauce, crustacean platter, spicy crispy beef, sweet and sour pork, a variety of seafood in abundance. I can't even get the right pick." He looked up and watched her. "What's so funny?"

She grinned. "The idea of you and Niyi meeting."

He smelled delicious. Some kind of soft tart and musk mixture with a very subtle hint of vanilla. She had noticed it when he'd paused to draw her chair out for her and was glad it was understated or it might have triggered a fit of sneezing.

All in all, she liked it. She liked him. So far. He had turned out to be the opposite of everything she had assumed after their social media war. Sneaking around with him was exhilarating.

His gaze dropped to the menu. "He's curious?"

"He is. Not sure I will be able to sneak out of the house again without him strong-arming me and making me give up your name."

He chuckled and put the menu down. "You think there will be a next time?"

"That's all you got from what I said?"

"Yes. Will there?"

She shrugged. "I don't know. Depends on the outcome of today."

"I'll be sure to listen well, so I'll have a fairly good idea what items to put in my next gift basket. They certainly paved the way for this one."

She grinned. "I think it was all the evening calls. They persuaded me to want to hear your voice some more."

"I'm glad my voice is persuasive. How are you, how's work?"

"I thought we said work was off-limits."

"You don't have to tell me the specifics, just a general idea. You enjoy working at One Tech?"

"I do. It's not Purple Chip, but it has its highs and lows."

"Any interesting work friends?"

"Lots." She was going to stop there, but she didn't know when she blurted out her thoughts about Sesan. "There is this one work colleague, so annoying, brilliant I have to admit, but so, so annoying."

Tomiwa leaned closer. "Is he asking you out?"

"Nothing of the sort. He's just an arrogant know it all. Sesan. That's his name."

"Sesan. Do you want me to arrange him? I know people."

Her eyes widened. "Are you serious?"

"If he is bothering you," he continued in a prevaricate intimidating tone of voice that had her struggling not to laugh.

"Please, don't do anything of the sort. I only meant he is thorough. Wants to be in on everything and on top of everything, back end, front end, presentations, everything has to be his way or no way. It's exhausting. But Niyi likes him and keeps putting us to work together. Despite everything, I'm learning from him. So, I'm not complaining."

"Guys like that are everywhere, even in Purple Chip."

"I know. It's just, he's hot and then cold and then hot, I never know what to expect with him."

Mide had been trying to get his 'have lunch with me' statement out of her mind the whole weekend, and she wasn't having much luck. It had come out of nowhere, and from a guy who seemingly wanted nothing to do with her.

"You should be careful with him," Tomiwa said, with concern.

"Why, so he doesn't ask me out?" was the first thing to come out of her mouth.

He smiled and proceeded to bestow her with a thoughtful gaze. "No, just generally. But then, you're pretty, so... don't let him ask you out. And don't say yes if he does!"

She saw concern in his dark brown eyes and melted. He was gentle, patient, and attentive. Everything she was beginning to like. "I won't."

"Good, so let's eat." He flicked his wrist upwards and studied his Samsung Galaxy smartwatch for less than a second before fitting her with his gaze. "What would you like? Boring me is leaning towards their Basmati rice and chicken curry."

The gesture had been both business-like and sensual. Her heart had leapt within its confines watching it. Her gaze dropped to the menu in front of her, and she perused it for options while thinking about his eyes on hers. "I'll have the rice, but with their beef and oxtail soup. Sounds interesting."

"We'll do interesting, then."

She closed the menu booklet, and he signalled for their waiter.

Sinking back into her seat, she studied him some more.

Definite upgrade, she decided. *And yes, I'd like to see him again.*

Chapter Twenty-One

IT WAS FRIDAY BEFORE they settled on how to make one solid presentation. Mide couldn't tell how the week had flown by so quickly.

Niyi was impressed with it but bothered about the errors still being thrown up by the trio of IT students he had hired during the week to run scenarios and test the application. He was worried their attempts at fixing the errors would scatter the codes in other fields, but Sesan assured him they wouldn't.

"There are almost thirty errors," he moaned.

"At least, your IT students are useful for something," Mide said to him and sneezed. "In truth, we can't be having this many errors so close to D-day."

"I thought you said your cold was gone!"

"Allergies." She fished her handkerchief out of her bag. "Something in the office, I don't know what it is."

"You want to step out and get some fresh air?"

She looked grateful.

Walking out of Niyi's office, she followed the short corridor to the pool and found everyone busy. The IT students had been assigned a supervisor each, and of the three, the female one was seated at Chuka's table.

Mide didn't have the strength to tease him. Whatever was triggering her allergies was stronger in the office pool. She sneezed once more and hurried towards the balcony.

"*Pele* dear, bless you," Chuka said as she passed by.

She was startled to find Sesan there when she walked out and shut the door. He had his hands in his pocket and was brooding at the sunny afternoon sky.

"Hi." She cleared the hoarseness in her voice. "Work all done or work not interesting? Everyone else is bursting their brains out inside, trying to move our project forward. You seem to be loafing."

He glanced at her and said nothing.

"Moody day, right? We all have them." She brought out her inhaler canister and took a long, slow drag. Then she leaned her head over the banister, breathed in deeply and slowly for a few seconds before she did it again.

"Asthmatic?"

She lifted her head and saw he'd been watching. "Not exactly an adjective I would use to describe myself, but yes. I often find I have to suck on this plastic cylinder to get clean, fresh air."

"Explains the frequent colds and irritating throat clearing. Doesn't explain the excessive giggles, though."

She wrinkled her nose at him.

"How long?"

"Since I ever knew myself."

She stared into the compound below them. She didn't want to talk to Sesan about living with asthma. She didn't want to think about it at all.

"Had an asthmatic friend once. Died three years ago."

She rolled her eyes. "Way to be encouraging. Talking about death by asthma to someone with asthma."

"I didn't say he died of asthma."

"You didn't specify. And for the record, it's a friend with asthma, not an 'asthmatic friend.' Calling someone asthmatic is kind of stigmatizing."

He ignored her chastisement. "There are herbs, you know. Natural African herbs that can help knock it out completely. Nothing like western medicine that gives you side effects."

"Can we not talk about asthma?"

He shrugged. "Sure."

"I know who is smoking in the office," he said a moment later. "That's what's aggravating this episode, right?"

"It's not exactly an episode, just mild wheezing and sneezing. Wait—why have you kept this from me? You knew I'd been asking."

He grinned. "I liked how it bothered you."

Mide rose to her full height and pocketed her inhaler. "I know you don't like me, but a little heads-up would have been nice."

"Now that I know it's a health risk, I'll fish him out. He doesn't do it in the office while we're around, just afterward, when everyone is gone. Or early in the morning, before we all arrive. Probably opens the window and just releases outside, thinking it'll go with the wind."

"I don't see the trip about smoking. It's the leading cause of half of the world's diseases."

"Leading cause is an exaggeration. I'd stake my claim on inactivity and obesity—they're more potent as leading causes of non-communicable diseases. Still, I'll fish out the smoker. We can't have you wheezing and skipping out on work." He turned around and stepped into the office pool.

Flabbergasted by his snarky comment, she followed him into the office pool and found him by Ross' table.

Ross! Shy, quiet Ross.

"Okay, gig's up!" Sesan turned and winked at her.

If she weren't already so surprised it had been Ross all the while, she would have widened her eyes at his out-of-character wink.

"What gig?" Chuka asked, causing Akin and Femi to look up.

"Smoking," Sesan said and wriggled his fingers at Ross. "Surrender all cigarettes and puffs and pots. Apart from aggravating Mide's asthma, we are all indirectly passively smoking!"

Chuka turned his chair around so he could look at Mide. "You're asthmatic?"

"Not a big deal. Plenty of people have asthma," she muttered and glared at Sesan before marching off to her desk. "You didn't have to announce it."

"Was that a playful or a real glare? With you, I can never tell," he replied.

"Take it however you wish."

"I prefer playful. Why don't you send that my way?"

Akin whistled. "Did I just hear the Dappler make a pass at Mide?"

Femi clicked his tongue. "The sun will have to rise in the west before that ever happens."

Sesan scoffed as Ross handed in his habit equipment. "The sun rising east and setting west is a generalization that happens only twice in a year. Rising and setting points differ daily northeast and southeast of the equator."

"Right," Femi replied. "We know there's an almanac downloaded somewhere in your brain, but how does that factor into what we're talking about?"

"It means the sun can rise any place it pleases and decide to ask Mide out," Sesan replied with a straight face. "Smoking items revealed. Smoking resolved."

Mide stopped all her actions and looked at him. "What's that supposed to mean?"

"Means he fancies himself the sun of this humble establishment," Femi answered.

"Point of correction," Chuka butted in. "Mide is the sun, you all are just passing planets. Ross, I think you should apologize to her."

"I'm sorry," Ross said. "I didn't know you were asthmatic."

"It's not a big deal," she replied, hating how everyone in the office now knew.

Sesan tossed Ross' pack of Marlboros and Tom Tom sweets into the bin and smiled at Mide. "No *thank you* for my detective skills?"

"Please return to your normal self," she said, grabbing a novel she'd been trying to get into and putting her phone in her purse. "You're making me nervous."

"Where are you going?"

"To lunch," she said, then walked out of the office.

———◉———

IT WAS DRIZZLING WHEN she got downstairs. Unfortunately, she had left her umbrella in the office.

"Shucks!" she muttered and stared at the falling rain.

The eatery joint she was planning to lunch at was a five-minute walk away. Besides, she didn't want to go back into the office and into any discussions involving her medical history or Ross' smoking habit. She was upset and trying not to be. Not at Ross—at Sesan, for spilling out her secret.

Jamming the novel above her head, she stepped into the drizzle and walked the short distance to the gate.

Unwittingly, she recalled the day she had begun to break up with Biyi. How his mother's birthday had been a blast till she had eaten vegetable soup and pounded yam. Everything had gone downhill from there.

Mide had discovered new things about herself. One, she loved being the centre of attention for everything other than being sick. Two, she was severely allergic to shrimps and crayfish. Three, potential in-laws were not favourably disposed to certain medical predispositions.

Her face and neck had swollen up so badly, she could hardly breathe. All would have been fine had Biyi's mum not insisted she wanted Mide to get a full report of her past medical history and every ailment she could inadvertently pass unto her future grandkids.

The asthma had come up, and Biyi's mum had not been too pleased. Being asthmatic was not a contagious infection necessitating alienation, but Mide would not do for her one and only son

Biyi's visits had cooled off and slowed to a bare minimum, and they had eventually broken up after a heated argument. She didn't even remember what it was they had been arguing about, but she knew the fight was being stirred underneath by his mother's bias towards her.

LIKE WHIRLWIND

Suddenly, Sesan's car slid to a stop beside her. She ignored it and kept walking.

He shot the car forward and slowed it to a stop again.

"Where are you going?" He leaned across the passenger side and peeked at her through the open window. "It's raining, and I'm pretty sure you're not supposed to be getting yourself wet for any reason."

She eyed him and kept right on walking. He followed with the car.

"Look, get in! Niyi has asked for updates, and we're nowhere near ready. We can look it over together during lunch."

She turned to him. "And why should I get in your car?"

"Because I'm buying you lunch, and we have lots of work to do."

"You had no right!"

"No right to what?"

"Share my health information in public without my consent!"

He looked baffled. "It's not like it was an AIDS report."

"It was none of your business!"

The rain dripped down her forehead and soaked her beige blouse, but she didn't care. Sesan had crossed a line.

"Look. You're getting wet, and it's raining. Get in the car."

"Apologize!"

"Mide—"

"Apologize."

For the first time since they had met, Sesan looked contrite. With one hand on the wheel and another on the gear, he stared at her. "I'm sorry. Come on. Get in."

She got into the car like a robot.

He handed her a handkerchief, and she dabbed at her arms and face without looking at him. He drove on, quiet.

As the rain hit the windshield glass landing with thick, fat splashes being wiped away now and then, she thought about her life.

What if she had another attack? What if she had it in the office in front of them all? How would they look at her? What would they think? How would she handle struggling for life in the presence of guys who had come to respect her?

"Mad at me? Don't think I've ever seen you this quiet." Sesan's voice broke the dull stillness in the car.

Mide wasn't the type to stay mute. "What you don't understand is, I don't want to be treated like an egg because of it."

"You're a very strong girl, and everybody knows that!"

"No one needed to know about the asthma."

"It was bound to come up."

"I don't want anyone judging me."

"No one is judging you." He glanced at her. "They all admire you."

"Well, I don't want anyone pitying me all the same."

"Listen to me. You are one badass female programmer, and knowing you have asthma makes me feel like shit. You won't ask why?"

She eyed him. "Why?"

"You have more excuses to fail at programming than I have because of it, and you're kicking ass." He squeezed his vehicle into an empty slot at the restaurant's car park and turned to look at her. "You built *Profit X*'s architecture before you got into school, and trust me, it's much better than that ugly *Purple Ledger*."

She smiled.

"Asthma is a no biggie, I agree, but judging by Niyi's prickliness over your health, it must have dealt with you a lot." He placed a hand over hers. "I'm sorry. I didn't mean to expose it."

She watched him exit the vehicle and marvelled that her feelings of despondency were lifting. Sesan had a soft side to him, and it was shocking to see. She opened the door and got out.

"We had to drive ten minutes to find the same thing that exists on the street where the office is located," she commented, following him up the steps of the building.

The rain had slowed further into a lighter drizzle.

"I like this branch." He drew the entrance door open and allowed her in. "They're neat."

"How much is the food again?"

"Affordable. Or do you want to eat *Mama Put* like Femi and the others? Remind me again where you were heading off to in the rain?"

She ignored him and stepped into a line made up of three people. Niceness with Sesan was always a fading fad. "How are we going to work without our laptops?"

He whipped out his phone from his back pocket. "I believe you've heard of such a thing as smartphones?"

"To code? Do you have all the languages on your phone?"

"To plan." He gave her a smug look. "You've got to plan first."

She wagged her head but couldn't help but smile at him. The angry ape persona she'd associated with him was lifting.

"Two wraps of *amala* with *ewedu,* and lots of fish," he said to the lady at the counter before turning back to her. "What will you be having?"

She perused the items on display. "Chicken and salad, thank you."

They got their meals and sat across from one another in a corner booth.

"Have you ever worked anywhere else before One Tech?" she asked.

"If you want to count IT stints here and there. This is my first regular job."

"Me, too." She beamed at him.

"I'm wondering, what were you thinking taking Purple Chip on?"

"The X threads?" She sighed dramatically. "I must confess, I wasn't."

"You're lucky they didn't sue you for defamation."

She wondered if Tomiwa had fought to prevent it?

"You all didn't need to drag them on X!" he said. "Those big-time firms are not worth the time. Besides, you wouldn't have gotten as much hands-on experience as you're getting with your cousin. I think that's the blessing in disguise."

She dipped her fork and knife into her chicken and added a bit of vegetable salad. "I always just hoped to get a place at Purple Chip."

"Scratch that. Purple Chip will tell you how to think. Niyi will give you wings to fly."

"Would have loved to find out myself."

"They'll work you so hard, you won't have time left for anything else. Good thing you're not in a relationship."

She exhaled. They were back on the topic. "Why do you believe I'm not?"

"Gift basket guy, or girl, hasn't shown face in the office. It's either you haven't given him an answer, or he hasn't worked up the courage to ask."

Tomiwa's image in the casual jacket came to mind. He hadn't asked her for anything, and there was no guarantee there would be a second date.

"Can we not talk about the gift basket person?"

"We can't talk about asthma or the boyfriend, and we can't talk about the gift basket. Which topics are not off-limits?"

"How about work? I thought that was why we were having lunch."

"It is." He turned his phone around on the table and opened up a Word document. "Listing all the things we still need to cover as regards the application should be the ultimate goal of this luncheon."

"You mean finishing up the documentation manual, addressing user clarity on language use, checking and cross-checking security log-ins, smart checking all functions, need I go on?"

Sesan looked at her like he was just seeing her for the first time. "I can see you've covered all the bases."

"I have been thinking about all the things left on our To-do list. What's our plan for ensuring all this is done?"

"Dividing and conquering. Should we do a coin toss?"

She lifted an eyebrow. "How about we just divide based on abilities?"

"I love a good coin toss."

"Suit yourself. It's just good to see you being cordial."

"I don't believe in mixing work with play. My work mode doesn't entertain any other function outside of work, and it kicks into operation the moment I step into the office. Are you going to say yes to your gift guy? I'm betting it's a guy."

"What business of yours is it? You already told me you hope I don't have a crush on you."

"Do you?"

"I don't!"

"Fair enough. It's still a wonder why you are not in a relationship."

"Why are we still on this subject?"

"Because you are an exceptionally beautiful girl, and I might be interested."

"Where is all this flattery coming from?"

"You think I'm being insincere?"

"Yes."

He dropped his fork and leaned back against his chair. "Why?"

"You just want to know who the gift basket guy is."

"Yes, because he should have made a show of coming over to say hi to your work colleagues to scope out potential competition and piss on his territory."

"Piss on his territory?"

"Mark you as taken."

She frowned. Tomiwa Oyinlolu walking into One Tech and stamping his claim all over her seemed like such a far-fetched and ridiculous idea. "He doesn't need to."

"It's a he," he said with triumph. "A very confident he."

"Can we get back into work mode?"

"No, I like this conversation."

She reached across the table and flipped an imaginary button on the side of his head. "Work mode. I can't believe I'm sitting across the table from you having a half-decent conversation for the very first time. It's a nice feeling."

He reached out to turn his phone around. "Work mode."

Chapter Twenty-Two

TOMIWA WAS LATE MEETING up for dinner with Mide the following Sunday.

When he got there, he found her banging away on her laptop at the private table he'd reserved for them both. Rather than pull out the seat opposite hers, he stood and watched her.

She was in a simple Ankara dress embellished with stones. Her braids were pulled into a ponytail highlighting the oval shape of her attractive face, and she was wearing the red-rimmed red frames which put a dash of seriousness to her sweet, cheerful demeanour.

She was ravishing. He knew at that moment Feyintola had been right.

Had they hired her, he'd have been unable to keep his intentions pure.

"It's a Sunday evening, and you're working," he said.

She glanced up, flashed him a small, guilty smile, and went on typing. "I just had a few things to wrap up before tomorrow, and you were running late."

"I apologize. Something came up."

"It's okay."

"You brought work to a date?"

"I was coming from work." She took off the glasses and laid them on the table beside her laptop.

"On a Sunday?" He pulled out the seat and slid into it as she glanced up at him.

Again, his breath got caught in his throat. Her eyes were beautiful. Bright, trusting, and full of hidden passion, prettier without the frames.

"Didn't you go to church?"

"I did. I just went to work afterward. A certain IT company is keeping us on our toes, and my boss will not like that I spent valuable work hours going on a date."

He grinned broadly, and she smiled back at him, taking his breath away. "Please, put that laptop away for the next hour or so, and give me the luxury of your time."

"I'm sorry. Something's just proving stubborn here. I can't think about anything else till I figure it out."

He leaned forward. "Something I can help you with?"

She bit her lip. "Wouldn't that be a conflict of interest?"

He paused as he stared at her. *Please, do not bite your lip in front of me. It's inviting.* "At all."

She seemed to think about his words. "I guess."

The night before, Feyintola had ambushed him at home with copies of all the materials Sesan had been able to gather from One Tech. He had blatantly refused to look at them. Now staring at her, he was glad he'd said no.

Not that Feyin hadn't gone behind his back and tried to corner Babs into using them. He wouldn't have been able to look Mide in the face had he done so. Besides, Babs was aware he would get fired if any material from those documents found its way in any shape or form into their presentation.

"I thought we said we were Ademide and Tomiwa whenever we meet. Zero conflicts, zero interests, just a boy helping a girl out." He shrugged his suit jacket off his shoulders and tossed it on a nearby table. "I'm seriously curious about what is putting your insides all in a twist."

He got up and walked towards her with his chair in tow.

She watched him approach for a second. "What are you doing?"

"Helping you out." He felt her stiffen as he lowered the chair into the space beside her and she was forced to scoot her chair over to make more space for him. "Plus, this is a great opportunity for you to show me how you intend to jazz up my codes. I did say we would discuss that."

She let out an edgy chuckle. "You knocked off all my complaints about *Compound*."

"I should thank you. We've been hitting higher profits ever since you decided to grant us free publicity."

"That was not my intention."

"I'm glad your original intention was destroyed."

"Ah. Then, you owe me share profits."

"I do." He turned and found his face close to hers, enough to fantasize about how much pleasure he could extract from her lips if she'd let him. It was getting worse, his need for her.

She pushed her laptop in his direction. "I'm ready to have you look at my work and tell me what's wrong."

Had she read his mind? Had she guessed he was thinking about kissing her?

"The cold sounds better," he said, hoping to disarm her and pace himself. She probably wasn't ready for all the things he felt ready for.

"To a large extent," she replied. "I still have a cold, but my voice is back to normal, as you can see."

He put his left arm around the backrest of her seat and turned to her monitor, eager to sort out her issues and move unto other things. "Tell me what the problem is."

"It's just a line in this syntax that I'm struggling with," she said, sounding relieved. "I've looked at it several times. I can't seem to figure out what I'm doing wrong."

"Hmm..." He peered at her screen for a couple of minutes. "Simplifying and optimizing is sometimes the key to a lot of these types of issues."

"I've tried to make the lines as concise as they can possibly be, but—"

"You don't have the right algorithm for what you want to do. Do you want to explain your logic to me?"

He caught her hesitant look. She seemed cautious about letting him into their application codes.

"Mide," he said gently, "I sincerely understand your unwillingness to trust me, but I only want to help. You don't have to mention it to Niyi if you think it'll get you in trouble."

She didn't say anything.

"I will only change what you agree to. Is it okay?"

She nodded.

He took his arm away from around the chair and turned the laptop a bit more in his direction. Unbuttoning his sleeves as he stared at the screen, he rolled them halfway up his forearms and settled his fingers above the keyboard.

"I see," he said, as he started to type into her carefully worded codes. "Let's define this in another function, shall we."

———⸺●⸺———

MIDE HAD TO SHIFT CLOSER to him to view her laptop screen.

He was quiet and focused, typing with a level of slowness that made her nervous. What was he looking at? What was he thinking? What was he doing? What if he planted a bug in the codes, what would she do?

She had broken protocol by allowing him to work on their application. The same one in competition with his. Niyi would kill her, Sesan would berate her, and Chuka would chastise her for handing a man she'd verbally bashed several times in the office access to their source codes.

It would be ridiculous that he would want to steal them. From the little she had seen, he didn't strike her as an unscrupulous person.

Yet, she wished she could stave off the anxious fluttering in her heart as she watched him work, but it wasn't to be helped.

Her unease had less to do with her seeming betrayal and more to do with the overpowering sense of his presence beside her. He'd invaded her mind and buried so many of her initial reservations in an avalanche of his never-ending sweet behaviour, she had become addicted to him.

Her long-standing admiration for his work and her recent encounters with him in person had merged into this intense magnetism she couldn't shake.

She'd met guys, but he was different.

"I see this is exactly like this line in this function, and both are cancelling each other out. Shouldn't a comma be here?" He scrolled up the page and inserted the necessary comma.

As she leaned over to look at the laptop screen, her breasts mistakenly brushed against his upper arm. She leaned back, alarmed at her unintended action and its resultant effect. He kept typing, but she couldn't ignore the tingling sensation the contact with his arm had initiated within her.

Get a grip, she said to herself, closing her eyes. She couldn't let him know his nearness was scrambling up her brain and her insides.

"You missed a line here."

"Do you believe I looked through that several times, and didn't see it?"

"Sometimes, you need to close a page and come back to it with fresh eyes."

She nodded.

"Always remember to use clear variable and function names for each line of code you write before you comment on them. Helps you to remember what code does what and helps you figure out where you're replicating. Just changing a little word even by a symbol throws everything you're writing out of whack. And I know you know this, but in a myriad of syntaxes, tiny mistakes are inevitable. And unforgiveable, because they can become huge bugs."

"Right," she whispered as her mistakes came sharply into focus.

"Plus, you can format your fence codes as stack traces. Open them with exactly three backquotes or three tildes, and close with the same. Then enter 'stark trace' in the opening line to set the language and then just copy and paste. With that, you have references to your source codes set up as links. This way, you can find them whenever you need to. Try it."

Taking his arm back around her chair, he turned the screen of the laptop so she could see it better. Then he sat back and pointed out a few more modifications she could make to the codes.

"Hope I've helped?"

"You have. I would probably have to run a couple of scenarios to test it, though."

"Go ahead. I doubt you'll find any issue. I am a god at programming, remember?"

She glanced at him and chuckled. "Don't get too cocky!"

"How about we bet on it?"

"With what?"

"Money. I'll give you a million naira for every error you find."

She turned to him. He was straight-faced, perusing her eyes intently.

"Are you serious?"

"Dead serious!" He reached over and typed a few more commands into her codes. "I don't want you ushering at any party, anywhere, for any financial reasons. I'm willing to pay you to find my errors. If you can."

She stared at him. He seemed pretty serious. "And if I don't find any error?"

"I'll require a kiss." He didn't look at her. "For your impudence."

She sniggered. *Her impudence, was he serious?*

"We have like—" He leaned over to count the number of pages. "Five pages I worked on. For every single error you find, I'll give you a million naira. That's a promise. Regardless of how many you find on a page. For every error-free page, you'll give me one kiss. Sound fair?"

What kind of ridiculous game— She stared at him. The heat from his gaze was unsettling and pleasurable. His lips looked soft and plump, ringed around by a well-groomed beard. *A kiss?* She hadn't been kissed since she'd left Biyi, and Tomiwa was not bad to look at. Plus, they were in a private seating area, no one would see.

"Sure." She pulled the laptop towards her. "I'm game."

"Great!" he said quietly as he scrutinized her face. "Go ahead."

She dove into the codes, anxious, yet not anxious. Determined, if ever, to find at least one error. A million naira in her bank account would be god-sent. Five million would be a lottery.

Was she crazy to accept a challenge that in hindsight, she probably couldn't win? Was he really going to give her a million naira?

He looked at his watch. "I'm setting a time limit. You have two minutes."

"Two minutes is not fair!"

"Three."

"Ten."

"Fine. I'm sure If I gave you a day, you'd still be kissing me."

Gosh! He was so cocky! "Just keep quiet and let me find them."

He laughed and relaxed into the chair.

"And stop looking at me!"

Ten minutes later, she was still looking. Her confidence took a hit, yet, anxiety had never felt so good. She was losing a bet, but by some crazy stroke of whirlwind luck, she was getting to kiss a guy she'd come to admire.

"Found anything?"

The comment felt like a tease. She wasn't going to find anything in those codes, and they both knew it. "I'm not giving up yet."

"Take your time," he said, sounding unconcerned.

She gritted her teeth and leaned into the screen like the gesture would help her find something. There was nothing.

Oh, kiss him already! You know he's good.

"Anything?" he asked as his arm dropped from being loosely draped across the edge of her chair rest to being placed solidly around her waist.

"You're distracting me!"

"You won't find anything, anyway," he murmured, his breath warm on the side of her face.

"I'm not giving up."

"I guarantee that five kisses will be a lot more interesting than trying to find one error. Either way, I'm willing to wait."

"This isn't fair."

"What isn't? The fact that I'm not giving you a million naira, or the fact that we're kissing?"

"I wanted the million naira!" she said with a pout.

He put his other arm around her. "Trust me, this is better."

Sandwiched between his chest and his arm, she weakened and leaned into him. There was no point pretending she didn't want to give up. None pretending she wasn't giddy at the thought of having his arms around her.

He took her glasses away and dropped it on the table. And in a gentle move that made up for all the anxiety of the wait, he lowered his head and merged his mouth with hers.

She closed her eyes at the sudden burst of pleasure from it. The tiny bristles of his facial hair brushed against the skin around her lips, electrifying every cell in her body and erasing every thought in her head as he tasted her lips softly, nibbling at them and teasing her senses to oblivion.

He had said five. They were still on the first one, and she was a quivering mess. Four more kisses like this, and she would be unable to say no to anything he proposed.

A moment later, mouth fused with hers, he scooped her out of her chair and transferred her unto his lap, sending heat tumbling into her with the fervency of his touch. His earnest hands wandered with perfect ease along the gentle contours of her body, folding her to him and then cupping her neck as his lips parted hers for more access. She didn't object. She wanted to be as close to him as she could get as their lips hugged and slow-danced to the attraction she knew had been there from the moment he'd sat next to her.

Lost in the sweetness of the entire moment, her heart tittered on the brink of sprinting out of her chest. She could not—was not meant to—be kissing Tomiwa Oyinlolu, but his mouth fought to elucidate the reason why being with him was not wrong.

Everything his hands were saying to her, his longing, acceptance, and need for her, she sensed and wanted in that moment. Pulling apart felt like torture. But she needed to. She needed a minute to breathe and process her feelings.

"That's what I'd been wanting all evening," he whispered huskily.

She gazed down at him, the sight of his mouth filling her with quiet dread and an unbridled yearning. "Do you frequently take your female applicants out on dates?"

"You would be the first."

"This is just our third date. I don't think we should be—"

"Kissing?" he replied, cutting her off. "I lose all sense of reasoning whenever I'm with you. Besides, you lost a bet. You still owe me four kisses."

For the first time in a long while, she was short of words. She leaned down and kissed him again.

Four kisses—it would take them a while to order for dinner.

Chapter Twenty-Three

TWO DAYS TO THE PRESENTATION day, the One Tech office was a blur of activities. Orders were sent back and forth with accompanying yells and frustrated expletives. Tempers had clashed and rained sour words, and Niyi was sure his blood pressure had risen by a few millimetres of mercury.

Mide was constantly having to ask him to calm down, but everything that could go wrong just kept going wrong.

At first, her laptop contracted some kind of online virus that scattered her files, rebooted her whole system, and eventually wiped off everything she had on it.

"Tell me you had the presentation on an external drive!" Niyi begged, eyes frantic.

"I didn't. Thank God I emailed the final copy to you. Besides, it should be on the cloud, so chill, relax. Everything will sort itself out."

"Just download the thing and let me breathe air that's not steeped in worry," he said, switching on his laptop and searching for said email.

When they had the system up and running, it developed new bugs which thankfully Sesan was able to fix without compromising previous data. Then Chuka had gotten the pages of the documentation manuals they had printed mixed up, and they'd had to unbind and rebind the copies all over again.

"All thanks to your constant drooling over Mide!" Akin chastised. "The girl has a boyfriend, back off already."

"If I reach you there and cut that your goatee!" Chuka threatened.

"Heaven no go fall!" Akin replied cheekily.

Mide understood Niyi's frustration. This was his first major break, and they couldn't afford to make a mistake with anything. She was handling the first part of the presentation and had rehearsed it from top to bottom severally.

As she rehearsed in front of everyone, Sesan kept stopping or cutting her off for one little mistake or the other. Despite her usually pleasant disposition, she was close to yelling at him.

"Project! Project! Project your voice!" he repeated. "The people at the back of the room need to hear you."

"I *am* projecting!" she yelled, near tears. "I'd like to see you do your part."

"I can do my part pretty fine," he growled back, piercing her with a gaze that returned his old moody self to the office in all its glory. She was not impressed.

"Sesan, go easy on her," Niyi called in from in front of his laptop. Oddly, he had calmed down.

"She can't keep looking at the screen behind her while speaking to people in front of her, and she can't keep fumbling through the sheets in her hands," Sesan said, slightly exasperated. "You've got to make eye contact with the audience. That's the only way you're going to know when you're losing them."

"Mide, you want to take it from the top again?" Niyi asked quietly.

She took in a deep breath and gave a bright smile, opting to start again.

"Lose the excessive smile. You're not trying to charm them. You are trying to convince them to trust your application."

She gave Sesan a quizzical tilt of her head. Seated beside Niyi, Femi gave her thumb-up signs.

"And don't use sentence fillers!" Sesan warned.

Her phone rang, and she was happy to take the call. "Okay, I'm going out to get some much-needed break from you all."

Sesan threw his folder on the table in a huff. "Can't take a little criticism. We are on a clock here!"

She stuck her tongue out at him and sauntered to the balcony, shutting the heavy door behind her. She had never been so glad to see the Lagos evening sun and hear the sound of cars blaring their horns as they inched through the traffic on the streets below.

Most especially, she was glad to pick up the call.

"Hi."

"How are you doing?"

Tomiwa's warm, easy voice filled her ear through the phone's speaker and massaged every part of her being, making her heart soar.

"Good. And you?"

"Not bad," he replied. "How is the prep for your pitch presentation going?"

"As well as it can. Hectically."

"Hectically?" A smile tinged his voice. "Please ensure you get enough rest. I read that stress can trigger asthma."

"You've been reading up on asthma?"

"Anything and everything I do these days is about you."

She could feel intense heat creeping up her neck and making its way up to her face. "I am doing my best to take care of myself. How's prep on your end?"

"I would say we are more than ready."

"Oh, good."

She worried. A while back, she'd been too confident her cousin could outperform Purple Chip, and she had thrown her energy into everything in a bid to outbid them.

Now, she wasn't so sure. Not with everything going colossally wrong at One Tech, and Tomiwa sounding more than over-prepared.

"I am happy to hear that," she added.

"Are you, really?"

"Of course. And may the best man win!"

He chuckled. "I'd like to take you out tomorrow night."

The smile on her face faded into dread. A delightful kind of dread brought on by the thought of being with him. She had only been able to suppress the memory of their kiss by burying herself in work. Now he was asking to take her out again, the memories were flooding her mind in all their delightful glory. And they had come with feelings and pleasurable tingling touring her innermost core to set her heart on fire.

"You do know—" she began, basking in the emotions, "—that tomorrow is the day before the pitch presentations."

"I know. And based on experience, I have discovered that a good night of relaxation is necessary for a prime performance in the morning."

"So, you want to take me out and make me forget everything I have spent the whole week cramming into my brain?"

"Hey, if you know the material, you know the material," he murmured, his voice sounding like a soothing piece of music in her ear.

"I don't think that's a good idea. Us, fraternizing the night before a bidding."

"I'm arranging dinner on a boat. You don't want to miss it."

Dinner on a boat! Her eyes grew round. She had never been on a boat, much less eaten a meal on one. Tomiwa was definitely pulling out all the stops.

"I would love to have dinner on a boat. Can we do it after the presentation?"

"Nope. It's a limited-time offer. Thursday evening or nothing at all."

Gosh, you and your time limits!

"Are you sure you are not trying to make me mess up our presentation?" She put a hand over her mouth. Revealing she was the one doing the presentation was giving the other side too much information. She needed to get off the phone with him.

"I'm not trying anything, Miss Akinseye. I just want to see you."

He sounded like he hadn't even heard her, but she knew he had. He knew she was the one giving the presentation on behalf of One Tech, but she didn't know how he could use it to his advantage.

She wanted to say no, but she wanted to see him, too. Their last date had started out awkward but had turned out great because of the eventual dinner conversation. He was a great listener. Attentive in every way that appealed to her, and economical with his responses. Plus, he let her get away with a lot of nervous chattering.

"I promise I will not kiss you until afterward," he said as if he'd read her mind.

She shut her eyes, shuddering involuntarily as she recalled the taste of his insistent lips plying hers open and willing her to kiss him back. And she had. Had enjoyed it, too.

"Promise me you will not kiss me at all," she said, eyes still closed.

"I can't make that promise, I don't trust myself. But if you have dinner with me, I'll have you home by nine. That, I can promise."

Mide opened her eyes, clearly conflicted but leaning towards dinner with him.

"Are you still there?"

"Yes," she whispered, conjuring the image of his face.

"Yes, to dinner?"

"Yes."

"I'll pick you up by five."

"No, I'll meet up with you." She didn't want to risk him coming to the office and being spotted by anyone.

"Great. Thursday evening, six to eight, dinner on a boat. Please don't stand me up, or I'll be forced to come looking for you."

She chuckled. "I won't. I promise."

So it was that after a gruelling day of final touches to the whole of their presentation, Niyi selected Femi and the female IT student, Abigail, to accompany him, Mide, and Sesan to Jules Incorporated on Friday morning for the pitch.

Mide shut down at four and declared she needed to take a break to rest up for the presentations. The others had followed suit, but Niyi had preferred to stay up in the office tightening things up.

She had taken a Bolt ride and met up with Tomiwa at the Blue Water Hotel lobby by five-thirty, and he had taken her to the jetty point in his vehicle. She had on a blue jean jacket over a red dress and blue Sketchers, recalling how the air conditioning in his car got next to frigid.

He, on the other hand, was dressed in a casual off-white, long-sleeved shirt over grey slacks and a grey sleeveless pullover. She couldn't tell what the brands were, but the quality of the fabrics spelled the word expensive in full.

When they alighted from the car, the air outside was warm. She started to take her jacket off.

"Don't," he said as they walked down a wooden dock towards what looked to her like a huge ship. "Curious as I am about what you have on underneath that jacket, you should leave it on. It'll be cool on the water, and I don't want you to catch a cold."

"I won't catch a cold, don't worry," she said, slipping out of the jacket. "The humidity around the water will be better for me."

The jean jacket went off to reveal a red, short-sleeved dress with a deep V-neckline made with a fabric patterned after dry lace.

"So, someone came up with the idea of having a restaurant on a boat."

"Someone did."

"And I'm having dinner in it." She turned to him. "With you. What if I get seasick?"

"You will hardly notice the movement of the boat."

"And the dinner?"

"Just like any other dinner on land."

She nodded and folded her jacket over her arm.

There was a waiter at the end of the dock who took her hand and helped her down into the boat. Once inside, she couldn't believe she was not on land.

The whole deck area had been transformed into a restaurant with tables, chairs, table cloth, cutlery, and everything she could ever imagine would be in a restaurant on land. Paintings hung on the walls, a live band strumming out the tunes of favourite songs from the eighties and nineties. The saxophonist was especially good.

"Oh my god!" she exclaimed, putting both hands together as she looked around the place in glee. "This is awesome!"

"I'm glad you like it."

They were seated next to each other at a table and a comfortable sofa for two.

She was too overjoyed to worry that they were so close, their knees were practically touching.

"I can't believe this is happening, and I can't gush about it to my sister-in-law. I'm in a restaurant, on a boat, on water, and it's really pretty awesome. I can tell her afterward, can't I?" She leaned across to say to him.

"If you want to."

Her face lit up. "I want to."

"You want to take a picture?"

"Yes! Oh my god, this is so surreal. Thank you. I am glad I didn't say no."

He laughed out loud.

"I told you not to miss this," he said, slipping out his phone and pulling her into himself for a selfie image of them both against a magnificent backdrop of dark blue water.

She couldn't help the grin on her face. "I'm so glad I didn't miss this."

"The boat is going to loop around the inland lake about two or three times while we dine," he said, folding one knee over the other. "You'll get to see an overview of Victoria Island at night with parts of Lekki and its famous Link Bridge."

She beamed at him. "Thank you."

"You're welcome." He looped an arm around the sofa headrest, invariably around her, too. Then he leaned into the backrest as the waiters brought their drinks as well as platters of beef *suya*, chicken strips, and fries.

One waiter paused to pop the bottle of wine while another set wine glasses down in front of them.

"I took the liberty of ordering." He watched her face for signs of disapproval as he reached for the open bottle of wine. "Hope that's fine."

"I'm fine with anything, really. You have great taste."

He paused on his way to pouring out some wine for them both and turned to look at her. "Even in women?"

She saw his face had taken on a comical look, and she let off a short burst of laughter. "Especially in women, yes."

"Wow, you are not vain at all."

"I'm so not vain."

He put the bottle down and turned into her. "Tell me more about yourself."

Her smile dipped. "What do you want to know?"

"I don't know," he replied. "Everything. Everything about you that I don't already know. Where you're from, where you schooled, primary, secondary, best friends, childhood crushes, current crushes, past boyfriends—"

"Current crushes!" She laughed out loud and covered her face with her left hand. "Do you really want to know who I'm crushing on?"

He saw the inside of her left wrist and stalled.

"Yes." He stared purposely at the wrist and his smile faded. "What's that?" He reached out a hand and grabbed her left forearm, turning it over.

She trembled involuntarily at the touch, especially when he looped his thumb over the inner part of her wrist to feel the thin line of scar overalying it. The touch was halfway towards caring and distracting, sending her pulse soaring.

"It's a scar," she said, managing to hold his gaze.

His hand was warm and large, fingers long and slender as they held onto her wrist. He wouldn't stop fingering the scar as he perused her face for an explanation.

"I can see that," he replied quietly.

She didn't want to talk about the scar. She hadn't even thought about it in years. He had found it, however. Seen it because he had been looking. Most people didn't. No one looked this closely. It was obvious now he spent quite a lot of time examining her from head to toe, paying attention to the little details everyone else missed.

LIKE WHIRLWIND

She knew he knew exactly what type of scar it was.

"It's an old scar," she said.

"A sad one," he added.

She nodded without attempting to take her hand out of his. She didn't even want to. She liked having it nestled in his. It gave her some form of comfort and ease, and for some bizarre reason, she wasn't averse to opening up to him about what had happened. Few people had seen her have an actual attack. Fewer knew there was sadness behind her exuberant cheerfulness. And, hardly anyone knew the reason for the scar.

Her relationship with him had been topsy-turvy from the beginning, and she had talked more about asthma with him than she had with any other person outside her family. Even Biyi. But the scar...

"How old is it?"

"Fourteen years."

"Fourteen." He waited to hear her speak some more. "You don't have to tell me if it makes you uncomfortable."

"I—" She wrinkled her nose and shook her head, eyes on their hands. "No, it's okay, it doesn't. I was just in a really dark place back then. Physically, socially, and emotionally. I was hospitalized all the time. There were needles, medication, and the works, almost every day. So, I was in pain. Tired often, cranky, angry, sick, and sick of being sick."

"The asthma?"

She nodded. "Sometimes, I could hardly get out of bed. I missed months of school. I was placed on this drug, Leukotriene modifiers. Had to take it for months."

She glanced at him. He was listening.

"I practically died inside. I don't know, I guess I lost the will to live, or fight, or even breathe. I told my mother several times that I was going to just give up, that I wouldn't tell her when the next attack came. Told her I wanted to die, and I didn't want to fight anymore. One day, I just took a knife and..." She shrugged. "I cut. I didn't know how much it broke her heart. The worst thing was, I didn't even care. I just—I wanted to end it all."

There were tears in her eyes when she stopped talking. When she reached up to wipe them, he raised his hand and let the back of his index finger swipe the tears away before he finished off with his thumb.

"I'm sorry," he said. "I shouldn't have let you relive that."

She sniffed. "It's okay. We found out months later it was just the side effects of the medication. Everything went away when they took me off them. They found another way to manage me, and I've never been back in that dark hole ever again. But I have this scar to remind me of how close I came." She raised her eyes to his. "How everything in life is to be valued. Why I should always be happy."

He lowered his hand and covered hers with it, then he slipped his fingers into hers and linked their hands. "I'm sorry. We will never, ever speak of that again."

"I had a great psychologist, and he taught me how to see the funny side of all things. Now I can't seem to stop, and someone compared me to a hyena the other day."

"What! That is just cruel!" he said. "You're not, you're an eagle. Rising above this huge challenge and surviving. We will never speak of this again."

She nodded. "That would be—that would be great, actually."

"Let's eat. I brought you here to relax and get away from all things stressful. Let's not do anything else but eat and talk about pleasant things."

"Pleasant things," she replied, forcing herself not to think about the time in the past when she was something of an enigma in school and no one wanted to have anything to do with her. For fear of triggering her symptoms and catching the illness. "I'm game."

"Okay, dig in," he prompted, letting her go as the saxophonist burst into a soft medley of popular Nigerian afrobeat songs by the latest artists. "You were telling me about your current crush…"

She smiled and turned to lean into him. "You are my current crush."

Later, they stood in a corner of the boat, with the open starless sky above them and black depths of water below them, talking about life in general. Two hours had disappeared, and it was time to go.

Mide experienced a weird sort of sadness at the idea of parting from him, and he seemed just as reluctant to leave the deck. Even though he'd paid their bill and tipped the waiters.

"So tomorrow, you should be calm. Relax into the questions, and focus on how you think your application can benefit the Jules."

She was leaning against the wall of the boat with her elbows on the railing running across it. "You're giving me business advice."

"I'm giving you presentation tips. I want you to do well. I want you to blow them to smithereens."

"Speaking of doing well, I should be well-rested the night before. You promised to have me home by nine."

"I did."

"It's a quarter past eight, and there might be traffic."

"I know," he said, and leaned into her, face inches from hers. "I'm just having difficulty letting you go."

She smiled and studied his face in the moonlight. "We both have work tomorrow, serious work that we need to prepare for."

"I know," he said with a regretful sigh as he stepped back and held out his hand for hers. "Let's go."

She gave him her hand which he tucked into the crook of his elbow as they walked across the deck to the exit and up the stairs, back unto the dock.

"What kind of questions am I going to get tomorrow?"

"They will want to know your reach as a company, basically if you've provided this kind of service before."

"And if we haven't?"

He shrugged. "Then you need to convince them that you can."

"With what? The number of experienced staff we have?"

"With a solid project management plan."

"What else?"

"Competence. Confidence. Good communication skills." They had reached his car, so he swung around to face her. "Honesty."

"Thank you for a wonderful night," she said, knowing what was coming next. The anticipation tickled her insides.

"You're welcome. I'm glad you enjoyed yourself. John will take you home now, and I'm sure you'll be home before nine, or around nine. Ten minutes, give or take."

"Without you?"

"Without me," he said with a smile and leaned down to brush her lips with his for what was mere seconds.

Mide felt a jolt of electricity hit her insides for those few seconds. She had expected it to linger longer. "Tomiwa—"

"We both have work," he whispered. "All the best tomorrow."

He then stepped back to hold the door open for her to get into the back seat.

She did with hidden disappointment.

She had hoped they would sit in the back seat on the way home. That he'd ignore her admonition not to hold her. That she would lean into him and he would wrap his arms around her, and they would cuddle in the backseat all the way home.

She had a lot to focus on, though—she had the presentation. Thinking about him was already a major distraction, and she didn't need this.

But he was all she could think about, and the kiss didn't happen.

Chapter Twenty-Four

MIDE HAD HER ARM LINKED to Sesan's elbow.

They were walking around the open hall, making new acquaintances and enjoying the cocktail party mixer Jules Incorporation had put together to announce their new project and the companies they would be signing on to partake in it.

Most importantly, they were happy. The presentation had happened without a hitch.

Each company had been invited for a two-hour meeting at different times on the same day. One Tech had gone first. Mide had been hoping to catch a glimpse of Tomiwa before going in. To her surprise, the Purple Chip team hadn't been anywhere around in the building. She'd been too keyed up to be disappointed.

Their presentation took place from about nine in the morning to about eleven, and Niyi had been pleased with the smooth way everything had gone. He'd taken the whole team out for a celebratory lunch afterward.

"We shouldn't count our chickens before they hatch," Femi warned, but Niyi said he was feeling quite optimistic. The Jules Incorporated team had been very impressed with them.

Sesan, too, had been impressed by how Mide had handled herself. He'd taken to becoming rather cordial and friendly, offering to pick her up from her home for the mixer.

Niyi had agreed. In some way, she knew he'd assumed her mystery friend was Sesan.

"Here we are—" Sesan was saying into her ear, "—mingling with the rich and famous, sniffing the air of opulence, drinking white wine and eating caviar, about to be awarded a contract that could potentially take Purple Chip Professionals off the winners' board and wipe that conceited smile off their CEO's smug face."

Mide nodded. She was thinking about Tomiwa, too. From what she knew of him, he was anything but smug.

She had seen him in the room when they had first arrived, and they had shared a look that had spoken a thousand words to her. He was going to ask her out again, and she was going to say yes. She was going to say yes because she had realized after their last date, something special was happening between them.

"What do you think?" Sesan let go of her arm and turned around to face her. "This is your chance to get back at the people who didn't think you were good enough to be in their company. How do you feel about that?"

"Hmm..." She kept smiling. She didn't think she wanted to get back at Tomiwa when he had been nothing but nice to her. "What I think is that you have amazing emotional flexibilities."

His face blanked out. "Meaning?"

"To think you can go from hot to cold, and from smile to frown, in less than a second, is a phenomenon I should definitely study. To think that you couldn't stand to have me sit beside you when we first met, and now, you have my arm in your arm, and you're being genuinely happy that I am going to get my revenge on my enemies, is nothing short of a miracle. I'm grateful."

"You're neurotic. Funny and beautiful, but definitely neurotic."

"What is that word, who's teaching you English?"

He laughed out loud. "I'll allow your insults today, if you agree to go out with me after the mixer."

"My goodness, you can actually laugh. Wow!" Mide's exaggerated exclamation was an attempt to ignore how alarmed she was at his words. She could not date Sesan. "That will be the first time I have ever heard you do that in the whole period of our acquaintance. That's awesome! That, my friend, is progress."

He laughed again, and she joined him. When he looked behind her, he touched her elbow lightly. "I have to go and see someone about something for a bit, but don't go anywhere. We need to continue this very interesting conversation when I get back."

"Me, I'm not going anywhere." She watched him brush past her and walk away, then looked around the hall for her cousin.

"Hey, there you are," Niyi said when he saw her. "Have you eaten something?"

She looked in his face and raised her eyebrows. "You are anxious. I can tell."

"I'm not." He fussed with his tie and looked around.

"You should relax." She helped him adjust the troublesome item of clothing. "Even if we lose this, we are already getting a reputation as a great tech company, so—"

"We are not going to lose," he snapped. "I can't afford to lose this, Mide. I need the money," he added a little harshly.

"I know," she replied quietly. "Just try to relax and enjoy the party."

"Hey, I see Mr. Ladi. I'll catch you later, dear."

"Sure."

She watched him hurry away, a part of her worried they would lose. He truly needed the bid to keep his company afloat, but he also needed to be prepared for an alternative result.

SESAN HAD GOTTEN FEYINTOLA'S note the moment he'd stepped into the party, but it had taken him a while to find the opportunity to slip away from Mide.

"I had no idea you were ready to let everyone know my true identity," he said to her when they met at the rooftop balcony of the event centre. "What's up?"

"Kenny is telling me he hasn't made up his mind. He should have made up his mind by now. Did you really give us everything from One Tech?"

He paused in front of Feyintola and pushed his hands deep into his trouser pockets. "You asked me to join up with One Tech, I joined up. You asked me to date the pretty cousin, she's hanging on my arm now. You asked me to give you their pitch presentation and IT solution template, I've done that. What more do you want? Is it my fault if after all of that, Jules refuses to give you the account? You should take it up with him and quit questioning my loyalty."

"The girl is hanging onto your arm, and you are laughing with her like she is the world's first human female. Are you in love with her?"

He turned down the corners of his mouth and gave an exaggerated shrug of his shoulders. "You asked me to date her!"

"I asked you to date her, not fall in love with her. What's to say you haven't crossed over to the other side?"

"In that case, I'll leave you guessing." He turned around and started to walk away.

She watched him go for a moment. "Come back and stop acting like some big hot-shot. What do you want? You haven't told me. We never talked about it."

He stopped and turned back. "Is that why we're here? Or are you still trying to leverage to ensure I delivered on my promise?"

"Sesan, the fact remains that I don't know if you are telling me the truth or not. You are a loose agent. You could swing either way. Who knows?"

"At this point, I don't think it matters anymore. Jules is going to make his decision tonight, and we have done all that we can do. You'll just have to trust me, and wait and see."

"Oh, the waiting!" Feyintola sank into one of the deck chairs on the balcony. She looked formidable in her plum-coloured evening gown, a huge contrast to Mide's short-sleeved, knee-length dress. Mide was the only good female programmer he knew who still managed to look feminine, and it set her apart because it was deceptive. The first time he had met her, he had thought it a joke that she was a programmer.

"Dappler, sit with me a while."

He felt sorry for Feyintola, so he sat with her.

She was beautifully fierce and running herself ragged trying to ensure she won a contract that was already hers by and large. He felt a certain kinship with her, though. The daredevil streak in him had come from somewhere, and she had it, too.

She should have been the boy and the other two should have come as girls.

"I want to go for my masters," he said to her. "Can you make that happen?"

"Of course. Anywhere you want."

"I already got the admission. It's the funds I need."

She stared at him. "Even better."

MIDE FOUND HER WAY from the open hall to the swimming pool area. She needed a quiet place to think. In another thirty minutes, the cocktail mixer would end, the contract would be awarded, and Niyi would know his fate.

Where would it leave her and Tomiwa?

They'd had an hour to mingle and enjoy the buffet the Jules had set out for all their competitors. People were meant to meet, make new contacts, and forge new business opportunities. It wasn't such a bad event as they had initially worried. Niyi had already gotten two new clients, but Mide had been unable to eat anything.

She didn't know what Tomiwa would do the moment her cousin got the contract, or how she would really feel if he won instead of them. The fairy tale dates would be over, things would be more awkward than they currently were, and he probably wouldn't want to have anything to do with her anymore.

The thought made her morose.

Why did I accept that first date? She groaned as she placed her forearms on the metal banister separating the terrace from the swimming area. *Why did he have to be the one around when I fell sick?*

If she'd never gone out to try to get a job with Purple Chip, she wouldn't have met him, and she wouldn't feel so conflicted about the whole Kehinde Jules account. It wouldn't have mattered so much if he lost.

"I've been looking for a way to get to speak with you all evening."

She swung around, startled. "Hi."

"Hey, I didn't mean to scare you." He lounged past a row of swimming pool deck chairs and walked up to her. "You look nice, as always."

"Thanks."

She'd gone with a white and dark blue polka dots dress with a deep vee neckline and a wide dark blue belt for the event. The shoulders were Grecian-styled, the bottom flared out into a full skirt. The belt accentuated her small waistline.

You look like you're from the fifties, Derin had joked when she, Sesan, and Niyi had headed out.

"Thank you, for the date two nights ago," she said to him.

He lifted his shoulders in a brief shrug.

"I enjoyed your company. And all night, I've been jealous of the company you're with."

"That's just Sesan, the guy at my place of work I told you about."

"You seem quite close."

"He's just a friend." She was aware of the pressing need to explain she was free and unattached. "Work colleague, more like. We've presented, and all the pressure is off so he's become quite cordial."

He nodded and kept his eyes on hers. "I'm happy to hear that."

She glanced at the pool. "I was wondering...on the off chance that we—that my cousin—wins, does it mean we can no longer be friends?"

"No, gracious me, why would you think that?"

"Well, because, I'd..." She looked at him. "It would be awkward, and I—"

He frowned. "There will be a billion other contracts. On the contrary, I'd be relieved. Because then, I would be able to tell you the things I want to tell you, without being—" He stopped and was quiet, staring at her. "Well, without making you think I was trying to distract you from One Tech so that I could win this particular contract and have you hate me forever."

She envisioned their kiss for a second. "Is that what you were doing? Trying to distract me?"

"Of course not."

"Really?"

"I promise you, that was not what I was doing."

She bit her lower lip with a solemn face. "So why not tell me? Whatever it is you want to tell me."

"If I win, would I still be able to ask you out on a date?"

She wrinkled her forehead at him. "No! I'd be mad at you."

He laughed and took a step closer to her. "I wasn't expecting that answer. Why?"

"Because I want One Tech to win. We need the money and exposure that you already have. To be honest, I wouldn't be very happy if you got it, and we didn't. I know it's childish, but…"

"Whatever happened to us forgetting you are One Tech and I am Purple Chip? What happened to two individuals getting to know one another outside of work?"

"That would have to take a backseat for a while."

He sighed. "Why? What if I didn't want it to? What if I'm not willing to let it?"

She folded her arms. "If there is anything you want to say, you should say it before the results are announced and things get awkward."

He began by stepping closer to her. "I wanted to ask you a question, and I don't want the answer to be dependent on the outcome of this mixer."

"Okay." She kept a straight face.

He reached out to pry her arms apart and hold her hands in his. She stared down at their hands together, and when she looked up, he was right in front of her. So close, she could see the tiny hairs that made up his well-manicured beard. She liked him. So much. She didn't want him to lose, either.

"I'm in love with you. I saw you in the elevator that morning of the test, and I was drawn to your enthusiasm and friendliness. I don't usually talk to people in elevators, but you just wouldn't stop talking, and you were so pretty, I was forced to listen."

He let go of her hands and slid both his arms around her waist, drawing her closer. "Now I've gotten an opportunity to spend time with you, I want more. I crave more. I want us to be friends beyond the contract. I want to date you exclusively. I want the chance to be able to see you when I want and kiss you when I want and come down to One Tech and take you out whenever I want without your cousin biting my head off."

She reached both arms around his neck and pulled him into a hug.

"I want to see your career progress and take off. I want you to succeed. I don't want to see you with any other guy," he said with his lips against the side of her head.

"I want the same," she whispered.

His hands tightened on her form, pressing her closer. "You do?"

"Yes, I do. You know everything about me, and you still want me."

"I've wanted you for weeks."

"If I hadn't seen your company come for recruits in UI, I wouldn't be in tech," she said. "I wouldn't have been motivated to push myself, and I wouldn't be where I am today. I'm sorry I dragged you on X. I understand that you had to do what you had to do."

He chuckled. "I don't think I want to upset you for any reason."

"You can't. Not anymore. You are the most down-to-earth rich guy I have ever met. And your encouragement is gold to me."

He exhaled as his arms tightened around her. "I love you. Regardless of what happens tonight."

She nodded.

"Will you go out with me tomorrow night and every night after, no matter what the results say?"

She drew in a deep breath. "I will."

"You promise," he said softly.

"I do."

"WELL, WELL, WELL," Sesan said to himself as he stood on the balcony overlooking the swimming pool area, staring at the couple embracing right beside it. "Look who's crossed over the wide divide."

Feyintola had left moments before, but he had stayed when he saw Mide come out to the swimming pool area. He'd been planning to go down to her, but Tomiwa had shown up.

"I leave you for five minutes, and you're kissing some other guy. I wonder what Feyintola will think of this little tête-à-tête."

He was angry as he watched Mide lean back and let Tomiwa Oyinlolu kiss her. The stupid gift box had come from him. There was no doubt about it. He was the hidden boyfriend.

Chapter Twenty-Five

WHEN MIDE AND TOMIWA stepped back into the party, they had an understanding. No matter what the results said, they would explore their friendship and make it work despite being on opposing sides.

For the moment, she was happy. She stole glances at him as he mingled freely with other guests and marvelled at how he was calm, hardly as anxious as her cousin seemed to be. He'd probably been at this point of expectation numerous times and had learned to manage it.

This was Niyi's first big break. It was understandably nerve-racking.

There were other aspects to the project. Other apprehensive parties like the companies supplying the hardware, the manual labour, and the contractors. Everyone was waiting for the announcements.

She looked around for Sesan—he had been gone a long while.

When he showed up, he was wearing a guarded look. Nothing like the smile that had been on his face when he had left earlier.

"Like I said," she said, grinning. "From smile to frown in one second. A phenomenon I should study. Someone has annoyed you, *abi*?"

He didn't smile. He just took her arm and turned her around. "I want you to meet someone."

"Oh—kaay." She noted his tight hold on her arm.

"This person knows all about my crush on you, and actually, he encourages it."

She turned sharply and stared at him as they wove through the crowd. "You have a crush on me?"

"Who wouldn't?" He let go of her arm and slipped his hand into hers, linking their fingers. "You are a very gorgeous girl, and I did tell you so on the date we had."

She narrowed her eyes. "That wasn't a date. That was you hijacking my lunchtime and making me work."

"Because your cousin gave us an assignment."

"During my lunchtime."

"Which I paid for."

"Which you offered to pay for," she corrected, wondering why he was acting weird. "Which I let you pay for because you were finally out of your terrible, sulking mood, and I didn't want you to go back into it." She watched him look around for a moment and slide his arm behind her back. "You're in a mood."

"I am. There he is. Let's go."

Sesan was leading her towards Tomiwa Oyinlolu who was getting a drink from the buffet table.

She blushed when he looked up and saw them together, then pushed Sesan's arm away from her waist, wondering what Tomiwa would be thinking seeing them together. He had already mentioned a fair amount of jealousy at seeing her hang out with Sesan. She didn't want to make it worse knowing she now had an understanding with him.

"Come," Sesan continued happily, apparently recovered from his moment of weirdness. "That's the person I want you to meet."

Mide dug her heels in and refused to budge.

"That's the CEO of Purple Chip," she said, feeling self-conscious as Tomiwa's gaze settled on hers. She didn't know she could still feel butterflies in her stomach by just looking at a guy. She thought she'd outgrown the ability. "I know him. I don't need to meet him."

"Yeah, about that," Sesan replied, staring down at her. "I think I should introduce you to him properly. You will like this, trust me."

She passed him a confused glance.

He placed his hand in the middle of her back and nudged her towards Tomiwa with a gentle push. She went reluctantly, noting Tomiwa had lowered the wine glass in his hand and was wearing a very straight face.

"Ademide, this is Tomiwa Oyinlolu, the CEO of Purple Chip," Sesan said with a bitter-sounding cheer in his voice. "The man who rejected your plea for employment. The man in whose face we are supposed to be rubbing our victory. The man who also happens to be...my older brother."

She wanted to laugh, but Tomiwa's eyes stopped her. He'd given a sort of cool, indifferent glance at Sesan and flickered his gaze back to hers. He wasn't acting like they had just been outside together and he had just told her he loved her.

He also wasn't acting like he didn't know Sesan, which was quite confusing.

"Older, half-brother, if I may correct," Sesan continued. "I don't bear the family surname, so I understand how things might have been a little muddled up. Bankole is my mother's maiden name, and Oyinlolu, my ungiven father's name. I am an Oyinlolu. I just don't own it."

Mide turned to look at Sesan, but he was looking at Tomiwa. Then she turned back to look at Tomiwa, expecting him to deny it. "I don't get."

"You do recall Ademide, don't you?" Sesan went on as Tomiwa's eyes went from appearing like they wanted to murder him to seeking hers. "Applicant at Purple Chip, cousin to the owner of One Tech." He leaned forward as if to whisper. "The one I'm supposed to date to get you guys some information and an edge over the securing of the Kehinde Jules bid."

"What are you doing?" Tomiwa's voice was ice-cold. He was looking at her, but his question was directed at Sesan. Mide could tell.

"What does it look like I'm doing? I'm clearing the air. You guys already nailed the bid, so what's all the pretence for? You can go ahead and kiss her in public. Let the world know how you really feel about her. Better still—" Sesan wagged a finger at Tomiwa and flicked it in Mide's direction. "Tell her the whole truth."

She kept her gaze on Tomiwa, trying to understand what Sesan was alluding to. "Tell me what truth? I don't get it, he's your brother?"

Tomiwa lowered his gaze. "Yes."

"As in, your biological brother?"

He nodded. "Yeah."

It took her a few seconds to ask the next question. "And you knew he was working at One Tech. With me?"

"It's a little more complicated than that."

"Complicated?" She wanted him to tell her it wasn't true. That Sesan was not his brother. That he didn't know Sesan was working at One Tech. That it was all a joke.

She wanted him to remain the person she thought he was. Unscrupulous.

But he didn't say anything. Her face went blank.

"I know what you're thinking," Tomiwa said instead. "But it's not what you think."

She took in a deep breath and let it out slowly. "It's not what I think?"

"Sesan being at One Tech doesn't—"

"Doesn't what? Absolve you of lying to my face, or spying on us? Your brother working at One Tech is not something you forget to mention. At what point would I not have found out?"

"Mide—" Tomiwa took a step towards her.

"I told you about Sesan, and you said nothing."

"I can explain."

"How?"

"Mide—" He reached for her hand.

"Don't." She stepped back from him and whipped around to find Sesan standing in front of her, hands in his pocket. "Get out of my way."

"You let him kiss you," Sesan said, visibly angry.

"Why are you telling me this now?"

"Because I'm a jerk." He shrugged. "And because your cousin is not going to get that contract. I made sure of it."

"Sesan!" Tomiwa warned, looking at him. "Stop talking."

"Keep talking," Mide replied. "What did you do?"

"Mide, there is an explanation for this, believe me—"

"Save your explanations," she snapped at Tomiwa without looking at him. "What did you do?" she asked Sesan.

"I gave them everything they needed to make a better pitch. I gave them our presentation slides, blueprints, system, literally everything."

She swallowed to steel herself against crying. "You did what?"

"Compared your solution with theirs. Gave them a list of your proposed industries. Fixed bugs in your codes so they don't work the way you intend them to. I pretty much sabotaged your pitch."

"Sesan..." Tomiwa's voice had grown a hard edge.

Mide pursed her lips and took in a deep breath so she could understand all the information coming at her.

"You fixed bugs in my codes?" she snapped, chest heaving. "Everything that went wrong the day before the presentation...."

"I need you to know who I am. Who we both are, before you fall in love with either of us, and pick one over the other."

"You're crazy. I am not in love with you. Or him."

Sesan exhaled and looked down at the ground briefly before looking back up at her. "Here I was, thinking we were settling into an understanding. Oh, sorry, that's how you are with every guy, isn't it?"

"That was not a date! And you know it."

"Sesan, stop!" Tomiwa growled.

"Laugh with them, bait them, kiss them if they get lucky, and then go right out and do it with someone else." Sesan stared at her like he was hurt. "I was going to ask you out. I had no idea you were seeing my brother."

"Don't even ask," she said. "You're a creep, and I don't want to have anything to do with you."

She turned around to leave, but Tomiwa grabbed her arm.

"Mide—"

She snatched it back. "Don't touch me!"

His eyes reacted with a splash of regret, but she ignored it.

"Please, let me explain."

"Save your explanations." She backed away from him and marched off in the direction of the exit.

She could sense him following, but her eyes were already blurry from holding back tears. She pushed through the guests who had all begun to gather together for the moment they had all been waiting for and searched for Niyi.

"Ademide—" Tomiwa caught up with her at the hall's exit into the hallway. "Please, let me explain what happened."

"I don't want to hear it," she said with tears in her eyes. "You're a liar!"

His face fell. "Ade. Please, let me tell you—"

"Don't tell me anything. You had several chances to!" Tears spilled from her eyes.

"Mide—"

"Leave me alone!"

She barged out of the hall, wiping tears as she weaved in between ushers, servers, and guests walking down the corridor. She was unsure where she was headed to or why, only that she wanted to get as far away from him as she possibly could. The idea of Tomiwa and Sesan being brothers was still confounding her. The idea he'd planted the boy in One Tech...

"Ademide—" Tomima's grip on her arm was gentle as he caught up with her and spun her around. "Will you listen to what I have to say?"

"No!"

She snatched her arm from his grip, but he put an arm on the wall behind her and backed her into it.

"I'm sorry. I am really sorry you had to find out this way, but I—"

"But you what? You forgot? You didn't know how to tell me? Or when to tell me? Or you were simply not going to tell me? Which excuse exactly would you have me believe? Which one is tenable? Which lie is going to come out of your mouth right now?"

"None." He was quiet for a second, looking lost for words. "None. I didn't authorize Sesan's posting to One Tech."

She started laughing, eyes averted from his. "I don't think you realize how ridiculous that sounds."

"I honestly didn't agree with it, and I wanted to tell you."

"You wanted to?"

"Mide—"

"Don't even—don't say anything."

"Hey, Tommy, I've been looking all over for you." Feyintola showed up in the hallway at that moment and stopped beside the two of them, eyeing him in confusion. "What's going on?" She glanced at Mide. "What are you doing here? Let's go. The results are about to be announced."

Mide lifted a finger and wiped a tear. "Go ahead. Don't worry about me. Go and get your contract."

She pushed his arm out of the way and marched away from him.

———◦———

TOMIWA DIDN'T WANT to look at Feyintola's puzzled face. He could only stare helplessly as the woman he had fallen in love with as she walked out on him.

He hadn't been able to bear seeing the devastation on her face. He'd wanted to wrap her up in his arms and beg her not to be angry, but he honestly didn't know where to start the explanations from.

"Are you seeing her now?" Feyintola asked.

"Not anymore."

"Not anymore, what is that supposed to mean? How could you—why did you?"

He exhaled, completely devastated. He'd been hoping to find a good time let her know.

"I told you what would— You know what, I can't even deal with this now. Let's just go and hear the results."

Feyintola turned around and headed in the direction of the hall entrance while he stood frozen in place trying to figure out how to repair the damage.

When they got back into the hall, Kehinde Jules Senior had announced the results.

The contract went to Purple Chip Professionals, but Tomiwa couldn't enjoy the victory. He could only watch from the other end of the room as Mide picked up her bag and files and left the venue with her cousin.

Chapter Twenty-Six

THE TAXIFY RIDE HOME was initially a quiet affair.

Mide was numb, trying to process everything that had happened that evening. Niyi's incessant rant about how stupid he had been hiring the Dappler, and how crazy he thought the Oyinlolu siblings were, didn't make things any better. Rather, it fuelled her anger at Tomiwa.

Anything and everything I do these days is all about you.

It had sounded so sweet and romantic when she had first heard it. Now, she understood he had meant something entirely different.

What's your relationship to One Tech?

Her heart plummeted. Her answer to that question had sealed her fate and got him planning horrible things for her and Niyi from the moment she had given it. And she had been too blind to see it.

"Good things don't just fall from the sky," Niyi continued. "And I knew that. When it's too good to be true, it probably is."

I'm not trying anything, Miss Akinseye. I just wanted to see you.

Liar!

She felt like her chest was about to explode. She was trying—unsuccessfully—to keep her heart from breaking, but the effort hurt. The only way out was to accept that Tomiwa had used her and played her from the very moment they had first met.

Being courted by him had seemed unnatural. Going for rides in his car and on the boat, as well as dining in the hotel restaurant, had felt too good to be true. And somewhere inside, she had known it. Why had she ignored it?

She placed her head against the door of the car and put her phone on silent. He was calling her again, but she didn't want to talk to him.

"I need to tell you something," she said out loud.

"Mide, it was not your fault. You couldn't have known who he was."

"I showed him the codes."

"I hired him. It was my fault," Niyi replied. "I was too lazy to check him properly, and I all but encouraged you to work with him because he is so good, and there was so much work to be done and so little time. I was so relieved to have help as good as him, I didn't vet him."

"I'm not talking about Sesan," she whispered.

Niyi looked mildly confused. "What? Who are you talking about?"

"The CEO of Purple Chip. I showed him the codes. I've been seeing him."

"Tomiwa Oyinlolu?"

She folded her lips together and nodded.

Niyi didn't stop staring so she explained some more.

"We went on a few dates, and one time when I was having trouble with a syntax line, I asked him. He told me what to do, then he kissed me. He probably asked Sesan to sabotage them, and he just—he was probably laughing at how easy it had been to fool me—and I let him kiss me. He was the one who took me to the hospital the night of the award ceremony."

"You said it was a friend."

"I couldn't tell you it was him."

Niyi looked perplexed. "The mysterious gift box—"

"Came from him. I'm sorry."

Niyi's gaze journeyed out through the window on his side of the car. He didn't say anything for a long while, but Mide knew he was very angry.

"I couldn't tell you. We most often didn't talk about work, but that's how I came about the breakthrough for the filters. He taught me what to do."

"He took advantage of you, that's shame on him."

She stared down at her hands on her lap.

"I was so stupid, so enamoured by the fact that a guy like him could be interested in someone like me." She closed her eyes and tried not to remember the pleasant feel of his beard grazing her lips the first time they had kissed. And every time afterward. "I didn't even see it coming."

She let out a sob. It was betrayal all over again, and it hurt from deep within. Her heart underwent a painful squeeze, the sadness washing over her as if it was never going to go away.

"Mide." Niyi leaned over and pulled her into his arms. "It's okay, dear. Don't think about it."

But she couldn't stop crying. Though she tried to keep it quiet, the sobs came from deep within, and she couldn't tell if it was her heart breaking or her rib cage being compressed by her anxious thoughts. She squeezed her eyes shut from the tension and gritted her teeth together as the pain began slowly and gradually built itself up.

"It's a lesson. Sometimes, you learn some lessons early in life before you hit it big so you don't lose money in a big way."

"Inhaler," she whispered as she extracted herself from Niyi's arms and leaned against the car door.

"Mide!" He grabbed her purse and reached inside it for her inhaler. "You need to calm down, please."

She pressed herself into the side of the door as the pain in her chest reached an excruciating point and she struggled to breathe.

He found the grey canister in her purse and handed it to her. She took a dose and waited for a second, and then took another dose.

Niyi held her hand. "Are you all right now?"

"A little better," she whispered but grabbed her chest as pain shot like a spike through it. Then there were several more. "*Aww!*" she cried, squeezing her eyes tightly as tears spilled beneath the lids.

He frowned. "You know the doctor said you need to be in control of your emotions. So, you need to calm down."

"I know," she whispered.

"This is what I'm telling myself right now. It's just a contract. There will be plenty more. There will be someone else, other guys. Don't allow yourself to feel it is all over just because a selfish guy—"

Niyi stopped himself before he spoke words he would regret.

Mide cried out loud again.

"Niyi," she whispered, her voice hoarse as she tried to inhale. "I can't breathe..."

HALF-LYING AGAINST the pillows of the hospital bed, Mide listened to Niyi goad himself for not having insisted she tell him the name of the guy she'd been seeing. She realized he was right. Telling him would have been good. Telling him would have probably prevented everything.

The door opened, and Derin came in.

"Hey," she shut it quietly. "How is she doing?"

"Better, but they are going to keep her overnight. This episode was a little severe. The emotional ones always are."

"Cheer up, dear. She'll be fine."

Derin leaned over and kissed his forehead before touching Mide's arm and dropping the package she had brought on the hospital cabinet. "I didn't know you were awake. How are you feeling?"

"Tired." In truth, Mide felt embarrassed. "My chest is heavy."

"Pele, try and rest."

"What of the girls?"

"I left them with Mrs. Koko. They're fine." Derin sat on a chair and turned to Niyi. "Have you called her mum?"

Mide shook her head and waved her hand at Derin.

Niyi took in a deep breath. "She doesn't want me to, and I agree. I don't feel we should worry the poor woman."

Derin took Niyi's hand and rubbed it. "I'm sorry."

"About the contract? You win some, you lose some."

"I should have allowed you to ask her some more about the guy who brought her home," Derin said. "I was just wanting to give her some privacy. Let it become more of a serious thing before we got involved. you know."

"I understand." Niyi looked over at Mide.

'I'm sorry,' Mide mouthed silently.

He squeezed his face and shook his head at her. "Don't be."

The phone in the room rang suddenly.

Niyi rose to answer it. "Yeah, who is it? Mr. Oyinlolu?"

Tomiwa?

Mide's ears perked at the sound of his name. She turned to look at Niyi, hoping to hear snatches of their conversation, but Niyi's face was contorted in anger.

"That's okay, keep him there. I'll come out and see him myself."

"Who is it?" Derin asked when he got off the phone.

He didn't answer.

"Niyi?"

"That selfish son of a bitch!" he bellowed, turning back at the door. "Telling me he heard she was in the hospital and was worried about her. How dare he?"

"Why don't you let him come in?" Derin said.

"Come in and do what? Come in and do what, Derin? He led her on, took advantage of her naïve goodness, and dared to plant a spy in my office? Who the hell does that? What does he want to come in and say?"

"He was her boyfriend."

"Boyfriend, my foot!"

"I think she deserves to decide if she wants him here or not, Niyi. It's not your call to make."

"I'm her guardian. It's my duty to protect her."

Derin ignored him and turned to her. "Mide, do you want to see him?"

She looked from Derin to Niyi and shook her head. There was no explanation for Tomiwa's callousness. There was nothing he wanted to say that she wanted to hear.

TOMIWA'S FOREHEAD WAS matted in a frown when Feyintola walked into his office.

"We won. Why are you looking so morose?" She took a seat opposite him.

He didn't answer. He just stared at his laptop and refused to look at her.

"Aww," she said. "Is it your little girlfriend? Had you told me you were involved with her, I wouldn't have sent the Dappler after her."

"That's not—" he started to say but gave up, shook his head, and dropped his gaze back to the open laptop.

"Do you see now why I didn't want to hire her? You wouldn't have kept yourself in check. You would have gone after her. You and Gori are so predictable, it's pathetic."

He ignored her tirade.

"Anyway, we have a meeting set up with Jules Junior for ten o'clock on Wednesday morning and celebratory dinner tonight at Three Centres. You and your team should start prepping for installation and support. I'll be with you until they pay the first instalment, of course, then I'll start looking for new prospects. We can use the list Sesan gave us of prospective industries we could target with our solution—"

"I'm not coming." He leaned forward and let his fingers fly over the keyboard.

Feyintola blinked. "To the dinner or the meeting?"

"Both."

"Why?"

"Because I don't feel much like partying."

"Tommy," she quipped, surprised. "Sinking yourself into some sort of depression over one girl is hardly the way to go, if you ask me."

"I'm not asking you," he replied. "I'm telling you."

She pressed her lips into a firm smile. "It's okay if you don't want to come for the dinner, but you have to be there on Wednesday for the meeting. You know how important it is."

"The next time we have an IT project, I don't want you on the team."

The smile dipped. "You can't do that. I am the Managing Director of Oyinlolu Incorporations!"

"And I'm the CEO of Purple Chip."

"As the MD, the onus falls on me to—"

"Back out of Purple Chip affairs."

He was satisfied to see the look of shock on her face. He had never used such a tone or pulled rank with her before, so he could understand why it was a little jarring for her.

"No, I won't."

"Yes, you will."

"No.'

"Cross me, and I'll pull out completely." Tomiwa's gaze held hers, resolute. "I mean it."

She blinked. "You can't pull out of the incorporation. Dad didn't—"

"Dad didn't found Purple Chip. I did. And I'm drafting a contract at the moment that gives me sole directory proprietorship. We remain a part of the Incorporation, but I make the decisions concerning the direction PC takes, and you have no say in it. You are too unethical, and I can't allow my company to keep compromising on values because you—"

"Tomiwa—"

"Counter me again, and so help me God, Feyin, I will destroy Oyinlolu Incorp and set up a new company."

They both stared at one another. He sensed she wasn't giving up, but the steel backbone she had was in him, too.

"We were never meant to run as separate entities. We are meant to be together. That was what Dad wanted."

"Dad's no longer here, and you run things like you're the only one at the top. I think I've sat back and let you take the reins long enough. No more."

Feyintola raised her head and pulled her chin out. "The Incorporation will still control fifty-five percent of the funds—"

"The Incorporation will do no such thing. If I pull Purple Chip out, you know what will happen. The stocks will plummet, and the hotels will gulp a lot until they stabilize. That is...if they ever. We all know real estate is not what it used to be, so in your own words, suck it up and get on board with the new program. I no longer listen to you."

Feyintola glared at him. "I know you didn't like my handling of the Jules account, but—"

"This is not just about One Tech and the Jules account. This is about you. You're unethical, and I need to distance myself from your style of leadership. I'm not going to let you take Purple Chip down that road again. I shouldn't have let you in the first place."

"Very well." She got up. "Suit yourself. But the agreement as per the Jules account still stands."

"Why, Feyin—" he passed her a sardonic smile. "We are not fighting. We're just marking territories. The contract will be on your desk by tomorrow morning, and you had better sign it."

"Yeah!" she said angrily and walked away.

TOMIWA KNOCKED ON THE door of the BQ and waited for his brother to open the door. The boy was surprised when he saw him, but let him in.

Slipping his hands into his pockets, he strode in and looked around. It was a typical bachelor's pad. Filthy, unruly, and shared by more than one person as he could see.

"What brings you here?" Sesan asked, slipping his arms into the sleeves of a T-shirt and throwing it over his head.

"You could have asked. We'd have paid for better accommodation."

Sesan laughed as he pulled the shirt over his hairy chest and down the rest of his torso.

"I thought you didn't like me. You didn't trust I was who I said I was." He reached for an apple on the desktop fridge. "This is the last apple; I'd have offered you one."

Tomiwa turned his nose up at the dingy room.

"I'm good." He turned his gaze to Sesan. "How did it feel?"

"To ruin your relationship? Pretty good, actually. But if I knew she was your girl, I'd have turned Feyin down. You didn't say, either. Great thing with the box, too. She really liked it"

Tomiwa's silence lasted only the few seconds in which he counted to five. "I'm not talking about that."

Sesan bit into the apple and then leaned against the table in the cramped apartment. "What are you talking about?"

"You don't become a dark web surfer without having a dark, deviant side to your personality." He took a slow walk around the room. "I took those words literally the first day we met. Safe to say I didn't trust you from one end of that conference table to the other."

Sesan shrugged. "Why are you here?"

Tomiwa stopped walking and faced him. "You know why I'm here. How much did you steal?"

"Steal?"

"I know your background in algorithms, so I wrote a code to catch your codes. The software you built tracked into my monitoring system, and the moment you plugged it in, it piggybacked such that I have you on fraud and racketeering."

Sesan laughed. "I only took what I needed."

"You didn't know our father." Tomiwa's calm look hid his anger. "He was charming to a fault, benevolent even, but not a nice guy. He dealt ruthlessly with scheming men. He did one thing, though. He paid enough forward to keep the necessary powers that be in favour with his children. The ones they know. That certainly doesn't include you."

"Are you threatening me?"

"I can get the police to do whatever I want with you," Tomiwa continued. "Think carefully about your options. You are going to give back the money you stole, and the grace extends for as long as I am in this room."

Sesan sniggered.

"I already have EFCC officials stationed outside, ready to move on my word. You're my brother. Let's not make this difficult."

Sesan threw his half-eaten apple on the table "You had everything growing up. All I wanted was a little something."

"You could have asked. We'd have given it to you."

"What? Peanuts? Out of a multibillion-naira empire?"

"You weren't entitled to anything legally, anyway. Your wolf cry moves no one."

He swallowed. "What gave me away?"

"It just makes no sense you would work for Feyin and spy on One Tech for money. You have no allegiance to us, and that crap about wanting to get back at Niyi for coming second in Longman was just what it was, a whole load of crap."

"There was some truth to it."

"I didn't give you access to my software. How did you get it to compare it with theirs? You should have just stuck with telling us about theirs, but you were trying too hard to impress. I had Babs watch our security codes like a hawk and set up hidden cookies. Like I said, you don't become a dark web surfer without having a dark, deviant side to your personality." Tomiwa paused. "I wasn't talking about you. You couldn't con me, even if you held a blindfold to my eyes. I set the bait and watched you take it. I'm going to enjoy seeing you rot in prison."

Sesan averted his eyes. It took him a while for the words to come out. "Three hundred million."

"Thank you for telling the truth. Now switch on your laptop, and start the transfers. Every single kobo from every single one of your fourteen different bogus company accounts! *Poko a Poko*, a little at a time."

He reluctantly grabbed his laptop from the desk and did as he was told.

Tomiwa opened the door and let Babs and Ugo in.

"Watch him," he said, "Like a hawk."

"You're not going to tell Feyintola, are you?" Sesan said as he typed. "I kind of like her."

"Why would I?" Tomiwa turned around to stare at the back of his head. "You are our brother, and little brothers are naughty sometimes. That doesn't mean we always have to tell Mum and Dad."

Ugo grabbed a bag and threw some clothes in it while Babs put down the monitor of his laptop and unplugged the charger cord.

Sesan leaned back and held out his hands. "What are you doing?"

Babs laughed. "You didn't think you were going to do it in here, did you? We have a one-bedroom apartment all set up to make you comfortable."

Ugo grinned. "Everyone knows you can't move anything above ten million naira from company accounts in a day, so we are going to be with you a few days."

Tomiwa waited to see the anger in Sesan's eyes before he left.

Chapter Twenty-Seven

KEHINDE JULES JUNIOR strode across the tiled floor of their office lobby and reached out to give Tomiwa a handshake.

"How far?"

"I'm good!" Tomiwa replied with a smile.

"Our meeting is not till tomorrow. I'm curious as to why you've been chasing me all over the whole place. You got the contract; everything starts next week Monday."

"I know that. Can we meet in your office, please?"

"Sure." Kehinde led the way. "How's your sister, and Gori?"

"They're good." Tomiwa stepped into his office. "How about your dad? I don't see him around much these days."

"Yeah, he's always out and about touring different countries. Retire young, retire rich, they say. My father lives the mantra." Kehinde motioned Tomiwa into a seat. "What brings you here?"

Tomiwa sat back and placed his forearms on the chair's armrest. "I want to start by saying thank you for your generosity in giving us the contract. I am grateful for the opportunity, and I realize it is a great honour that we were chosen out of all the companies vying for the job."

"No need to thank me. We love your brand. Everyone on the team was comfortable going for tried and tested."

He took in a deep breath. "I am sorry, I'm afraid I will have to decline it."

Kehinde frowned. "Good heavens, why?"

"Because I think you would be better off going with One Tech."

"But why? We love your ledger, and we think it will be in our best interest to work with a more experienced company."

"*Profit X* mirrors our solution well, and you're not losing out. I need to pull back the ledger."

"Why?"

"Personal reasons."

"Does Feyin know about this? Does she approve, or will she be sliding a knife across my neck?"

He chuckled. "Don't worry your head about Feyin, I'll handle her. I own Purple Chip. The final decision is mine, and I'm not giving you *Purple Ledger*."

"Why?"

"I'd rather not say."

"But you fought hard for this. What if we want to go for another company? If we can't have you, then I'm afraid—"

"You would be making a very big mistake. One Tech is good, and you know it. For us, there are other things we can do, but for them..." he trailed off. "Look, I know this is a crazy business decision and unwise in every way you can think of, but I don't want to be the big fish that swallows the little fish. The tech industry is huge and growing by the second. I believe there are other pots we can open easily that they will struggle to even find. I want them to have this."

Kehinde had his mouth open, looking at him. "Why?"

"Kenny. Do this for me as a favour. And give them the contract for the exact same amount you were willing to pay us."

"Goodness, Tom, that's—"

"I know they bid lower, but it's very possible, Kenny. I know you can do it."

"I don't know about this, Tomiwa. It's not done anywhere."

"Do this for me, and I will owe you. And I promise you, the *Profit X* solution will be a great investment. The guys that built it, they're good."

Kehinde Jules stared at Tomiwa, then he held out his hand. "It's a deal. I'll up their fees, but I will not give them what you billed. No. You know what I would like in return."

Tomiwa nodded. "I do.'

"Then, we're good."

They shook hands.

"Whatever you are doing this for, I hope it's worth it."

He was doing it for his conscience, to set things right, and maintain a clean record. But he exhaled and thought about Mide. "I hope so, too."

"HEY, ARE YOU OKAY?"

Mide looked up and saw Niyi at the door to her room. She was still on the mend after her discharge from the hospital three days prior, and she was glad to be home with the familiar. "I'm okay.'

"Feeling better?" he continued.

"Yeah." She watched as Derin ushered the twins off her bed and straightened the bedspread.

"Are the girls ready for school, can I take them?"

"Yes," Derin replied. "Okay, ladies, kiss your aunt bye-bye and let her rest."

Both girls climbed back into bed with Mide and gave her a hug each.

"Bye, munchkins. Enjoy school. Ensure you disturb your teacher."

"We love you, Aunty Mide, get well soon," the twins chorused.

She watched them run to their father and slip out of the room.

"I'll just stay with her for another hour before I go to work. You can leave."

Niyi saluted his wife and looked at Mide from across the room. 'Rest,' he mouthed.

"I will," she whispered, and blew him a kiss.

He waved but hovered by the doorway.

"Go!" Derin shooed him away and turned towards Mide who grinned at her.

"He wasn't looking at me, he was looking at you."

"I know, but he worries too much."

Mide nodded, hating to have put her cousin and his wife through so much. If Niyi always worried, it was because of her.

A minute later, Derin sat on the bed next to her and adjusted her petticoat over her nightgown. "You are going to get over this one day, I hope, you know. It will be a thing of the past."

"That's what the doctors told me when I was a child. I'm still battling."

Derin smiled. "I wasn't talking about the asthma, but then, don't ever give up hope. Miracles can still happen."

Mide's phone rang just then. She stared at it and let it ring out.

Derin picked up the phone and looked at the name against the missed call.

"Thirty-eight missed calls, today alone." She looked at her. "Why don't you answer him?"

"He's a liar. I don't trust him."

"Perhaps there is some sort of explanation—"

"There's none. He used me to get a contract."

"I'm guessing he is the one who sent the box."

"I've got it in mind to buy everything back that was in that box and return it to him."

Derin sighed out loud. "Sometimes, people do things that don't make sense for reasons we don't understand. And we won't, unless we hear them out."

"I don't care," she said as her phone began ringing again. "I don't think I ever want to see him again." She put the bowl of pepper soup down on the table beside her bed and turned to pull the covers up to her neck. "I am super glad Niyi didn't let him in at the hospital."

Derin placed the vibrating phone on the table beside the bowl and patted her on the arm. "Well, rest. I'm going to get ready for work, but I'll check on you before I leave."

"Okay," she said in a muffled tone as tears slid down her cheeks and wouldn't stop.

TOMIWA HELD THE PHONE in his hands and pressed the call button. Then he put it down on his desk and stared at it. It was just going to ring out. She wasn't going to pick.

"Mide, please," he whispered to himself. "Please, just pick up."

The door to his office burst open suddenly, and a visibly angry Feyintola marched inside towards him.

"Tomiwa, what the— how dare you?"

He looked up and then sat back in his chair to watch her rant.

"You upped and went behind my back and flipping gave the contract to One Tech. What in the world is wrong with you? We worked hard for that thing, we needed it! Do you know what the account statements look like? We'll go belly up in a year if something is not done about it soon. We need the money to expand Blue Water and buffer our shares. What on Earth were you thinking about? Your little girlfriend is pouting, so what? The rest of us should catch a cold because she sneezed?"

He reached into his drawer for a thick binder and threw it on the desk. "When you're done yelling, you can look at this."

Feyintola dropped her eyes to his desk and frowned. Then her eyes caught the name on the front page of the document. "Walter, Braithe, and Sons, are you kidding me? When did you do this?"

"While you were busy sticking Sesan into One Tech and spying on them."

"Oh, my goodness, when did they sign?"

"Yesterday," he said quietly.

Feyintola ran around his desk and wrapped her hands around him. "My darling brother, you are brilliant, you are the best. You just saved us."

She proceeded to give him a few kisses on the cheek, and he couldn't help but laugh.

"Let me go and work on this." She slid the binder underneath her armpit and ran out of his office.

His laughter waned with his sister's exit from his office. He turned to look at his phone and thought again about calling her. He knew, however, she wasn't going to pick.

One Tech was never supposed to have found out about Sesan. The boy was meant to have hung around long enough for the sting of their loss to die down, then found his way to the US and stayed there. But he'd been too greedy. And he'd ruined things for everyone.

Recalling the hurt in Mide's eyes when she had found out he had been less than honest with her, he picked up the phone and dialled her again. He didn't think she would be malicious enough to rant about it on X. He hoped so because his brand couldn't take another hit. But there were no guarantees with a woman scorned. In a month, it was possible she would start a thread about it.

Even if she didn't want him back, he wanted to do everything possible to right every wrong they'd done. He hadn't stuck Sesan in One Tech, but he'd been indifferent about it.

That had been his crime. His silent complicity.

Chapter Twenty-Eight

IT HAD BEEN A WEEK, and Mide was tired of staying at home recuperating. Though the chest pain had completely disappeared, she was still exhausted most of the time.

It had been drizzling all morning, and she had read all the novels in her arsenal halfway and thrown them all in her book bag. Romance novels were the last thing she wanted to read. They were hardly reflective of real life in any case.

Tomiwa's calls had waned, coming twice a day. She still refused to pick up.

At first, it had been due to anger at what he had done. Then, it had been fear. The fear of trusting him again. Of trusting her own ability to vet human intentions.

She longed for his touch and his voice, but she was scared of letting him off too easily. Of letting her guard down and being deceived again. She was scared of falling in love.

When the doorbell rang, she hoped, for some crazy insane moment, it was him. So, she got out of bed, slipped into a large warm sweater, and found her way down the stairs to go and check on who it was.

She wasn't sure yet how much anger she wanted to show to him, but she was finally tired of holding back her desire to see him and hear what he had to say. She wanted to jump into his arms and kiss him and ask if there was some part of him that had loved her and not the contract.

When she opened the door, it was Sesan standing there, hands in his pocket under the light drizzle.

Disappointment ate up her courage and placed a heavy stone in her stomach. What if Tomiwa had given up? What if he, too, had decided he never wanted to see her again?

She pulled the large brown button-down sweater more securely around herself and tried not to look worse for wear. "What are you doing here?"

"I'm leaving town. Can we talk for a bit?"

She looked reluctant. "Give me one good reason why I should talk to you?"

He sighed. "I'm sorry. You only ever tried to be my friend, and I ruined it. I'm here to make amends."

"You lied to us."

"I did. And I'm sorry. I came to tell you that I'm going away. Your cousin doesn't even have to pay me for the month I did."

She didn't smile. "Even if he wanted to pay you, there is no money. You knew that."

He nodded. "Just listen to what I have to say. You don't have to forgive me."

"I don't plan to."

She pushed the door open and stepped out into the light rain, following him to a spot under the carport. There, she folded her arms and lifted her face to his.

"I'm off to a two-year master's degree program at MIT."

"Why should I care?"

"Because I can't leave without clearing up a few things."

"I don't know what you are going to say that will more than make up for what you did."

Sesan shrugged. "Nothing, I guess. I hate sob stories, but you should hear mine."

She stared at him arms folded, heart dead set on not giving in to any form of persuasion.

"I don't care about your story. How are you his brother?"

"My father had me out of wedlock. I didn't know who he was till I was twelve. I didn't come looking till I was twenty-five and his communication stopped. Of course, I was angry to find them living large while I lived in penury all my years. Doesn't excuse what I did to you and your cousin, but—" he shrugged, "—life's what it is. I've always had to do what I needed to do to survive."

"To survive. At the cost of others."

"He tried to take himself out of the equation, Mide, but Feyin wouldn't let him. All the while, I was busy sabotaging your brother's Jules proposal, he was searching for another contract to replace it with. He wanted One Tech to get the bid. He wanted you to win."

She stared at him, eyes unblinking, a tiny frown on her brow.

"It hurts me to say this, but he loves you! And he can give you what I can't."

"And what's that, money? Fame? I don't want his money."

"Wholeness," he replied. "And love. And money. The things that you need. There's no money in that account, Mide, don't be stubborn."

"That's none of your business."

He shrugged. "I'm leaving anyway. It's none of my business."

She kept her arms folded, but her gaze dropped to the floor. "Suddenly, you're his best friend and lawyer. No more talk of wanting to sabotage them."

"Well, they've given me what I wanted, and I won't be coming back for a while."

"It's just as well. I wish you all the best."

"I spent a few days under house arrest for crimes committed. And we got to talk, iron out our issues and share a few meals. You are a great programmer. One of the best I've seen. You're a great girl, and he's one of the best men I've seen. Go and check on him. Not for me, not even for him. For yourself. I know how much you like him."

"I think you should leave."

He grinned. "Promise me you'll check on him, for his sake, too. Everyone's walking around on eggshells, and it's not good for the company."

She shook her head and didn't say anything or look up from staring at the floor.

"He's not even seeing anyone presently, but when you do decide to forgive him, his assistant Shile might be of some help. I gave him your number."

"You didn't need to."

"This is goodbye," he said. "I'm not sure I will keep in touch, I'm not very good at that."

"That's fine with me. It will take me years to forgive you."

He reached out and pulled her into his arms. Scared he had more in mind than a hug, she stiffened.

He didn't—he just held her for a moment in which she couldn't relax. She was still mad at him.

"I enjoyed getting to know you, Mide," he whispered. "And for the record, I ran to keep from getting attached because I was severely attracted to you. I wish you all the very best in life. Goodbye."

He let her go immediately and marched off into the drizzle.

AFTER ANOTHER COUPLE of bored days at home, Mide dressed up one morning and took a taxi to work. She was fed up of staying indoors and wanted to be out in the sunshine.

Chuka gave a whoop of delight when he saw her. "Why are you here? You should be in bed. *Oga* said you were taking two weeks off. We were expecting you back on Monday morning. What are you doing out of bed?"

She smiled. "I'm fine. I don't think I can sit in that house a minute longer."

"Seems like those high society parties don't agree with you," he continued with a sly grin. "You get sick after every one of them."

"They don't, *abi*?"

They both burst out laughing.

"And I heard who your mystery guy was."

Her face fell. "I'm—I was—"

"Don't worry about it," Chuka said. "He is a powerful guy at the top of his game. Who can resist that?"

"I owe the whole office an apology." She looked around the practically empty office. "Speaking of which, where is everyone?"

"Well, the Dappler's gone. The IT students have a school submission thingy. Akin and Femi had to go to Shoal farms and train their staff on the app. Kemi went to go drop off some letters, and Ross is going over some things with Mr. Niyi in his office."

"Mr. Niyi doesn't know I'm here. I should say hi to him."

"Sure."

He watched her walk away. "Hey, Mide. It's really good to have you back at work."

She nodded with a small smile and opened the door to the office.

Niyi's eyes grew round when he saw her. "What are you doing here? You should be at home, resting in bed."

"I couldn't take one more day of staying at home. Hi, Ross."

"But the doctor said—"

"I know what the doctor said. Fresh air, cross ventilation, warm soups, daily meds. I'll be fine."

"Miss Akinseye." A smile lit up Ross' face. "Welcome back."

"Thanks, Ross."

"Guess what came in the mail this morning." Niyi sounded excited. "A formal invite, and a pro-forma invoice for the Jules Account."

She stared back at him, confused. "But we lost..."

"They took the contract from Purple Chip and gave it to us!"

"They couldn't have just done that!"

"I don't know how. I don't care how. All I know is that I'm meeting with them on Monday, and you're coming with me!" He stood up and did a little dance.

Mide knew just then what Tomiwa had done—why he had been trying to reach her. She couldn't hear anything else Niyi was saying, just Sesan's explanations and Derin's voice in her head.

He wanted One Tech to get the bid. He wanted you to win. Sometimes, people do things that don't make sense for reasons we don't understand. And we won't, unless we hear them out.

Go and see him. Not for him, for yourself. To see if anything can be salvaged.

Chapter Twenty-Nine

THE EIGHTH-FLOOR RECEPTION office of Purple Chip Professional Services was a beautiful place. It was tastefully furnished and luxurious in design with a wide, open floor plan, a rich, dark-blue wall-to-wall rug, and window blinds.

The furniture was upscale and modern, the light fixtures aesthetic. Interesting oil paintings hung on the walls, giving a cheerful and welcoming atmosphere. Mide was wowed. Judging by offices, One Tech had quite a long way to go.

Sesan's exit meant Niyi had to do some hiring so it was not the time to rent a new office but the time to find competent, honest staff.

The bi-racial receptionist was pleasant when she asked to see him.

"I'm sorry, but Mr. Oyinlolu is not available at the moment. May I take a message?"

"I'd rather deliver it personally. If you tell him my name, he might agree to see me."

The lady pursed her lips. "I'm sorry to disappoint, but Mr. Oyinlolu is not available. So, I was just going to take a message."

"In that case, can I see Mr. Shile?"

"Your name again, please?"

"Ademide Akinseye."

"One moment. Please take a seat while I see if he's available."

"Sure, thanks."

Mide flashed her a bright smile and walked across the wide reception room to find a seat as far away from the nearest air conditioning unit as possible. When she looked up, she noticed the receptionist was watching her. She smirked.

She hadn't wanted to walk into Purple Chip looking shabby, but she didn't own any high-end designer clothes. She'd thrown on a sleeveless blue dress with red and green floral patterns made from fabric she'd had cut and sewn and paired it with black ankle boots. Her braids had been swapped for her Darling Caribbean curls wig, and she had put on minimal makeup.

She wasn't as fashionably savvy or as well-to-do as most of the women she had seen strutting up and down the building, but her tailor always managed to create half-decent clothes with her fabrics. Adding the grey, cashmere, off-shoulder sweater from Tomiwa's gift box had lifted the dress's value by a few thousand nairas, and she was glad he had gifted her with it.

One Tech definitely has to do a salary review, she was thinking. *At least add a wardrobe allowance.*

The exotic-looking receptionist was wearing a dress she was sure had come from a high-end store, and for a tiny moment, Mide felt jealous. This was a person Tomiwa saw every day. The whole building, it seemed, was filled with beautiful, well-dressed women who he saw every day!

For the life of her, she couldn't understand how or why their CEO had zeroed in on her.

He had stopped calling. She felt foolish because there was a whole building of replacements and she'd been giving him an attitude. She'd worn the sweater more to placate him than anything else. Now, seeing the competition, she was glad she'd worn it.

When she caught the receptionist scoping her out again, she imagined she could see the wheels turning round in the lady's head: the quizzical idea that the affluent Mr. Oyinlolu would ever associate with a simpleton like her.

For a second, Mide wondered at the wisdom of having come to his office when a phone call would have sufficed. She knew why she'd come, though—she'd wanted to look into his eyes and have him tell her why he had done what he did.

Also, she wanted to let him know she had missed him.

If it's not too late! If I haven't blown my chance with my stubborn pride.

A few minutes later, a young man in an office shirt under a sleeveless sweater approached her. "Hello. Miss Akinseye, I believe?"

"Yes."

"Great. I'm Shile, Mr. Tom's office assistant." He extended a hand.

"Ademide." She shook it and stood up.

"Mr. Sesan told me you were the antidote to Mr. Tomiwa's ailment."

She raised her eyebrows and chuckled. "He said that?"

"He did. I am more than very pleased to see you here, ma'am. May I take you to him?"

"Sure." She tossed a triumphant grin at the office receptionist and followed Shile out of the reception into the corridor.

"I hear you're also a programmer."

"Yeah, I applied to work here, but you guys didn't think I was good enough."

He gave a lopsided smile as he stopped by the elevator and pressed the up-button. "I don't make the decisions, but I'm sure they had their reasons."

"That's water under the bridge. I work for One Tech now."

"I'm aware."

"Where are we going?"

"Tenth floor. The execs have their offices there."

She nodded as the elevator doors opened up.

There was a young lady already in there who looked up the moment they walked in. Mide took in her stylish black dress with white line-trimmings crisscrossing the entire lower half of it and recognized her immediately. She was the lady who had coordinated the tests and handed her the question sheet. The lady in the killer red dress and stilts.

"Hey, Chioma."

"Shile."

"Good morning," Mide said with a bright smile.

"Morning," she replied, giving Mide a look from head to toe. "I'm guessing you're Ademide Akinseye."

Mide lifted her head in the beginning of a nod and tried to keep the surprise away from her face. It was definitely true word had gone round.

"That's an excellent memory you have there. I thought I was lost in the sea of applicants the other day. Didn't know you picked me out."

"I didn't," the lady replied. "I packed and sent the gift box on behalf of Mr. Oyinlolu. I hope you enjoyed the contents."

"Oh!" She felt foolish. The lady obviously recognized the sweater. "Thank you, it was...very helpful."

"I'm Chioma." She handed Mide a kind smile. "The sweater looks good on you."

"Thank you."

She turned around and watched Shile swipe his key card across the control panel and start their ascent.

"So, this ailment plaguing your boss—" she said to him.

"Is a mysterious kind of Jekyll and Hyde peculiarity."

Her eyes widened. "Excuse me, what?"

"He's pulling a good guy and a bad guy all rolled into one at the moment."

"Okaaaay..."

"Everyone is just worried. He hardly comes out of his office, and when he does, he's firing someone."

"Yes," Chioma added. "Two junior programmers have gone this week over issues the old Mr. Tom would have overlooked. Plus, he's doing all his programming himself these days, hardly leaving anything for anyone to do. If he continues at this rate, he is going to break down, and we can't have that."

"True." Shile took over. "No matter how good we are, we need his direction. It's like having a bunch of great drivers and mechanics with no road map and absolutely no clue where they are going."

"I understand," Mide replied. "You want him to come out of that office and not fire any more people?"

"If it's possible," Shile said.

"That would be excellent," Chioma added. "Everyone has tried talking to him. I'm hoping you can make a difference."

"I hope so, too. If he's not mad at me already."

"He's not," Chioma assured her. "He's just disappointed that you ignored his calls. I'm glad you came. We all want the old Mr. Tom back."

When they stepped off the elevator, Shile walked her up to the security guard on duty to get her registered and vetted. Chioma left, hurrying towards the last door on the right-hand side of the corridor.

Mide watched as Shile's eyes followed her. She had the loveliest fair-complexioned skin she'd ever come across and an attractive figure. Plus, she seemed to be close to Tomiwa and was another prospect he could explore.

Fear gnawed her insides. What if he'd given up?

"That's not our stop," Shile said, noticing her gaze. "That's the way to the Filex Property MD's office. We're going left."

"Lead the way."

The name plate on the door read 'CEO, Purple Chip'.

Shile gave a quick double knock and opened the door.

"Hey, boss," he said, peeping his head through the crack. "You have a visitor."

Mide bounced lightly on one spot. She hadn't seen him since the night of the mixer, and she was nervous. She had a combined total of eighty-three missed calls on her phone from him and several texts. If Persistence was a real human being, he would be Tomiwa. Yet, she wondered why she would believe he liked her when he had all these ladies working around and for him.

Her mind brought up the images of the pretty-looking receptionist and the assistant who had sent the gift box. Fear struck her again that it had all been a ruse to get information out of her to win the bid. It wasn't too late to go back home.

"Mr. Tom," Shile said again.

"I told you I didn't want to be disturbed."

Tomiwa's voice rang out and gnawed at her insides. She hadn't known how much she'd missed hearing it.

"Yeah, but you have a visitor—"

"I'm not seeing anyone."

Shile looked slightly frustrated.

Mide peeped in from behind him and saw Tomiwa hunched over his laptop in one corner of his office, a headset over his ears. His fingers were dusting the keyboard with lightning speed, and his brow was furrowed in concentration. He reminded her for a second of Sesan.

"Mr. Tom?"

He didn't look up and had apparently chosen not to reply.

She touched Shile's arm, and he let her step into the office. Then she waved him away. He nodded and shut the door behind them both.

She examined his office. It was a large, neatly arranged room, with long rectangular windows on adjacent walls that flooded it with natural light. Set up as a live-in slash work-space environment, it spelled privilege of a kind she wasn't used to.

Each item in the room was unique. The walls were painted a cream shade with the fixtures and window panes done in light, maroon tones. One corner housed a multi-gym equipment and a treadmill, the other had Tomiwa scrunched over his laptop. A large desk in the middle of the room had a fridge and a table with coffee or tea-making equipment by the side. The small settee and low oval table next to them stood above a rich-looking centre rug. Behind them was a cupboard and a wall to ceiling book shelf filled with thick, neatly stacked books.

She was awed for the few seconds she stood staring around, hoping her cousin would one day have a place as good as it.

"Shile?" Tomiwa's voice rang out from the corner where he had set up his laptop. "Don't let me put your name in that termination letter next."

She turned to him in alarm. He wanted to fire Shile. That was bad. It didn't seem like the man she had gotten to know.

"Mr. Oyinlolu," she said, but he didn't look up. "Tomiwa?"

This was her second time ever addressing him by name out loud to his face. It felt weird because this was a time when she was re-evaluating her relationship with him.

But the name possessed the appropriate level of intimacy she needed to win him back. Despite everything that had happened, she had missed him and wanted their relationship back to where it was before the mixer.

He looked up from his laptop momentarily to glance in her direction, then returned it and kept up with his typing. A moment later, he stopped typing, looked up at the wall in front of him for a few seconds, then swung his chair around to face her.

Mide stood in the middle of the room, staring at him. He looked tired and worn out. He hadn't shaved in days, and his eyes were devoid of the usual charming light that danced around within them.

"Hi." She gave him a small smile. "I heard you'd turned into a Mr. Hyde, hoarding up in your office, playing solo with your laptop and firing people."

He took the headset off his ears and placed them on the table beside his laptop. Still, he didn't say anything.

"How have you been?"

"Good," he mumbled.

She stared at his laptop. "You seem busy."

"I have a lot of work to do."

"You have a lot of staff."

"I need to prep before I involve them."

"You're running yourself ragged."

"I'm filling up my mind and time."

She knew what he meant, and in that moment, she just couldn't be mad at him.

"What are you working on?"

"A new solution," he said. "The one I got in place of the Jules account. Believe it or not, we need money, too."

This drew a smile from her. "Can I help?"

"It's classified. You work for One Tech, and it would be—"

"A conflict of interest. I get that."

"Sort of."

They went off into another spell of not saying anything. She realized then she hadn't gotten over him. She doubted she would ever.

"I didn't think you would come here."

"If you're busy, I can always come back another day," she said, worried at thelacklustre tone in his voice.

He didn't respond, so she turned around and started to walk away. He allowed her to get to the door before he spoke.

"Don't leave!"

She stopped with her hands on the door handle and turned back to him. He was still staring at her.

"Stay. I don't want you to leave."

She turned around, her heart crashing against her rib cage. *Will you hold me? That's all I want.*

"Come over here. Please."

TOMIWA'S EYES FOLLOWED Mide's movements across the wide office and round his large desk to where he was working. He couldn't believe she was in his office. He'd called, left a thousand messages, and finally resigned himself to the fate that he had lost her forever.

Her being in his office was priceless, and he wanted to take his time savouring every little detail.

He tapped his thighs, indicating where he wanted her to sit. She hesitated, then dropped her bag on his desk and walked the rest of the way over.

Placing her hands on his shoulders, she lowered herself into position across his lap, and he leaned back, adjusting the back seat of his chair, one arm wound around her waist so he could place her properly on his lap.

"I take it you're not mad at me anymore," he said as he studied every inch of her face.

She looped both of her hands around his neck and shook her head. "I think I punished you long enough."

He kept his gaze on her eyes. "I missed you."

"I started to miss you, too, after a while. I'm sorry I didn't pick up your calls."

"You had every right to be angry."

"I'm not anymore."

"I think I'm in love with you."

The words threw her. He could tell. Was it too soon to declare love? His feelings were juxtaposed between the idea that they had just met and he couldn't go a day without seeing her, but he was sure he was in love with her.

"I liked you, too," she said. "So much it hurt to find out everything."

"Liked?"

"I've forgiven you, but I'm still trying to determine if I still like you."

His eyes dropped from hers. "I'm sorry."

"I was so angry with you that day—"

"I love you." It was a sentence meant to silence all her complaints. "I think I figured it out when you walked out on me at that mixer. I'm so in love with you, I'm doing crazy things. You might decide to steal all our ideas and come up with rival software, and I would be powerless to stop you."

"What you did—"

"I understand. What I did was unforgivable, and there was no explanation. I invaded your privacy, lied to you, and did a whole lot of things I'm not proud of." He took his other hand off her knee and placed it around her waist, pulling her closer. "You can go ahead and punish me some more in any way that you want," he finished, his face inches away from hers. "I won't shrink from it. I won't even stop you. Just don't leave me."

"I'm over being mad at you. I saw what you did for my cousin. Thank you."

"Is this why you came?"

"I missed you, that's why I came. I was tired of being mad at you. I didn't pick up your calls because I was scared."

"Of trusting me?"

She lowered her head onto his forehead, and he felt the relief in the motion.

"I thought you used me," she whispered. "I was so mad because I thought you used me."

"I'm sorry. I'm so sorry."

He responded by crushing her closer to him, his hand spread wide across her back.

"I need you to know that I didn't use any of the things he gave us. Regardless, we didn't play fair, and the whole process was tainted."

MIDE COULDN'T BELIEVE all her anger towards him was gone.

"How did you get your sister to give up on the Jules account?"

"I found a replacement."

She detached herself from his embrace and stared down at him. "How?"

"Can we not talk about that?" he whispered, lowering his hand to her thigh and letting it trail down the lateral border of her knee and leg. "Let's talk about us."

She closed her eyes and tried not to react to the sensation of his fingertips moving lightly and slowly up and down her bare left leg. "You need a shower."

"I would be willing to take one now if you would be willing to take it with me." He leaned forward and placed his lips against the right side of her chin.

She chuckled. "I am not going to do that with you. Not today."

"Tomorrow?" He trailed her lower jaw and stopped at the base of her throat, kissing it gently.

"No!" she said, laughing.

"In the future?"

"Maybe. If I let you walk me down the aisle."

He leaned back. "In that case, I have a job offer. You were in here a few weeks ago, and my company snubbed you."

She smiled, eyes on his. "Can I retake the test?"

"Unfortunately," he drawled, his tone husky. "Those positions have been filled."

"Then why are you rubbing my face in it?"

"Coz there's another opening," he whispered, holding her gaze. "Twenty-four-hour lifetime job. Office address, my house; designation, my wife."

She laughed out loud and threw her head back, giving him an ample view of her neckline for a second before she brought her head down and scrutinized his eyes. "What's the pay like?"

"Unbelievably amazing! You set your salary, and you will be allowed to put your feet up all day and do nothing but sit and look pretty for show. Plus, I'll take you anywhere you want to go. Paris, Milan, New York... No more ushering gigs."

He was asking to marry her, and she was enthralled by the idea. "It's a very tempting offer."

"It's a great offer. Take it and make me a happy man. Let me walk you down that aisle so we can take that bath together."

She chuckled.

"But first, go out with me. You promised the contract wouldn't come between us."

"If you promise to get out of this chair, leave your laptop with Shile, and go home to take a bath, I'll consider your offer."

"The job offer?" He sounded hopeful.

"Let's start with the date."

"I'll take whatever I can get."

Chuckling, she lowered her forehead back onto his. "I'm glad this is over. I really like you."

"I really like you, too. I never, ever want to hurt you like I did, ever again."

Her smile waned. "I'm sorry I didn't pick up your calls. I'm usually not a mean person, but I didn't trust you anymore, and I didn't know if..."

"Ifemide," he said, quietly. "*My love has come.* I gave you a new name. Do you like it?"

"I do."

"You had every right to be angry. You are the sweetest, most beautiful person I know, and I'm honoured to have you sit on my lap and tell me you are not mad at me anymore."

Cheeks bulging, she lowered her mouth onto his with all the love she could muster. She wasn't mad anymore.

He hijacked her mouth and kissed her back fiercely, hands running gently all over her back while tasting her tongue with gentle probing motions. She allowed him. She didn't care if he hadn't taken a bath. Her nose wasn't offended. Her heart wasn't offended, either, because she had made up her mind about him.

"Go home with me," he said, when his mouth left hers.

"Here is what we'll do. You will go home, alone, take a bath, brush your teeth, and get dressed. I will go home, alone, and wait for you."

"Then I'll come and pick you up and we'll go out," he finished with a hopeful smile.

"Hmm, no, dear."

"No?"

"No. You will come and meet my cousin and his wife, and we will all have dinner together at our house, and then you can come by any time of any day and take me out."

"You're joking, right?"

She chuckled, got up from his lap, and picked up her handbag.

"Mide, your cousin detests me," he said, standing up.

"Seven o'clock. I'll expect you." She swung her handbag over her shoulder and strolled across the carpeted floor of his office.

"Mide, that man will murder me."

She turned at the door and paused to blow him a kiss before stepping out.

She came back in a second later. "Oh, and by the way, please, let's not fire any more people today, okay?"

He nodded, eyes smiling at her.

Epilogue

Niyi stood in the kitchen holding a bottle of Cabernet Sauvignon and peeping through the crack made by its open door.

He could see right through it to his living room couch where his cousin and Mr. Oyinlolu were seated, side by side, reading something off his phone and laughing quietly. The scene was innocent enough, and Mide seemed genuinely happy, but he was wary.

The CEO had his head and shoulder tilted towards his cousin as he made swiping motions across the surface of his phone with a finger. She was pressed to his side, arm looped around his elbow, comfortable just leaning against him and passing him syrupy looks.

I've been seeing him, he recalled her saying in the cab on the way back home, the night of the mixer. *The CEO of Purple Chip.*

He clenched his fist around the bottle. What in the world had he said to make her forgive him and fall prey to his charms?

He had been in a nervous state of unrest ever since he had opened the front door to his home and found the man standing in front of it.

"Good evening," the man had said, his voice annoyingly self-assured. "I'm here to see you."

Niyi had at first been surprised, then suspicious. Then a tad angry. The man had not looked in any way sorry for anything.

Rather, he'd looked fairly confident holding an unopened bottle of Cabernet by the neck. The suit he had on was made of an elegant-looking, light cotton fabric that seemed melded unto his frame. Niyi imagined he had stood idly by while the tailor draped the fabric and made it fit. Nothing he owned fit quite like it, but he wasn't about to let the tech magnate intimidate him in his own home. This was his territory.

"What are you doing here?" he'd demanded.

Tomiwa Oyinlolu had messed up badly, and he wasn't going to let him get away with it.

"I wanted to apologize in person about everything that went down between us. My company was unethical in their dealings, and our behaviour was unbecoming. I'm very sorry about it all, and I promise you it will never happen with you or any other company again."

"So, you think you can just walk in here and say you're sorry, and I'll just forget about everything?" Niyi had found himself saying.

His visitor had shaken his head. "I'm not expecting that to happen now."

"You think I'm an idiot? Is that what you think?"

The man had paused for a moment in which time he'd looked him in the eyes and Niyi had felt foolish for losing his temper.

Then he'd proceeded to talk. "What we—what my company did was wrong. Nevertheless, I take full responsibility for everything, It won't happen again."

"You cheated," Niyi had accused.

"We...did. True."

"Your brother sabotaged my app over and over again."

"Yeah," Tomiwa had said, worry lines appearing on his forehead. "He did."

"I know you didn't plant him in my office, but you could have told Mide about it."

"I could have. I'm not going to deny nor defend that."

"You hurt her feelings and put her in a hospital."

That had seemed to get a reaction out of him.

He'd taken in a deep breath, readjusted the wine bottle in his left fist, and looked him square in the eye. "I regret every action of mine that put Mide in the hospital, and I'm glad she is all right. Nevertheless, it wasn't my intention to deceive her. If you don't want me in your home, it's fine."

Niyi had still held the door open but had been conflicted on whether to let him in or not. "I said a couple things at the hospital that I'm not proud of, too, but I'm hoping you can understand my motivations."

"You were well within your rights," he'd replied. "I completely understand."

Niyi had wanted to say more, but he'd been out of steam and anger. He'd released a soft sigh and taken a step back, holding the door wide open. "Come on in."

"Thank you."

The CEO had bowed his head and entered with a humble kind of gait alien to rich, well-connected men like him.

Niyi had closed the door wondering why else the man had come.

After Tomiwa had shaken Derin's hand, complimented her and their home, and admired his twin daughters, he'd handed Niyi the Cabernet. Secretly thrilled about opening a bottle of wine he couldn't afford to buy on his monthly salary, he was grateful. He'd been adamant to find fault with his visitor, but the man had been surprisingly flawless in character.

At least in the short space of time he'd been in their home.

Despite offering him a seat, Tomiwa had politely remained standing. Then both of them had turned to see Mide flying down the stairs like an excited teenager introducing her boyfriend to her father for the first time.

"A little more gently down the stairs," Niyi had found himself saying before he recalled she was almost thirty and didn't need reprimanding in front of strangers. He'd been worried, though—any excess exertion on her part would bring on an attack. Mide was a young woman with boundless energy.

She had slowed down and taken the last two steps gingerly. Then she'd padded barefoot into the living room with a smile the size of the ocean for their mutual visitor. Dressed in a simple three-quarter-sleeved knee-length dress, she'd looked elegant even with bare feet and no makeup. He'd noted the look the man had given his young cousin when she'd hugged him and understood the CEO of Purple Chip wasn't in his home only to mend fences as he had earlier implied. He had come to court Mide.

He had wrapped his arms around her and placed his chin against the side of her head with closed eyes.

Then, they had both completely ignored him and Derin.

Now he was seated in the living room with her, Niyi couldn't keep his mind off the fact his younger cousin needed protection from the sly-looking wolf. He didn't trust the man for anything. As he loaded wine glasses onto a tray, he thought about how best to force him to come clean about his intentions.

"They're waiting." Derin goaded him in the back with her elbow as she put peppered chicken, snail, and gizzards onto paper plates to serve.

"They're more interested in themselves than in us."

The moment he saw Tomiwa take her hand and raise her fingers to his lips, he froze. The fingers remained on the man's lips for a long moment, forcing joyful laughter from Mide. "My goodness, look at her. Are they having relations?"

He didn't know he'd said it out loud.

"Niyi!" Derin sounded irritated with him. "He seems like a nice guy. A very rich, nice guy who is in love with your cousin. Behave!"

"Then he shouldn't have done what he did."

"For goodness' sake, he's apologized."

"She hugged him, right in front of me. And he holds her like he's put his arms around her many times. What is he really doing here? Do you know if they've had sex?"

"Calm down, and take those wine glasses outside!"

Niyi grudgingly took the tray to the living room. He opened the bottle of wine with cool, methodical motions while giving his guest murderous looks. They were still seated side by side but with an element of space between themselves now he was there. He eyed their entwined fingers briefly, worried about his inability to determine Tomiwa's true motives.

"So," he began warily as he uncorked the wine. "Why did you step down for One Tech?"

Tomiwa sat up and gave him all his attention. "I wanted to give you a chance."

"You don't think my application is good enough?"

"I didn't say that. Your application is very functional and addresses all their needs. Believe me, if I didn't think it was worth Jules' investment, I wouldn't have stepped down. But I thought it was exactly what they needed, and they thought so, too. We used our influence to get ahead of due process because your app is great and it scared my sister. That's why I stepped down."

"But you let it happen. If Mide hadn't found out—"

Tomiwa sighed. "When you have a board of directors and a company under incorporation, a few decisions get tossed out of your hands. In truth, I knew about the deception, but I didn't agree to it, and I can assure you such will never happen again. At least not under my watch."

"You want me to believe that it's not because of Ademide that you're giving me the contract?"

The cork popped at that point, and Mide stared at her cousin with widened eyes.

"Niyi!" she said, her tone full of laughter. "Don't be ridiculous!"

Tomiwa just looked at him and smiled. Then he turned his head to look at her. She held his gaze in amusement while Niyi watched the two of them stare at each other. He worried his cousin was falling into another trap.

"Maybe," the Purple Chip CEO said and squeezed her fingers. "But maybe more because I see your company doing great stuff, and I want to help in any way that I can. I'd like us to work together on a couple of projects that are coming my way soon enough because I think it would be a great way to mend things."

"What kind of projects?"

"Something you'll like, I guarantee you."

Niyi didn't. "So, what happens when you both have some sort of fight, and you decide to call off this...this relationship. What happens then?"

Tomiwa lowered his eyes and took in a deep breath. "My intentions towards your cousin are nothing but honourable."

"And I don't doubt that," he said as he poured wine into their glasses and Derin appeared with more snacks. "You start this relationship, you and I go into partnership, and then what? We have a falling out as most often happens with partners, and your relationship with Mide suffers. Or you disagree with Mide, and all of a sudden, you're hiding jobs from your partner because you don't want to have anything to do with his cousin."

"I don't mix business with pleasure, and I'm not proposing a partnership. I'm saying we can work together on different aspects of the same job, and it will be a mutually beneficial plan, regardless of what happens with Mide and me."

Niyi offered Tomiwa a wine glass.

"I'm sorry," he said, "but I'm going to have to decline."

Tomiwa looked at him for a moment and then nodded once as he accepted the wine glass. "That's fine. I respect your wishes."

Both men sat back and watched one another carefully for the rest of the evening.

The ensuing conversation was light and balanced on both sides by Derin and Mide, and they had gone on to have a few laughs. Niyi was able to relax somewhat towards Tomiwa, and he wasn't sure the Sauvignon was not to be implicated.

When Tomiwa got up to leave, he thanked them profusely.

Niyi felt compelled to see him to the door.

"Thank you for coming." He held out a hand and shook Tomiwa's own.

"Look," he said just before he stepped outside their house. "Your cousin means a lot to me, and I love her. Very much. I need you to know that I plan to treat her with respect and dignity and take care of her in every way that I can."

Niyi shrugged and looked at Mide. She had an arm in Tomiwa's elbow. "I really want to trust you, but you haven't given me a lot to go by."

"I know that, and I'm hoping I can rectify it."

"Niyi," Mide said. "The only way we are going to get past this is to try. You have to try and let everything go."

"I'm trying."

"I know you are," she replied. "But Tomiwa is a decent guy, and you'll never know it till you let him in."

Niyi held back his scowl and looked from one to the other.

"I fully expected you to throw me out of your home the moment I showed up at the front door, but you didn't, and I respect you for that. The offer will always be open. Call me anytime you change your mind."

"Sure. Ademide is a very precious girl, and we may not have as much money as you do, or live in a big house, or come from a well-known family. Know this, however. I am going to go out on a limb and trust you with her. Don't disappoint me."

Tomiwa chuckled. "You have my promise."

"Mr. Oyinlolu." Niyi held out his hand and shook it once more. "It was nice spending an evening with you."

"Likewise."

So saying, Niyi nodded at both of them and went back into the house.

TOMIWA TURNED TO MIDE. "I think your cousin just gave us his blessing."

She smiled and wrapped her arms around his neck. "I think he did."

"Your father..."

"Is dead," she said. "Big deal."

He stared at her for a long moment as an overwhelming urge to protect her washed over him. He reached his arms around her waist.

"It's a big deal, from one fatherless child to another, and trust me, Niyi is doing a great job of filling in for him. Please, go easy on him."

"Uuh, see who's on Niyi's side."

He laughed.

"Thank you for coming."

"Can I go ahead and take you out now?"

She laughed out loud. "Yes. Anytime. So that I don't have to sneak out and avoid telling anyone where I'm going."

He stared at her for a long time.

"If you ever need anything…" He left the statement hanging.

"I think I have everything I need," she replied.

"Me, too," he said, smiling down at her. "My little whirlwind. The one who upended my life and heart with drama. I love you, Ademide Akinseye, and I want to spend the rest of my life loving you."

She reached up to kiss him.

THE END

Extended Epilogue:
Like Sandstorm Intro

It was about eleven in the night when Tomiwa got back home. He'd spent most of the evening with Ademide in his car, but he was just glad everything had been sorted with Niyi.

She hadn't wanted to go anywhere. He hadn't, either, so they'd spent the rest of the evening cuddling in the backseat of his car, away from Derin and Niyi's scrutiny.

He had missed holding her, and he had needed to make it up to her for abandoning her the night before the Jules presentation. The night they'd had dinner on the boat. It had been agonizing for him to leave her, but the need to be a gentleman had far outweighed his desires.

He was just about getting into bed when his phone rang. It was Chioma.

Earlier on, she had sent him a feedback message on her meeting with Babatunde Rollington, a client just getting his business signed up on their app.

The meeting had run late, and he had instructed Chioma to let him know when she got home. Lagos at night was not a safe place, and it was his work that had kept her out so late. He always needed confirmation from his staff they were back home in one piece.

"Home?" he asked, wondering why a simple text hadn't done the job.

"Sir." Chioma's voice was high-pitched. "Your brother is in my flat, bruised and most likely shot in the shoulder."

He froze. "What!"

He looked at his phone and clicked on the app that verified caller IDs and filtered AI scams. It *was* Chioma. *What the heck is Goriola doing in Chioma's place?*

"He's bleeding, and I'm scared. He doesn't look too good, and he won't let me take him to a hospital."

"What does he mean?" He jumped out of bed and strode to his bathroom so he could find a decent shirt and a pair of jeans to change into. "Take him to the nearest hospital immediately. I'm on my way."

"He told me not to."

He found a shirt. "Is he serious at all? Put him on the phone and let me talk to him."

"I can't. He fainted a minute ago. Said to tell you the word vulture."

Tomiwa pulled the shirt down and froze again for the second time that night. *Vulture? Code Vulture?* "Is that what he told you?"

"Yes. Sir, he needs a hospital!" The girl seemed panicked.

"Don't take him anywhere. I'll be there in thirty minutes."

"I don't think he'll hold on for that long," she cried.

He pulled off his pyjama trousers and hurried into his jeans. "I'll be there in twenty. Whatever you do, you can't take him to a hospital."

"What? Why? What if he dies?" Her shriek had become a sob.

He didn't respond as he grabbed his car keys, barged out of his room, and ran down the stairs.

"Mr. Tom!" Chioma sounded like she was crying. "There's blood everywhere."

"Calm down." His voice was soft, but he was already getting into his car and starting the engine. "He's not going to die."

"He needs a doctor. I am not a doctor!"

There was another reason why Chioma was panicked, and he was the only one who knew it. She had a huge crush on Gori, but what he was doing in her flat was a mystery. Had they somehow gotten together without his knowledge?

"I'm going to cut the call now and call you back in a minute. Keep the phone on loudspeaker, so I can tell you what to do."

Chioma sniffed on the other end of the line. "I have a friend, she's a doctor. She can be here in two minutes."

"Can she be discreet?"

"Yes, sir. She keeps all my secrets."

"Fine. Call her," he said. "No one else."

Thank you for reading LIKE WHIRLWIND by Feyi Aina. Support the author by rating and leaving a brief review on the site of purchase.

Want to know about the next book releases and special offers, sign up to our mailing list at:

https://www.loveafricapress.com/newsletter

About the author

OLUFUNMILOLA ADENIRAN writes as Feyi Aina, a Christian author and poet, crafting contemporary inspirational women's fiction as well as historical stories infused with an African fantasy flavour.

She is a Physiotherapist by day, a writer by night and the author of several short stories, and novels including **Love's Indenture, Home Cooked Love, Love Happens Eventually**, and most recently, **AYANFE**.

Her short stories have appeared in Brittle Paper, and in several anthologies, most notably **Hell Hath No Fury, Healing Hearts and Hurts** as well as **Roses Aren't Red**. Her stories feature strong male and female lead characters in *'what if'* scenarios created to epitomize good moral conduct while showing off the beautiful process of falling in love.

Olufunmilola lives in Lagos with her husband and children. She is the RWOWA 2019 Author of the Year winner for her novel Love's Indenture. Her short story, THE RIVER GOD, was sampled in the textbook *Nature, Environment and Activism in Nigerian Literature,* by Prof. Sule. E. Egya.

When she's not reading or writing, she loves cooking, traveling, and scouring the net for information about art, history, and ancient civilization.

Her e-books can be found on the following platforms: Amazon, Bambooks, Kobo, Scribd, Smashwords, Selar, and

Waterstone. Physical copies exist in popular bookshops across the country.

Website – www.feyiaina.com[1]

---

1. http://www.feyiaina.com

Other books by Love Africa Press

Schemes N Love by Jomi Oyel
Locked In by Opemipo Omosa
Against the Run of Play by Kiru Taye
Nila Princess of Sheba by Mukami Ngari
CONNECT WITH US
Facebook.com/LoveAfricaPress[1]
Twitter.com/LoveAfricaPress[2]
Instagram.com/LoveAfricaPress[3]
SIGN UP TO OUR NEWSLETTER
https://www.loveafricapress.com/newsletter

---

1. https://www.facebook.com/LoveAfricaPress

2. https://twitter.com/LoveAfricaPress

3. https://www.instagram.com/loveafricapress/

Milton Keynes UK
Ingram Content Group UK Ltd.
UKHW031305251024
450245UK00004B/269

9 781914 226618